The SMELL of RAIN

Alyson Hope

Renaissance.
Diverse Canadian Voices

PressesRenaissancePress.ca

First edition 2023

Cover art by Alyson Hope
Cover design by Alyson Hope, Rachel Boyd, and Nathan Frechette
Interior design by Éric Desmarais.
Edited by Shawn Brixi, Joel Balkovec, and Molly Desson

Legal deposit, Library and Archives Canada, November 2023.

Paperback ISBN: 978-1-990086-50-2
Ebook ISBN: 978-1-990086-61-8

Renaissance Press - pressesrenaissancepress.ca

Renaissance acknowledges that it is hosted on the traditional, unceded land of the Anishinabek, the Kanien'kehá:ka, and the Omàmìwininìwag. We acknowledge the privileges and comforts that colonialism has granted us and vow to use this privilege to disrupt colonialism by lifting up the voices of marginalized humans who continue to suffer the effects of ongoing colonialism.

Printed in Gatineau at
Imprimerie Gauvin
Depuis 1892
gauvin.ca

For Marguerite and Annette

PART I

Chapter 1

Grief is like a rock that you drop into your pocket. At first, the rock is jagged and brittle, poking holes in the lining and scraping your skin. As time goes by, it becomes worn and smoothed. While it is almost exactly the same size and weight, the rock becomes easier to overlook. That is, until one day, you innocently reach into your pocket — perhaps for a set of keys or a book of matches — and instead, you pull out the rock. There it sits, in the palm of your hand, existing as the centre of your universe.

When Rachel's cellphone rang early one Monday morning, she was in the middle of a dream about a boat. The boat was the size of a poppy seed.

Rubbing her blue eyes and pushing away a few strands of blond hair, Rachel sat up, at first mistaking the phone call for her morning alarm.

When the sound stopped, Rachel was surprised, reaching over to see what was the matter. When she read the name of her mother's nursing home under *missed call*, her heart sank. She hated the idea of intuition, preferring the concept of coincidence, but in that moment... she knew.

It was incredible, how short the phone call was, how little time it took the head nurse to declare that her mother, Nina O'Connor, had passed away in her sleep. It was being decided, at that very moment, whether any of her tissues or organs could be harvested for donation. It was doubtful, said the nurse, as she had died of pneumonia. Rachel had no idea that her mother had wished to be a donor, but the nurse assured her that it was indeed her intention. All of the necessary paperwork was in order.

Rachel hung up the phone. Then, she laughed aloud at the absurdity of the whole thing: how could her mother, who had been so selfish in life, be so benevolent in death?

Once the final vestige of her smile faded, Rachel felt herself become sad. It was hard for her to tell what bothered her more: learning of her mother's death, or the mourning of what could have been but never was — and now, could definitively never be.

But there was more to her grief. Rachel had reached into her pocket to drop in a new rock, only to brush against the one left after her father's passing.

Rachel knew that she had to advise her siblings before she had time to process the news.

First, she tried calling her younger sister, Claire. Upon receiving no response on her cellphone, she dialed Claire's home telephone number. It rang and rang.

Rachel hung up, then clicked on her brother's contact. He picked up on the second ring.

"Hello?"

Rachel could hear a child fussing in the background. "Uh, Tom..." she said. Her breath caught in her throat.

The line went silent for one heartbeat, and then another. Rachel felt sure that Tom knew. She waited for him to speak.

"Sorry, Rachel, did you say something?" asked Tom after a few more seconds. The ambient noise returned. "I dropped the phone into my lap."

"Tom, it's about Mom," said Rachel. "I just got off the phone with her nursing home. Tom... She died in her sleep early this morning."

"Are you sure?" asked Tom. As soon as the words came out, he felt silly for having uttered them.

"Well, I haven't seen the body yet, if that is what you're asking..." said Rachel quietly.

"Oh," said Tom, his hazel eyes filling with tears.

"They say it was pneumonia..." added Rachel. She felt her palms become warm and damp. Her scalp prickled. "I don't think it was scary for her, Tom..." she said, searching for a way to comfort her older brother, "... since it was in her sleep."

"Yeah..." said Tom. Rachel could hear his voice break. "I'm... I'm going to go and tell Zandra. Does Claire know?"

Rachel explained that she was not able to get a hold of her.

"Okay, just... let me know when you do," said Tom.

"Sure," said Rachel. She hung up, exhaling deeply.

"God dammit, Tom, I've been calling all morning, and I still haven't been able to reach Claire," cried Rachel as she paced across her apartment, inspecting the floor tiles for imperfections, namely specks of dirt or discarded strands of her golden hair.

Frantically, she bent over, pressed her fingertip into the little grain of sand that had somehow evaded her past scrutiny, and dropped it into the garbage can.

Tom breathed his irritation in the form of a sigh into the phone. "Why not just drop by her place?" he asked.

"Who knows where she could be? Maybe she's actually out, doing something productive with herself. Working, maybe? That could explain why she isn't answering her telephone... I tried her apartment phone, and her cellphone too... Nothing. Not even a text back."

"You don't want to drop by her apartment, just in case?" asked Tom.

"I would, but by the time I would get from Ottawa to Montreal..." It was not a sincere offer, and both he and his sister knew it.

"I don't have time to go by at this point, Tom. Adil is the key speaker at the Multidisciplinary Earth Science Conference, which begins this afternoon. I have to be there for him. Actually, I have to go get ready now, or I'll be late."

Tom sighed again. "Well, do you have Robin's number?" he asked.

That was a clever idea. Rachel was irritated. "I should have thought of that myself," she said. "I'll call her. I'll let you know."

They said goodbye and hung up. Rachel called Robin, who answered on the sixth ring. She left a brief message with her sister-in-law. It was almost 11 o'clock.

Rachel had very little time to waste. She jumped into the shower turning the knob to the extreme right. All hot. No time for cold. The water was blistering. At least in the shower she could lie to herself about crying.

Rachel washed her hair twice. It was a matter of routine. Maybe she could get away with washing it once, but she did not want to risk it. The routine was comfortable. Safe. Predictable.

She dried herself quickly, hydrated her bright red, flaking skin — a condition which she knew to be aggravated by the scalding heat of her showers — and dressed quickly.

Rachel looked herself over in the full-length mirror hanging on the back of the apartment door. She had opted for a moderately fitted, professional-looking grey dress and black heels. Her thick blonde hair was half pulled up into a perfectly round bun, the bottom half brushing just below her shoulders. She turned to the side: her profile was unobjectionable. Time to go!

Buttoning up her coat, Rachel grabbed her handbag, turned off the lights and stepped out into the hallway. It was almost noon. Adil was scheduled to begin his talk at 12:30. She would be there just in time.

A dusty golden spring sun shone through the grimy windows of a third-floor apartment. In the bedroom, a lacquered red rotary phone sat on the floor, ringing on and off.

Finally, after several hours, the brassy chime of the telephone leapt through the crypts and caverns of the world of dreams and into the conscious mind of the sleeping brunette. Without getting out of bed, she reached over for the receiver and nearly fell to the floor in the process. "Hello?"

"Claire!"

Claire sat up in bed and rubbed her eyes. She brushed her thick bangs out of her face and glanced at the old-fashioned clock perched upon her mid-century Formica bedside table. Five minutes to noon.

"Robin?" she asked, her voice rough from too much sleep. "Are you okay?"

"Claire, I have tried to call you all morning. I —"

"Yeah, sorry, I was working on something..." said Claire, rolling her dark brown eyes.

Like any person, she had a long list of things that irritated her, and one capital offence was the criticizing of her sleeping habits. She was not *lazing around* in bed at noon. Certainly not. What an outright *vulgar* suggestion. Sleeping late was simply part of Claire's artistic process — as was drinking, smoking, and cursing, for that matter. Perhaps in other professions those habits were a sign of sloth, but that was of no concern to the young painter.

"Whatever," said Robin with a sigh. "Claire, you have to listen to me. Rachel has been trying to reach you all morning. She called me around 11. Listen... She needs you to call her."

Claire felt her stomach contract to the size of a walnut. "What's going on?" she asked, her voice no longer rough, now hardly making any sound at all. Her throat had dried and a stale taste overwhelmed her tongue.

"I don't know, Claire..." she said. "Listen, I have to get back to my patient."

"You don't know, or you don't want to tell me?" asked Claire. There was a silence on the end of the line that said more than any words ever could. A presence most felt by its absence. It hurt.

"Robin?"

"It's not my place, Claire. I'm hanging up. Just call you sister, okay?"

"Okay," she finally whispered. "Okay."

"I love you, Claire," said Robin, the sound of dentist drills and suction tubes whining in the background.

"Me too, Robin."

Rachel sat on the Metro picking at her fingernail, trying to focus on anything but what had happened earlier that morning. She walked into the giant hotel conference room just in time to grab a spot at the front before the lights were dimmed. Her eyes searched for Adil, who was usually quite easy to find. She spotted his tall, exceptionally thin frame on the side of the stage and waved. Seeing Rachel, Adil smiled and waved back. She gave him a thumbs up. He returned the gesture.

A phantom female voice with an English accent was telling everyone to turn off their cellphones and to refrain from taking photos. Reaching into her pocket, Rachel clicked her phone into silent mode, then pulled it out just enough to check her screen for text messages or missed calls, casually, in the way that all people of the 21st century do. Indeed, there were four, all of which were from her sister: two from her home telephone, then two from her cell phone number. Rachel went to swipe the notifications away when a text came in.

please please call me I'm freaking out

Rachel hesitated, but eventually responded.

I'll call you in about an hour.

Then, she added *Actually, call Tom.*

Adil's session was about the biogeochemical cycle of inorganic mercury in the St. Lawrence River, which was the subject of his PhD thesis, but despite the engaging topic, Rachel was having trouble staying focused. Suddenly, everyone around her was standing, applauding, so she shot up and did the same.

Suddenly very cold, Rachel shrugged back into her emerald green felt coat. She followed the ebb and flow of the crowd out into the hall. Standing awkwardly near the conference room door, she awaited her fiancé.

"Rachel!" came a singsong male voice, peppered with an Indian-English accent.

The couple hugged and held hands. "Congratulations, Honey, it was even better than when you practiced it last night," said Rachel as she stretched herself upwards to kiss Adil's stubbly brown cheek.

"There's wine and cheese in the room back there, did you want to come?" he asked.

Rachel accepted the offer and they made their way through the crowd, arm in arm. It was a slow process, because people were continually stopping Adil to shake his hand, ask him further questions about his research, and compliment him on his skills as an orator.

"Is this your wife, then?" asked an elderly gentleman with a puff of white hair.

"Fiancée," said Adil. "Her name is Rachel Rossi."

The man nodded amiably. "How obliging of you to come to the conference for your fiancé. It isn't too hard to follow the subject matter?" he asked brightly. "For someone who is not in the field, I mean."

Rachel's scalp prickled and she held her breath.

Adil laughed. "Rachel is currently doing postdoctoral research on pro-inflammatory immune responses."

"My focus is on the role of immunomodulation of estrogens," said Rachel, dryly.

"Oh, very nice," said the man, his head wobbling about. He was clearly not listening, but what did it matter? "Excuse me." And with that, he was gone.

"Sorry about that," said Adil, eyes wide, as he took Rachel's hand to continue through the crowd. "Your hand is like ice. Is everything alright?"

Rachel dismissed his concern and they continued into the next room. Platters of cheese, fruit, and crackers slathered in pink, white, and grey all bobbed along the room on the arms of the black-tie waiters. Rachel's eye dismissed all of the food — who knew how many dirty hands had manipulated those little food bites — and searched instead for the drinks. Flutes of champagne and glasses full of reds and whites were neatly lined up along a table at the back of the room.

"I'm going to grab a drink," said Rachel, letting go of Adil's hand. "Can I get you something?"

Adil shook his head. "You're drinking?" he asked, his eyebrow questioning her unexpected choice. "You never drink…" He searched her slate eyes for elucidation, but came up to the surface empty-handed, as always. "Rachel… What is it?"

His low whine grated on her eardrums, but before she could respond — or more specifically, blow him off — a group of wide-eyed admirers were upon him. Rachel seized the moment and made a break for the champagne.

Almost an hour later, Adil finally found Rachel sitting at a small table alone. There were no less than seven empty champagne glasses in front of her. "Hello Croc-Adil," she said as she chuckled to herself. "I have been practising to say that. Get it? Like *crocodile*? Ha!"

"Rachel, you need to tell me what is going on," he said as he sat down next to her. "What is it?" he implored.

"She died this morning," said Rachel.

"What?"

"She's gone, Adil. My mother is gone. She died." Rachel shrugged, putting on a cool front in response to his mouth which twitched into a frown. "It was the pneumonia..."

"I thought that she had taken a turn for the better? Didn't it look like things were better? Isn't that what they said last week?" He was busy trying to bargain with reality when the deed was already done.

He pulled Rachel into his arms and she finally surrendered. Mascara leaked down her face, then onto Adil's perfectly pressed white chemise. "Rachel, Rachel, Rachel..." he whispered into her ear.

Claire clicked on her brother's contact in her phone and waited, unable to breathe.

"Did you speak to Rachel?" asked Tom as he picked up.

"Will someone just tell me what the fuck is going on!" exclaimed Claire.

She was trying to pull a t-shirt over her naked body, but when she finally got the shirt over her head, she realised that it was both backwards and inside out. She pulled it off in a quick, angry thrust and threw it at the wall with all her might. It grazed the wall lightly before gently tumbling to the floor. "I called her a million times. She texted me to call you. So just bloody spill it."

"Are you... are you sitting down, Claire?" asked Tom, his voice wavering. Instead of a response, he heard a loud clanking sound, then nothing at all. "Claire? Claire!"

He listened as hard as he could. Nothing. He listened harder. He could hear her. She was sobbing.

"Claire... Claire, I am so sorry... Claire!" He stayed on the phone for several minutes listening to his baby sister weep for the loss of their mother in utter impotence. He was only 200 kilometres away, but he might as well have been on Neptune.

Finally, she picked up the receiver. "We're orphans, Tom..." she whispered, still crying. "Adult orphans, but orphans all the same."

Tom tried to comfort her, but Claire was inconsolable. They hung up.

Claire was still lying in bed, on top of the messy covers when her wife arrived in her green dentist scrubs. No words were exchanged; they cried, holding each other until long after the whole city was swept into darkness.

Chapter 2

"So, this is the box that we put together of your mother's personal belongings. We would have let you come in and clean through the room yourself, but, you know...there are a limited number of beds, and new patients to fill them every single day..."

Rachel nodded as the nurse thrust the brown cardboard box into her hands. It was remarkably light. Too light, indeed, to carry the totality of the final belongings of a (former) human being, especially someone whose life has been as ardently lived as that of Nina O'Connor.

"Again," said the nurse, looking at his watch, "we are so sorry for your loss."

The box was brought home and dumped into the storage shed of a back balcony. It was done so not out of disregard for its contents, but simply to keep it safe. Safe for a better time, for a more practical time, when it would need to be sorted through and parceled out. No more than a few days, or a few weeks, at most.

But time has very little interest in its promises.

Like dusting the ceiling fan or organizing piles of old magazines, that task fell to the wayside until it was almost forgotten about entirely.

The three siblings had already spent weeks in their parents' home, when their mother was first placed in the long-term care centre, combing out each and every drawer, closet, and shelf. They had called their maternal grandmother, Shelley, to take part in the process, but even though she promised to be there several times, she never did turn up.

Each time that the siblings felt that they had made good progress, it felt like yet another complicated task fell into their lap. The house was to be sorted, banks were to be called, envelopes were to be sent to the government... It was a most exhausting process. There had been arguments, not about heirloom jewelry or Persian rugs, but about more practical issues.

Thomas, the eldest, was the most sentimental of the three, trying to fill his SUV with as many possessions as possible. He seemed to forget that he needed room in his vehicle in order to drive it from Montreal, where the rest of his family lived, to Ottawa, where he lived with his spouse, Zandra, and baby daughter, Laci.

Rachel was far more practical than her elder brother. Not only did she resemble her mother physically, she was also very similar minded: practical, effective, stoic. For Rachel, objects were objects, and although they did indeed remind her of her late father, Elvis, and sick mother, she did not equate keeping the items to loving her family. For Rachel, dropping a broken chair and old cookbooks into a garbage bin did not make her cold, only pragmatic.

The youngest sister, Claire, often found herself stuck in between. She did want to respect her parents' earthly belongings, but, at the same time, she did not think that it was necessary to take out and examine every single utensil from the drawer in the kitchen before placing it in the 'give away' box.

Tom wanted either to keep everything — or, if the item was really not necessary to him, to give it away to people in need. Claire and Rachel, on the other hand, wanted to sell some of the nicer furniture and appliances to help pay for their mother's stay in the care centre. Nina's room was not cheap, and they had no idea how much time their mother would spend there. Whenever the topic was broached, Tom would get worked into a fit and storm out of the room, categorically refusing to talk about their mother's rapidly deteriorating state. Claire said they should discuss it, but only briefly, because she did not want to attract any negative energy to their mother. But since she did not have the money to finance a decade or more of care, she did agree, in the end, that selling things online was a wise idea.

Tom was adamant in not taking part in the sale of any of the items, so the sisters had to do the dealings when he was at home in Ottawa, during the week. When Tom would arrive the next Friday or Saturday to continue with the cleaning and sorting, he would refuse to acknowledge whatever piece of furniture that had disappeared over the week.

Once the entire house was cleared out, it was time to scrub it, paint it, and put it on the market to be sold. The large, two-floored, brick house was, in fact, not a house at all, but a home, *their* home. All three had grown up in that home, taken their first steps there, played hide and seek in the dark on stormy summer nights, stolen their first kiss, nursed their first broken heart...

To make matters even more sad, it had been their mother who was supposed to sell the house herself. Nina had had a successful career as a real estate agent, profitable enough to work only part-time in her fifties while she planned her impending retirement. She had always said that her home would be the last that she would sell, a symbolic act, taking the earnings and travelling the world with her husband, Elvis, until they died in each other's arms on a quiet, starry night in the Gobi Desert, or on the rickety porch of a stilt house in Vietnam.

Planning for the future may give a sense to one's life, but, in the end, no matter how skillful the hand, it is life that holds all of the cards.

It was mid-December and a light snow was dancing down from the sky. The streetlights glowed orange, casting an amber glimmer over the whole world. Their work was done. The house was ready to be sold. On a nostalgic whim, the siblings decided to order in pizza and have one last picnic meal on the floor in front of the fireplace before handing the keys over to the real estate agent. While they were waiting for their food to arrive, Claire trekked out into the crisp night air to get a bottle of soda and some spiced rum.

At least their mother was still alive, they said as they sat around the fireplace together, and they tried to find comfort in the fact that she was in a place where she could be cared for appropriately. The onerous task of closing the chapter on their mother's life as an autonomous person was definitively completed. The sisters and brother quietly whispered about their shared relief at the job being over, but their sense of accomplishment was dwarfed by the sense of guilt that they could not shake off, no matter the way in which they examined the situation. The process — including the emotional storm which it generated — left them heavyhearted and exhausted.

And so, when Nina O'Connor died quietly in her nursing home bed six months later, Thomas, Rachel, and Claire wearily pulled themselves together again to draw up the funeral arrangements. They tried to contact their maternal grandmother, but found out from a woman with a strange accent who answered Shelley's phone — and who, incidentally, was subletting her condo — that Shelley was deep in the Costa Rican jungle studying the mysticism of trees, and that she would be unreachable for an undetermined amount of time.

Between running after the legal pronouncement of death, to obituary writing, to closing bank accounts, to notifying the tax people and credit card people, the siblings were caught up in the finalizing of their mother's passing for several more weeks — as though her no longer breathing was simply not a true enough death, in and of itself.

Nina was 67 years old when she died of complications brought on by the skulking, silent villain that is Alzheimer's disease. Her final belongings — a fuzzy, itchy, punch-coloured sweater; three pairs of pewter pants with elastic waistbands to make changing her diaper simpler for the orderlies; a few colourful, oriental-styled, half-empty tins of loose-leaf tea; a cloth-bound journal, its pages dog-eared; and a spider plant in a cheap, juniper-coloured plastic pot — were dropped into a brown cardboard box.

The funeral came and went, and so did the seasons. Things changed, but mostly, they stayed quite the same.

In the back of an outdoor storage unit, gathering dust and mustiness, sat the unremarkable cardboard box, branded with the insignia of a no-rinse moisturising body wash.

Chapter 3

Rachel scanned down her to-do list for the hundredth time that day. There were only 72 hours left before her flight was due to take off, and she still had several errands to run, items to purchase, and papers to sign. To ease her mind, she tried to calculate how many items she would have to do an hour in order to finish them all on time.

Via a university website, she had found a student from France who was studying in Montreal for a year. She wanted to rent Rachel's apartment fully furnished, which made things both more simple and more complicated: on the one hand, she did not need to find storage for her large furniture, but on the other hand, she had to find a place to pack away all of her personal items that she would not be taking to Myanmar with her.

It was a sweltering June day, and when Rachel opened her back door, the humidity felt as thick as a slice of smog-flavoured mousse. She had meant to re-organise her storage unit — it had been on her to-do list since March — but she had to face the fact that she would simply not have enough time. It irritated her, but she consoled herself with the fact that she had written the task in green ink, the colour code indicating that it was a non-compulsory chore.

Rachel was about to dump a pink plastic bin full of winter clothes into the outdoor storage closet when a cardboard box sitting right in the middle of the floor caught her attention. Her mind flashed back to when she had last been out there. She could not remember. She bent over to pick up the box. The nagging sensation tugged at her brain: that box!

Where had it come from? Suddenly, the pesky feeling transformed into cutting fact: it was from the care centre. Her mother's death house, as it were. She carried the box into the apartment and dropped it next to the front door.

Then, she went back to her list.

"What's all this?" asked Tom as Rachel walked through the front door of the first-floor apartment. He took the cardboard box — feather-light — and a fabric grocery bag — heavy as lead — from his sister's hands.

"The bag is food for Claire, stuff that I can't possibly eat alone before I leave. And the box is just a bunch of stuff we have to go through together," said Rachel as she kicked off her straw flip flops.

"Keep those on," said Tom under his breath.

As she stepped back into her flip flops, Rachel looked through the entryway and into the hallway, quickly sweeping her gaze over the floor of Claire and Robin's apartment. The orange-tinged hardwood floor was covered in multiple unidentifiable solids and liquids — mostly dry.

Unfortunate, she thought, looking around. It was a nice enough apartment, if you did not consider the junk, the furniture, or the décor. The building had been erected at the turn of the century, and had all of the exposed brick, wide windowsills, high ceilings, and nooks and crannies archetypally associated with such constructions. If only her artist sister were capable of keeping the place uncluttered and clean...

Claire's tanned face appeared in the entryway from behind the stained-glass inner door. She was wearing an off-white linen t-shirt dress adorned with a kaleidoscope of small paint splatters. "For me?" she asked as she extended her arms forward. She was by far the shortest of the siblings, and the darkest: a feminine, nymph-like version of her late father. She wore her dark hair in a short-banged bob, and her high cheekbones and little button nose projected an aura of childlike innocence.

An *enfant terrible* to the bone, Claire was anything but innocent.

"Stuff we have to go through," said Rachel. She leaned forward to hug her sister. It was an unfamiliar gesture. Claire accepted the sign of affection as though it were an everyday manifestation.

"Is it stuff to go through now, or after the party?" asked Claire.

"After," said Rachel. "The bag is for now, though," she said, taking the bag from the floor and handing it to Claire, who peeked inside. "It's a bunch of food, stuff I can't eat or bring with me to Myanmar. You'll have to be attentive about the best-before dates, some of it will be going bad soon."

Tom dropped the box in the room to the right of the entrance hall, which was Claire's atelier.

"We've set up the drinks and snacks on the back balcony," said Claire.

Rachel sighed. "I hope there is shade. The last thing I need is to get a huge sunburn three days before hopping onto a transatlantic flight. The reprocessed air already wreaks enough havoc on my skin..."

Most people who met Claire and Rachel were doubtful that the two could be biological siblings. Whereas Claire was dark, small, and plump, Rachel was light, tall, and slim. Only the people who had met both of their parents could understand the enigma. Claire had inherited the Rossi's Calabrian genes.

But Rachel... she was pure O'Connor. Rachel did not look like her mother: she was her exact replica. She had porcelain skin which burnt even from watching images of the sun on television. She had shoulder-length blonde hair which she often wore in a low bun. Her eyes were the colour of a brilliant sky in the middle of spring.

And yet, despite the obvious — and numerous — dissimilarities, if one were to look at a photo of the sisters in black and white, one could find something vaguely comparable between the two: the angle of the eyebrow bone, perhaps, or the profile of the nose, or, maybe, the shape of the eyes. Blink back into the world of colour, however, and all similarities would vanish, leaving one looking into a set of dark, playful, softly scintillating eyes, and a pair of light, logical, critical eyes that seldom saw value in anything further than hard scientific facts.

They made their way through the winding labyrinth which was Claire's apartment, first brushing past a section of wall covered in coats which were hung on hooks that extended halfway to the ceiling, then stepping over a faded, rolled-up carpet further down the hall leading to the kitchen, its brown, linoleum flooring awash in toast crumbs and abandoned grains of uncooked rice. The door at the back of the kitchen, next to the large walk-in pantry, was the point of access to the shabby-chic second-floor balcony. The large outdoor space had been fitted with a bright-green, faux-grass shag, its thick plastic bristles tickling their bare feet.

On the balcony were Robin, Zandra, and Shelley, with two-year-old Laci in her arms, chatting away on the wrought-iron patio set. Rachel was relieved to note that there was a large yellow parasol planted in the centre of the table, like a big sunflower straining to meet its maker.

Robin, seated facing the door, was the first to rise.

"Hi, Rachel!" she said, reaching over and giving her sister-in-law a hug. She was wearing a blue romper with small white flowers, and her wavy red hair was loose, a fiery mane framing her freckled face.

"Thanks for having everyone over here," said Rachel, smiling genuinely. "My place looks like a pigeon's nest right now..."

"I somehow doubt that," said Tom.

Zandra stood next, and went over to embrace Rachel.

"Congratulations, Rachel, I am so happy for you!" she declared in her charming Brazilian Portuguese accent. Zandra was tall and dark, and her eyes shone with passion and secrets. It was clear, despite her casually trying to disguise it behind a white flowing tunic, that Zandra was at the outset of expecting her second child.

The last to embrace Rachel was Shelley, her maternal grandmother, the decades-older mirror image of herself.

"Oh, Rachel," exclaimed Shelley, her hand on her chest, poised for her performance — for Shelley never spoke if not to give a performance. "How, how on earth, are we going to get on without you?"

Rachel held back the urge to say *just fine*, and instead smiled. Baby Laci squawked and put her hands out for her father, who took her into his arms.

"How are you doing, dear?" asked Shelley, moving closer to Rachel. "How are you *really* doing?"

She squinted, looking into Rachel's eyes, as though that would give her a better sight into Rachel's cerebellum.

"Pretty bu —"

"No," said Shelley, putting a palm up in protest. "On the inside... How do you *feel*?"

"I'm not sure what you're getting at..." said Rachel. The conversation, if it could be called as such, had already dragged on long enough to create an awkward silence on the sunny terrace.

Robin cleared her throat. "Drinks, anyone?" she asked.

Tom, Zandra, and Claire agreed. They went to the table and filled a few glasses with homemade lemonade, Laci waddling around behind them, playing with a yellow metal dump truck.

"I know what it is like to gallop about the world, looking for love, and happiness, and even self-acceptance. And let me tell you one thing, Rachel..."

She looked off into the distance, making eye contact with an inexistent camera. She waited for the camera to pan forward, framing her face.

"Just know, everything that you will become, everything that you want to become, you already are, Rachel. *You already are...*" she added in a mystical whisper.

Rachel frowned, nodded, and went to turn away.

"I also broke off my first engagement, you know," said Shelley, her hands clasping Rachel's bare shoulders. She simply could not let her foil walk away until her piece had been said in its entirety. "He was madly in love with me, but I... I was looking for something bigger. Something more meaningful. I was too young to be tacked in one spot. Too green."

"Adil is the one who broke off the engagement... He said something about irreconcilable differences..." said Rachel. Her voice was soft, low, and only barely bearing the inflections of regret. He was the most reliable and predictable person that she had ever met. When he knew what he wanted, he went for it. And when he changed his mind, there was no going back.

Rachel had been taken by Adil since they met. When she found out that he was in a serious relationship, she was both disappointed and enticed. The two began spending more and more time together, working on school projects, preparing presentations, and filling out paperwork for various grants. It was all innocent, as far as Rachel was concerned... Or so she told herself.

Then, out of the blue, Adil announced that he was single, and very quickly, he asked Rachel on a date. They saw each other every day, and quickly, Adil was introduced to the family. Caught in a candied cloud of delight, Rachel did not hesitate when Adil asked her to marry him.

After their engagement, they wined, they dined, they took weekend trips to precious little bed and breakfasts... Rachel wanted to take their relationship further. She was ready to move in together, but Adil refused. First, they had to be married, he said, and then they had to buy a place together. Never, ever, could he consider moving into a woman's home. Rachel had things that she wanted to achieve before getting married, but Adil was growing impatient.

In the end, it was his rigidity that spoiled everything.

"Oh, Rachel!" exclaimed Shelley, her voice at near crescendo.

Rachel was torn from her thoughts and back to the present. Shelley pulled her granddaughter into a hug, her palms open, tapping her sinewy back.

"*I had no idea!*"

Each word was spoken in a sentence of its own.

"Lemonade?" asked Tom from across the patio. "Extra rum?"

Rachel nodded and meant to break off the conversation for a second time, but her grandmother was not quite through with their talk.

"How did it happen, dear?" asked Shelley, her eyes turned into giant blue saucers. "I assumed that since you were leaving for the East..."

"*The East...*" repeated Tom, letting the Old World feel of it roll over his tongue. He handed a blue plastic cup to his sister, its outer wall drenched in condensation.

Rachel took a sip, grimaced slightly, then took another. She wiped her wet palm on her jean shorts.

"Shelley, if you must know, Adil didn't want me to leave for Myanmar. And he didn't want to accompany me, either. That was what broke it all off. He admitted that he was waiting for me to finish my current research, then to get married in a hurry, and you know the rest... He supported my studies, my career, but only until it got in the way. It boiled down to a timeline, a timeline that — apparently — will continue its countdown, whether or not my name is on the graph."

"Men!" exclaimed Shelley.

"Bittersweet, or bitter, or sweet?" asked Tom.

Rachel leaned back against the brick wall. "I had been preparing my files for Mandalay University since just before Mom died," she said.

"So, over a year, then..." said Tom. His gaze went inwards for a moment, thinking about how strange a feeling it was to talk so plainly about their mother's passing. When he returned to the present, a mere few seconds later, he noted that Shelley had mysteriously disappeared. "And... was Adil part of your plans, back then?" he asked.

"My plans included Adil, obviously... But when it became obvious that he wasn't coming, well... I was glad to see his veritable self before it was too late. One cancelled airplane ticket is hardly the tragedy of a lifetime."

"Cheers to that," said Tom, offering his own purple plastic cup to toast his sister. "Anyways, this going-away party, it isn't about court-martialling the past, is it?"

Rachel smiled. "Cheers again," she said with a sigh. "Now let's go sit in the shade before my skin begins to boil..."

As the handful of Rachel's closest friends trickled in, an awkward separation of family vs. social network was felt with increasing intensity. The situation was amended when the food began to be served.

The sun grew rounder and rounder until it became too heavy to be contained in the sky. As the sun sunk into its nighttime bed of feathery clouds, it left the air charged with heat.

Zandra was the first to leave the patio, taking Laci inside to wash up and go to sleep, exhausted and only too happy to join her daughter in bed. Shelley followed her out.

Robin lit candles, the lemon-scented ones she used to ward off the mosquitoes that had begun their own feast. Either the citronella burning was effective, or the alcohol levels in the victims' blood had become too elevated for the insects.

Hours melted into minutes, and minutes flowed into hours.

Much later, according to the clock, the last three of Rachel's friends were shuffling clumsily down the outdoor stairs and into their cab, shouting loudly about how they expected postcards and emails, and how they were certainly going to come visit their friend when they had the chance.

Rachel, who had accompanied them down to the car, closed the door softly.

Slightly buzzed from the day's sunshine — in the sky and in their veins — Rachel, Tom, Claire, and Robin went back inside. In a consensus that need not be said aloud, they turned right, walking solemnly into Claire's atelier.

Claire plugged in a set of yellow-white globe-shaped string lights that were hung at random intervals along the ceiling of her atelier. Everything in the room seemed to be in a half-finished state: aquarelle paintings teetering on wooden easels, pastel outlines in thick spiraled sketch pads, patchwork collages on heavy cardstock, pencil sketches on scrap bits of paper, mugs of coffee with almond milk and honey, grilled vegetable sandwiches, bowls of mildewy strawberries covered in sugar...

"Come, sit," said Claire as she moved a stack of magazines off the velvet olive-coloured loveseat. Rachel and Tom took their places as Claire put the box at their feet. Robin stood in the doorway of the room, her long orange hair blazing in the dim light.

"*Edwina's No-Rinse Moisturising Body Wash*," read Claire as she sat, folding her legs over a Japanese-style straw-woven cushion. "Chic."

The three siblings looked at each other, absorbing the significance of the moment, not knowing what to do next. Or what to say next. If anything.

It was Robin who broke the silence. "If you don't need me, I'll be off to bed now. I'll leave you all to it," she said. She walked into the room, stooped down, and planted a soft kiss on Claire's forehead, and then was off.

The room was silent again, save for the sound of the shower running in the bathroom, and the buzz of a frantic housefly bumbling about on the windowsill.

"You should open it, Tom," said Claire.

"Why me?"

"You were always Mom's favourite child," she answered. "Her only boy."

Tom smiled sadly.

"I'm pretty sure you were her favourite, Claire," said Rachel.

Tom nodded in agreement.

"I don't want to..." said Claire. Her voice shook. Her chin shook. She felt sad, vulnerable, and suddenly, very cold. She folded her legs up against her chest, pulling down the hem of her t-shirt dress, cradling her knees.

"I'll do it," said Rachel after a few moments of silence. "Can I?"

Her brother and sister nodded in agreement.

Rachel put two fingers from each hand into the small space in the middle of the flaps and gently coaxed them upwards. The cardboard unfolded itself with little resistance. The flaps were warm, malleable, humid.

She peered inside and pulled out a dead houseplant. "Can you grab a garbage bag or something?" asked Rachel.

A muscle in Tom's neck tensed.

"Let's just empty the box and then decide what to do with the stuff," said Claire, reaching for the thin plastic pot. The dried leaves crumbled as Claire set the plant on the flat lid of the steamer trunk to her right.

Rachel reached back into the box and pulled out a sweater that looked ruby-red in the dim light. She held it up. It seemed so big. "Was this really hers?" she asked. "I just can't imagine it."

Claire reached for the sweater. It was itchy and caught on her gnawed cuticles and torn fingernails. She found herself hoping that her mother had not worn such an uncomfortable sweater.

Rachel rummaged around in the box and pulled up more clothing: three pairs of dark-coloured pants. Claire took those and added them to the small pile.

"Anything else?" asked Tom.

Rachel reached in and grabbed something small. Something that fit into the palm of her hand. Metallic. Square.

"What is it?" asked Tom.

Rachel brought the container closer to her eyes. "I can't read it," she said finally. "It's written in Chinese characters, or something."

She pulled at the square lid with her fingernail. It popped open, and if by magic, the room was filled with the smell of jasmine flowers and chestnuts.

"Tea," said Claire with a sad smile. The building nostalgia stung her heart.

Rachel pulled out four more tins of various size and colour.

"That's it," said Rachel as she tipped over the box for dramatic effect. To her surprise, out fell a thick notebook. She picked it up from the floor, turning it over in her hands.

"What's it?" asked Tom with bated breath.

Rachel cracked the cover open and flipped through the pages.

"A journal," she concluded. "Should we burn it?"

"*Rachel*!" exclaimed Claire. "Why would you even say that?"

Rachel turned to her sister, irritation etched upon the creases in her forehead. "This is a private journal, Claire. We have no business reading it."

"I wonder what she would want..." whispered Tom. "That is what we have to figure out, right? What Mom would want?"

"She would *absolutely not* want us to read this," declared Rachel. "No way. These are her private thoughts. She was always so cagey... We have to get rid of it... There is no way that she would want us to read it."

Tom agreed with Rachel.

"Well, that is all fine and whatever, but I won't let you do it." Claire stood up in front of Rachel, extending her hand. "Give it to me. I want it." She thought back on the immaterial quality of those days when her mother had first been diagnosed. Although initially, it was hard to digest, after the passing of a few days, or no more than a week, the A-word was forgotten all together. Life had shrugged back into its normal coat, and her mother's absent-mindedness was again viewed as simple inattention, the affliction of a person with too many daily distractions and preoccupations. Claire had no idea the degree to which the disease was already gnawing its snaggy teeth on her mother's brain.

"Okay," said Rachel, relinquishing the journal to her sister. "You don't have to get upset about it."

"I don't know..." said Tom quietly. "I think that Rachel is right. Mom wouldn't want you to read it, Claire."

"How could you know what she would want?" asked Claire. "Maybe she would want this to be her legacy."

"Unlikely," exclaimed Tom, sounding like a toddler no older than his daughter. "There is no way we should be reading that!"

"Mom and I talked a lot that year, you know, the year before we put her in that home, Tom." He and Rachel looked up at Claire, suddenly very quiet. "I think that I know why she started writing the journal. So... I want to read it." Claire flipped through the pages absentmindedly. "In fact, I'm sure she would want us all to read it."

"It's not like she would know either way," said Rachel.

"Rachel..." grumbled Tom. "You always know just what to say. And anyways... I thought you agreed that we need to get rid of it?"

"I changed my mind. She's dead, Tom! What does it matter, in the end? If Claire wants to read it, if it will bring her some comfort, well, let's let her read it."

"It won't hurt anyone if I keep it," said Claire.

"Will you just keep it, or read it?" asked Tom.

Claire snorted. "I don't know!" she shouted, a little more loudly than she had anticipated. "I have to think about it."

"I have to go to bed," said Rachel, looking at her watch. "It is almost three o'clock in the morning." She stood and stretched her arms above her head. "I'm calling myself a cab. You enjoy the rest of your evening, kids..."

"If Claire is going to read it, then we all should read it too," declared Tom.

"Pass it on to Tom when you're done, then," said Rachel. She pushed her hands against the small of her back, arching her body forward. "I'll read it when I come home for the holidays."

"No!" said Tom, abruptly pulling Rachel out of her stretch. "We need to read it together."

"Like... holding hands, or sitting in each other's lap?" asked Rachel, the incorrigible cynic.

"What if we just read a few pages now, and see how we feel about it?" asked Claire. "Aren't you the slightest bit curious?" She flipped through the pages, lifting the journal to her nose and breathing in the musky paper odour.

Rachel sat back down on the couch, followed by Tom. "Frankly, I'd rather not know what's in there..." she said. "Mom had a lot of skeletons in her closet. The less bones I see, the better off I am..."

Tom nodded in agreement. "Not to mention the deterioration."

This time it was Rachel who agreed with her brother. "It would be kind of perverse, wouldn't it?" she asked. "We read her journal and watch as her brain slowly corrodes, as she unlearns how to write in the English language... Her second childishness, *sans everything...* That's fucking miserable."

"We can see it in two different ways though, can't we?" asked Claire. "What if, instead, we read the journal from the perspective of revisiting Mom's last words, her final thoughts... Tasting the bitter, we can't help that, but especially savouring the sweet?"

Tom shrugged. "I still don't want to do this. But if you do, then we need to do it together."

"Rachel?" asked Claire. "Your vote breaks the tie."

PART II

January 1, 2016

The first time that I realised that something was off was when I lost my keys. It was a few months after Elvis's death. It is not that losing my keys was exceptional, that happened often enough. What is strange is where I found them.

My keys were in the oven. The oven was off, thank goodness. The blessing, of course, was that I had also forgotten to turn on the oven.

Then I remembered having gone outside.

I trudged to the car being sure to step in my very fresh, slipper-made footprints. It was cold, and I was wearing only a thin nightdress.

There it was, on the driver's seat. My potato casserole. I grabbed for the door handle, but it was locked.

"Where the hell are my keys?"

It struck me. They were still in the oven.

Coming back outside (for what was the... third time?), I was intercepted by my neighbour, May. May is a sweet girl who has lived across the street from us for as long as I can remember. Her parents had her when they were older, so when she turned 30, they gave her their house and went off to their home in sunny Florida. May was also Claire's first serious relationship.

"Nina?" she came closer. "Nina, aren't you cold?" She stood there at the bottom of my driveway wearing a long t-shirt and leggings. And fluffy, pink boots.

"No more or less than you are, I suppose."

"It is October. There is snow on the ground... You should be wearing a coat."

"I don't see how wearing a coat would change the fact that there is snow on the ground." I fiddled with my keys, but had trouble finding the right one in the dark.

"Nina, do you want me to call Claire? Or is Thomas is town? Or should I call Rachel?"

"That won't be necessary! It's just that I forgot my potato casserole in the front seat. I'll be right back inside when I grab it. Don't you worry about me," I said.

She looked at me strangely, nodded, then backed away.

So the first big 'event' was this one, back in October or so.

As it turns out, May did call Thomas... and Rachel, and Claire too.

The diagnosis happened pretty quickly after that. Rachel came over two days later, putting on her *how-I-hate-to-have-to-mother-my-mother* airs. She tried to be forceful, which of course, did not work. She stood in the doorway to the living room, her hands on her hips. She was tall and graceful, like a ballerina, her blond hair pulled in a tight bun. She was beautiful — stunning even, with the brightest blue eyes — but she always looked so cross that most people probably did not even notice her looks. I never understood where she got her attitude of extreme arrogance... At times, she irritated me to an extent that I could not put words.

"Rachel, I'm 66, which makes me damn well old enough to decide whether I want to see a doctor or not."

She threw her hands into the air. "Mother, this isn't about what *you* want!"

"It is time for you to go now, Rachel. I am expected at Harvey's place."

"Harvey?" she asked.

"Take it easy, Rachel. Yes, Harvey. Our neighbour. My friend."

"Dad just died and —"

"And he would be happy to know that I don't sit at home all day and wallow in self-pity. Goodbye, Rachel. I'll see you next Tuesday."

The next day, Thomas came. He drove straight to Montreal from

Ottawa, even though is girlfriend was eight and a half months pregnant. He put on his airs too.

"Mom, Rachel said that —"

"Since when do you care what Rachel says?" I was standing in the kitchen making myself a cup of tea. I put the kettle on the stove and went to sit with Tom at the wooden table. I felt silly for keeping all six chairs, when most day I sat alone, but I could not bring myself to put them into storage. It reminded me of the precious times we spent together as a family. I had always struggled to keep my house from looking like children lived there: toys in the bedroom only, no silly plastic cups or plates... And for what? I sighed.

"What is it, Mom?" He may have been a grown man, but he was still as sensitive as when he was a small boy, much more emotional than his sisters.

"I was remembering when you all were little," I said. I smiled. Tom reached for my hand. At 37, he was a handsome young man with his father's dark skin, but tall like me. Like Rachel, he had my light eyes.

"Mom... It is perfectly normal that there comes a time when people... Older people... Should not live alone. It's not like we'd send you to a hospice... It is a home for cool, retired, funky —"

"You had me at funky. No, really. I'll get in line first thing in the morning. Now go home, Tom. Zandra needs you. Laci could be born at any moment."

The kettle went off.

"Mom, I wished that I lived closer... I am always so worried about you. When May called, I just didn't know what to do..."

"I am fine, Thomas. Really. And you don't need to live in Montreal. Rachel and Claire live here. And anyways... I don't need my children to babysit me. So I got a bit mixed up with my keys... It's not like I did anyone any harm!"

"No, but you could have..."

"Tell me that you have never forgotten something in the car? Come on, Tom. Haven't we all?" I said.

He nodded, shrugged, but physically, he did not change his mind.

We made some small talk, and he left not long after having arrived.

Claire strolled in Sunday morning.

"Mom, I have the worst hangover. Can I make myself some waffles?"

"At 29, you are too old to be hungover every weekend, Claire. Don't you have a career?"

"Mother," she said, raising her eyebrow at me. "I am a painter. I must sell my art. And where is art sold? In art galleries. And what do they serve in art galleries? Expensive champagne. And how much do I have to pay for this expensive champagne? Nothing. It is the only advantage to being an artist. Now waffles. You want any?"

"Yes. The chocolate chips are in the pantry in the soda cracker box. Let me get them..."

Claire shifted her eyes suspiciously. Of all the children, she was the only one who really looked like Elvis: dark eyes, dark hair, short, compact.

"Mom?"

"What? I have to hide them there. You know Rachel. If she knew I still permit myself the odd chocolate chip, she would bitch about it from kingdom to high water..."

"From what?" asked Claire.

"That expression, you know... Forever. She's a control freak."

"Kingdom come? From hell or high water? Neither of those mean that, Mom..."

I grabbed the bag of chocolate chips from the box of soda crackers and threw them at Claire's face. She ducked.

"Mom! You almost hit me in the face! What the hell!"

"Claire, you complain a lot for someone who *isn't* making chocolate-chip waffles. I'm going to take a shower."

When I returned, Claire had made an exceptional mess of my kitchen. Over half of the light granite countertop was covered in batter... But there were waffles, so not all was lost.

I sat down at the table. "Claire," I said. "Sweetheart, I know what you're here."

She raised a studded eyebrow at me and served each of us a waffle. Mine appeared to be raw in the centre.

"I'm only 66," I whispered. "Isn't that too young for... Alzheimer's?"

She let her fork fall. It clattered onto her plate.

"Rachel called me. You're right, she's a bitch. But she was worried. And Tom is worried. And I'm worried too, Mom. I know that some stuff has been... Kind of sliding lately. I'd just like for you to get checked out. That's all. See your doctor, see what she has to say, then we figure things out. I want you to be safe. Other than that, fuck Rachel. Totally."

"You shouldn't talk about your sister like that," I said. I pulled at a chuck of cooked waffle. "So I see my doctor, get whatever tests done, then you all leave me alone?"

"Yes. We're just worried about you, Mom. Thomas wants you around for Laci's high school graduation. Rachel wants you to watch her become more and more miserable as she slowly educates herself to death. I want you to help me plan my wedding. We love you, Mom. All you have to do is see Dr. Lee and follow her advice."

"When is your wedding again?" I asked.

"Valentine's Day, 2018, Mom. I wrote it on the chalkboard near the phone, Remember?" She pointed to the wall next to my phone.

A few weeks ago, she came over with chalkboard paint and did some redecorating. Her wedding, their birthdays, emergency phone numbers...

"Why are you waiting until 2018? Why would you want such a long engagement?" I asked.

"Because I'm poor and cannot afford it any time soon. And Robin is still in school. And... Did I mention I'm a painter?"

I followed through with my promise to Claire.

The diagnosis process was pretty quick after that.

Dr. Lee called me into her office.

"Okay, I can see why your children would be concerned. Tell me about your patterns of forgetting things. Go back as far as you can remember. But before you do, I am going to give you a series of words. You must remember them, in order, if possible. *Berry. Sand. Triangle. Rabbit. Seventeen. Maple. Fork.* Okay? Now tell me about your forgetfulness."

I told her. She asked me about the series of words. I had forgotten five.

"Okay, Mrs. O'Connor. I'm going to give you this referral for an MRI. Just to make sure that all of the nuts and bolts are in place, you know? Just take it to the clinic in the B wing. You give them the paper, they call you back in two or three months. I'll get a nurse to take you."

"That won't be necessary," I said.

"I insist!" said Dr. Lee. "The nurse would be glad to help —"

"No. I mean I have health insurance. I'll go to a private clinic and have the results sent here."

I called Claire from the car. I was just sitting there, in the hospital parking lot, with the fateful paper on my lap.

"How did it go, Mom?"

I looked down at the paper, but my focus was off because it was hard to see through my tears.

"Mom?" asked Claire.

I read her the information which had been printed onto a tiny square of paper:

PATIENT: NINA W O'CONNOR

MRI - brain

RE: Alzheimer's disease

"I'm so sorry, Mom," said Claire after some time. "But is it a sure thing? How can Dr. Lee know for sure?"

"She doesn't. There are just a few hints at it... We'll know more after the MRI."

There was silence on the other end of the line.

We'll see, Claire. One step at a time. My MRI is tomorrow at nine."

"Which hospital are you going to?"

I explained to her that I had made the decision to go to the private clinic. We chatted, but not for long, and then we hung up. I drove home.

Claire was waiting for me in front of the clinic the next morning.

"White tea?" she asked, extending me a paper cup.

"Thanks Claire. You can go home now. It makes no sense for you to waste your time here, already I have to be here and waste mine."

"It was either me or Rachel. Now shut it and march."

I took the cup from her hand and went into the clinic, barely opening the door so that it closed in her face.

"Funny," she said as she joined me at the receptionist's desk. "I see what you did there, letting the door close in my face. Real mature."

For those of you who are on a waiting list for an MRI, I don't suggest you look into it. Bottom line, you're stuck in a giant — on the outside, but tiny on the inside — tube for the longest 45 minutes of your life. And even though the technicians can see everything, they won't say a word about the scan.

By the end of the week, I had my diagnosis. Alzheimer's disease. Mild cognitive decline. Those are scary words.

I spoke to the psychologist who I had been seeing since Elvis's death.

"I am so sorry to hear that," he said, leaning back into his leather chair on wheels. "The early stages of dementia can be subtle, so it is good that you have caught it right away. I am glad that you're being followed by the right specialists now."

Alzheimer's is a scary word, but *dementia* is plain ugly.

"Here are some pamphlets and other documents," he continued, not missing a beat. "You will want to share the information with your children."

I shrugged, taking the papers and stuffing them into my oversized handbag.

"Are you planning on continuing to live on your own?" he asked.

"Yes. Of course."

"In that case, I have a few suggestions for you."

The psychologist gave me lots advice, especially about writing stuff down, since he was convinced that my memory of recent events was already decreasing. Make grocery lists. Order a daily paper to create a healthy routine and to be sure I know the date. Write everything on a calendar. Keep a journal. At the time, I just was not ready to write about my experience...

So here I am, January 1, 2016 — about six months after my initial diagnosis. I have finally found the courage to write.

I don't know how I will like this, writing about my life. But I have always liked writing. I guess it will be fine, as soon as it becomes part of my routine.

What's the harm, anyways? No one will ever be bothered.

January 6, 2016

When Elvis died, I thought that I would die too. I had no reason to believe that, I just did.

I had always told Elvis that if he died before me, I would cash in for a new, younger, sexier model. He knew that he was advised to do the same.

I met Elvis when I was 28. He was 30.

I had built a career for myself as a real-estate agent. I was proud of myself, proud of my small, designer home, proud of my exotic vacations every January. I had no wifely ambitions, no motherly ones either.

Truth be told, Elvis was one of my clients. I should say that he and *his wife* were my clients.

They were shopping for a two story house and were open as to its location, so long as it was on the island and near public transit.

I showed them a few properties, but honestly, I did not have much hope. There were not the types of places that young couples were interested in. Too much work required. Elvis called me that night.

"Hello, this is Nina O'Connor."

"Hi, Elvis speaking..." he said. "Are you busy?"

"Is this regarding business, or pleasure?"

We started a friendship, which blossomed into an infatuation, which matured into a genuine romance, which eventually became a serious relationship.

"Elvis, either you leave her or I go. And by the way. I'm pregnant."

I had just turned 29. I never thought that I would have children, and there I was, a mistress *and* with child.

Elvis probably lied to her — he never had the nerve to displease anyone — but either way, he had the divorce papers signed and approved before my third trimester began.

When I met him, Elvis was a short, chunky, dark, balding Italian Quebecer. When he died, he was a short, fat, bald Italian Quebecer. Elvis was always known for his consistence.

We had 36 turbulent but sweet years together as a married couple. Then he died of a heart attack in our bedroom on a Sunday morning in July of 2015.

It was about a quarter to eight in the morning. We were both in bed. I was reading a magazine and Elvis was asleep. I felt him stir.

"Nina?" he whispered.

I looked over at him from above my glasses.

"I don't feel well. My stomach hurts. And not like usual..."

He was pale and sweating. Under regular circumstances, I would have told him to quit whining, that of course his stomach hurt, with the amount of eating and drinking that he did... But that morning I sensed in my heart that he was not well.

"Elvis!" I grabbed his hand. It was trembling. I let go and ran for the phone in the sitting room. I do not regret much in my life, but I do regret that one choice.

When I returned to the bedroom with the cordless phone, talking to the 911 operator, Elvis was very still. My heart tore in two. I did not need to check his pulse. After 36 years, one does not need a physical sign to prove death. I had let him go gentle into that good night all alone. His last memory of me was seeing me walk away from him, of me turning my back on him. I hated myself.

His funeral was modest. His family — i.e., his mother — had wanted to give him a ridiculous opulent Catholic eyesore of a funeral. I refused. The whole family was more than welcome to be there, but if they came, it would be on my terms.

Elvis and I had bought one of the houses that we had visited when he was married to his first wife. It was a fixer upper, but one that called more for style enhancements than for any serious plumbing or structural work.

The kitchen had to be done first, as it was the room which was most important to me and to Elvis. We had one wall taken down, the one between the kitchen and the dining room. What a difference that made! We pulled up the tile ourselves and put down some white, blue, and green Moroccan tiles with bold designs. We called in a team to take care of the cabinets and had light granite countertops put in. The walls — which had been yellowed by the original owners from abusive amounts of cigarette smoke — we painted white. Almost four decades later, the kitchen is the room which underwent the least amount of change. The other room which has stayed the same throughout the years — and the one that took the longest to create — was the master bedroom.

I designed everything in our room around one central theme: an Italian nautical outing. I stayed away from the tacky buoy, the glass balls, the thick rope accents, the big brass ship wheel, the anchor... The inspiration which came to me was far more subtle, just of a hint for the colours (off-white and navy, a few pastels) the textures (thick canvas-like material, metals, wood) and the patterns (organic and flowing, bold stripes).

When I lived alone, before Elvis, I had gotten into the habit of changing all of the linens at least once a year, which included the bed, the rugs and the curtains. It just made me feel so... current. Fresh. It all quite horrified Elvis, who was raised in a rather poor home in rural southern Italy.

"Leave it alone, Nina! I like what I like," he would say, grumpily.

"Okay." I turned the page of my design magazine. "But do you like this?" I would ask, showing him another picture.

"No!" he would shout, without even looking. "It is a waste of money, and you know that it takes me too long to get used to new things. Just leave it alone, will you, Nina!"

The other upstairs rooms changed, of course, as the children were born. Elvis had wanted a study, as he planned on going back to school to train as a chef: that room was first to go, when Rachel arrived. He never was accepted into the program. After, we made the last spare room into a home gym, because Elvis wanted to get buff to join the fire department. That did not happen either, and the room was quickly transformed into a big boy room for Tom, so that newborn Claire could sleep in the nursery.

The living room had been left by the former owners as a wall-papered calamity. The first layer was a beige and pink floral print and the wall underneath was a burnt-caramel. After days of scratching, we finally had removed the wallpaper and were ready to paint. We were going with a baby blue colour, which was very *en vogue* at the time. Even with primer, it was terribly difficult to cover the orange walls. After a few coats that looked more like vomit that cotton candy blue, we finally gave up and wallpapered the whole thing in a white-beige-bright-green-palm-tree pattern. Since then, it has been changed multiple times. Most recently, we had a team of professionals come in and paint the whole thing white. The living room furniture was all imported from Madagascar, through a connection that I had made with work. We reupholstered the cushions a few times, but the furniture is still the same today as when we first brought Tom home, swaddled in a tiny car seat.

All three of our children had grown up in that home. So when Elvis died, there was no question in my mind.

"Today," I said as I stood before the small group at the funeral home once the short ceremony was over, "I take my husband home with me." I held up an opaque glass urn full of ashes. "Elvis loved our home, he died in our home, and now I will return him there."

I had bought a Japanese lilac tree to plant in the backyard. When a Japanese lilac tree is in full bloom, in the early summer, it looks like it is covered in snow. Elvis loved the snow. Thomas, Rachel, Claire, and I dug the hole for the tree ourselves. It took an entire exhausting morning. It was a hot and humid day, typical of a July in Montreal.

Once the hole was big enough, we stopped to say a few words and to empty out the ashes.

"Thank you dad, for making me the man I am today," said Thomas. His face was streaming with tears. He was still wearing his black suit pants from the funeral and his white button-up shirt was rolled up and soaked with sweat. "You were a man who loved with your whole heart and who had a serious sense of humour. And who had the most ridiculous hairy chest. My friends always made fun of your gold chain necklace. And you would always laugh too. You never took life too seriously. I don't know that I remember seeing your face without a smile on it." He took the glass urn, unscrewed the lid, and poured about a quarter of the ashes into the hole.

Claire spoke next. "I will miss you too, dad. And your smile. But I know that Elvis has only left the building... You'll be back. You have to. A spirit like yours doesn't die... It can't. Until then, please do not rest in peace. It is not your style." She blew her nose into a dirty tissue. Her dark skin was covered in beads of perspiration and smudges of dirt. She took the urn, poured out another quarter, then placed in on the ground at Rachel's feet.

"Dad." Rachel cleared her throat, wiped her hands on her gardening apron, then took out a small square of paper from her pocket. "You taught me the value of a good smile and a well-placed lie. You taught me that any mistake I make doesn't matter, so long as I learn from it. You taught me how important it is to start a project and stick to it. I miss you already, it is digging a hole in my chest. But you live on in our hearts. So long as we are here, you are here too." She folded her paper and put it back into the pocket of her dress pants. She put her gardening gloves back on, then picked up the urn, poured out some ashes, and handed it to me.

"My Elvis," I said, choking back a sob. I was not used to crying in front of my children: Elvis had always been the more sensitive one. "Elvis. My best friend. I am only sorry that you had to go alone." I was having trouble speaking. I looked at our three children, all crying, all watching me, worried about me. I cleared my throat. "I am sorry I walked away... I know it is silly. I know that you're gone, that you can't hear me, that your energy is slowly becoming something new... But I need to say it. I wish I had stayed in bed with you that morning. I wish I had held you in my arms and accompanied you as your life slowly flickered out. You did not deserve to be all alone." Breathe. Air in, air out. "I miss you, Elvis. I am lost without you. I don't know how I will cope, and this part of my life is only just beginning. I miss you so much already..."

Thomas reached over to me, but I moved aside. I needed to finish. I needed to stand alone. No matter who we are or what kind of life we lead, we are always alone in the end.

"Being with you was not always easy," I continued. "But who cares about easy? Easy is boring. And you were worth the trouble. You threw my world upside-down when you came into it... I should have known that you would do the same upon your exit. I should have loved you better at the start."

I poured the rest of his ashes into the pit. The tree was lying on its side near the hole.

"Why did you choose a Japanese lilac tree?" asked Rachel.

"Because it will help bring up the value of the house," I said.

She gave me a sharp disapproving look.

"I'm kidding. Your father always wanted to go to Japan. It was our retirement plan. So..." I felt my eyes sting.

"Do you think that his DNA will become one with the tree?" asked Claire.

"Shut up, you idiot," said Rachel.

We struggled to get the tree upright. Tom, the tallest in the family, held it in place and the girls and I shoveled the dirt back. The day was becoming ever more sweltering, but the physical activity felt good. It was numbing.

The tree was upright and stable. We looked at it in silence. It was beautiful. The air smelled of dirt and lilacs. Of new beginnings. Of the slow process towards moving on...

"Let's go inside," I said. "There is food in the fridge left from the service. And I bought beer."

We went into the house through the solarium. Entirely walled with windows and filled with plants, the solarium was my favourite place in the house. Elvis and I used sit there in our big rattan chairs for hours, reading and dozing off... It was the newest addition to the home, *our* home, the final renovation that we undertook before I had planned on retiring.

I kicked off my shoes on the kitchen carpet, then went to the refrigerator.

"Aren't we a little messy to be walking through the house?" asked Rachel from behind me. She took of her shoes, then her gloves and apron, folding it and placing it neatly on the carpet.

"I don't care, dear." I grabbed four beer bottles and went into the living room. The air conditioning felt terribly nice.

"Do you mind if Zandra swings by now?" asked Thomas. He was sitting on the floor next to the couch, beer in one hand, bottle opener in the other. He was filthy.

Zandra, a giant Brazilian Glamazon, arrived about an hour later.

"So, does anyone have any good news to share?" asked Thomas. We were all sitting in the living room, finishing up the sandwiches that had been left over from the funeral. You know the kind, cut into neat triangles and arranged with cherry tomatoes and parsley. The bread had already started to become rigid.

"I have some good news," said Rachel. She was sitting on the leather footrest, determined not to dirty the cream-coloured couch. She sat up even straighter than usual. "I will be taking another seminar in the fall. It is about the biology of calcified tissue."

"Don't you already have a PhD?" asked Thomas.

"Hence the *postdoctoral* seminar!" said Rachel, rolling her eyes. I swear, if it were not for her attitude, she would be an absolute catch.

"What about you, Thomas?" asked Zandra with her thick Portuguese accent. "Something you would like to share?"

We all looked at him expectantly.

"Zandra is pregnant. Mom, you will be a grandmother in January!"

I looked at him, entirely shocked. I could not muster a smile. I was not ready to take such a huge step without Elvis. It was too soon. I wished he had not said anything. Not yet.

The silence dragged on. All eyes were on me.

"Aren't you happy?" asked Thomas, his voice reverted to that of a little boy.

I began to cry and left the room. I locked myself in the bathroom. The kids had the common decency not to come knock.

January 9, 2016

It took me much longer to warm up to being a grandmother than I had anticipated. I am not a monster. I had not wanted kids, but as it turned out, my children made me incredibly proud. They surprised me with their humour and intelligence. Their hopes and dreams became mine too. Well, I had not wanted to become a grandmother either. Not really. And certainly not alone.

I was dusting the massive wood bookcase in the living room when the phone rang.

"Hello?"

"Hi Mom, how are you?"

"I'm alright, Tom," I said. I could tell from his voice that something was off. "Thanks for calling. How are you?"

"I'm okay. I wanted to talk to you about what happened last week..."

"What do you mean?" I asked, sitting down on the cough. "About your father's death?"

"Indirectly. Listen, I just wanted to talk about the baby."

My stomach fell.

"Okay, Tom. What do you want to talk about?"

He was crying into the phone.

"Aren't you happy for us, Mom?" he asked, his voice small and frail.

"Well of course, Tom. Of course I'm happy. You and Zandra will make wonderful parents."

"Mom," he said. He caught his breath. "Mom, I hope you are. I didn't mean to offend you when we told you. We were sitting around together, drinking and eating. The funeral was over. We really thought that it would lighten the atmosphere..."

"I know, Tom. Like I said. It is good news." I felt terrible. "I just didn't know how to react."

"I know. I don't know what I expected from you. It's just... She'll be your first grandchild. It is a special moment. We were excited to share it with you."

"A girl?" I asked. "That is lovely, Tom."

"Yeah. We're going to call her Laci."

"That is a pretty name."

"Mom, you sound out of it. Are you okay?"

I could feel my frustration building. Of course I wasn't okay. I was only 65. I was partially retired, almost entirely retired, and I was going to travel the world with my husband. Then we were going to waste the next 20 years of our lives just being together. Just the two of us. Our hard work would finally pay off. And then in one instant, that plan went to hell. I was allowed to be angry. I was allowed to be disinterested in all other human life. I had just lost my husband of 36 years.

"Mom?"

"I've got to go now, Thomas. Give Zandra my love."

"I know that you lost your husband," said Tom, as though he were reading my mind. "Well, I lost my father. He wasn't supposed to die. He will never know what it is to be a grandparent. I am scared to become a dad without him being here to teach me how. I'm sad too, Mom, but I am trying to move on."

It hurt me. I did not want to move on. I did not want any of this.

"I'm sorry, Thomas. I am feeling a little selfish right now. Can you understand that?" I was speaking a little too loudly. I took a deep breath. "I am drifting along, all alone, in this sea of the world. I have organised the last 36 years of my life around this one person, and one day, he is gone. Just like that."

"I'm sorry, Mom."

"We didn't always get along. We had our issues, Tom. There were times when I hated him as much as I loved him. But I *loved* him. So much. And until you have to start talking about your best friend in the past tense... You just can't possibly understand. I loved him so much, Tom. But it turns out I miss him even more. I didn't think that my heart had the capacity for such sadness."

"For the record, Mom, I am 37 and fatherless. For what it's worth, I am dealing with this pain too. It is not the same as yours, but it is real. I am sorry. I wish there was something more I could do. Something to make it hurt less. Mom..." His voice broke. "I would take all of the pain from your heart and bury it in mine if I could. I hate to see you so... so damaged."

Damaged. Apt expression.

"That is not your job, Tom. I'm sorry. I should be consoling you. This is a tough time for you too."

"We lost two babies in the last three years."

"What?" I was confused by the sudden change of subject.

"Zandra and I. We lost two. 10 weeks, then eight weeks."

"Why didn't you tell me?" My stomach fell. I felt hot. "I am so sorry."

"So this time... We're nervous, Mom. 13 weeks, 3 days. We count the days. Because each day counts. Each day our baby girl is stronger and stronger. Each day we believe in her a little more. She's the size of an egg now. She can almost breathe on her own... We're excited. But we're also afraid, Mom. Because what if we love her too much? What if she leaves us too? There are no guarantees, even now!"

Silence.

"All I wanted to say is that there is suffering all around us, Mom." His tone was sharp. He was angry. "People live their own personal tragedies every single day. That doesn't mean you can't be happy when something good happens to other people. Or at least seem happy. Pretend if it's not real... For their sake. Dammit, Mom. Feel how you want. But you don't have to be so fucking insensitive."

January 13, 2016

POEM: (BEING DIAGNOSED WITH A TERMINAL ILLNESS)

Everyone knows they are going to die.
Without death, what sense is there to life?
The only difference is that I know what will take me.
Unless I get hit by a bus.
But then, so could you.

January 16, 2016

Something unsettling happened today. I was scared. I'm just glad to be home now.

I sat down in my car. I was at the grocery store. I had gone in for something, but had forgotten what that thing was because I had put the list in the pocket of my other coat...

So I walked around the aisles, aimlessly, for too long. A young lady employee came over to me and asked if I needed assistance.

"No, thank you. I am just trying to remember what I needed."

"Okay, let me know if I can get you anything..." she said.

I was frustrated with myself. I can have all of the best intentions in the world, but if I cannot keep myself organized... It was so cold in the store, the airconditioning was cranked too high, especially for January!

So I got back into the car. I felt like a moron. I sat there. I cried in anger.

I decided that I wanted to go home. I looked at the steering wheel, at my feet on the pedals... But for the life of me, I could not remember what I needed to do to turn on the engine. I was confused. Discouraged. I felt tired.

A car pulled in next to me and a lady go out. I saw the keys in her hand. That was the lightbulb that I need.

I looked through my bag for my keys, but could not find them. I looked in my coat pockets. In the console between the seats. My eyes rolled forward... My key. I had gone as far are to put my key in the ignition. I turned the key and the car turned on, the fan blowing out cold air noisily, the radio droning and scratchy.

"Why doesn't the heater work anymore?"

I drove home without a problem, as though I were on autopilot. I took my keys and let myself into my house.

When I walked into the kitchen, I stopped in my tracks.

"Are you okay, Mom?" asked Claire. "Did you get the flour for Rachel's cake?"

Flour. Chocolate cake. Rachel's birthday.

"You were gone for all of that time, but you forgot to get the flour?" she asked.

I nodded.

"Let me make you some tea, Mom." She tried to veil the worry in her voice, but failed. She grabbed the kettle, filled it with water and put it on the stove. The whole time, I could feel her looking at me from the corner of her eye, watching me, analyzing me, evaluating...

"Don't you have a neighbour who can lend you a cup of flour, mom? It may be simpler than going back out."

"Ask May," I said. "She'll be glad to help."

January 13

Yesterday was Claire's birthday. We celebrated it at her apartment. She had a bunch of her school friends over. Claire and I brought her the cake that we had made together the night before.

"Hi Mom, hi Claire," said Rachel as she greeted us at the door. "Thanks for coming."

We took off our shoes and walked into the small apartment. It smelled like cooking, but not any scent of food that I recognized.

"You can put your coats on the bed," said Rachel.

We did. Rachel's bedroom was a perfect mirror of Rachel as a person: neat, tidy, void of emotion. It looked like a hotel room, mostly white with stainless-steel accents. Like a hotel room, or like a hospital room?

"So, Mrs. O'Connor, how are you doing?" asked one of Rachel's friends. He was tall, thin, and dark. He reminded me of an Arabian prince.

"I am well, thank you."

"You remember Adil, right Mom?" asked Claire.

"No," I said. "I don't think we've met."

"We saw each other at Rachel's MA graduation ceremony," said Adil. "But there were so many people. And I was wearing a cap and gown myself..." he said. "Anyways, with how much you and Rachel look alike, I would have known that you are her mother even without an introduction."

"Who's hungry?" asked Rachel as she came through the separation between the small kitchen and the rest of her open-air living space. A general grunt came from the dozen people standing about.

Rachel brought out a platter of vegetables, nuts, and some grey dips of an origin unknown.

The conversation revolved mostly around scientific university gibberish, grants, and internships.

We sat down at the table. The meal which followed consisted of waxy round beans that you have to squeeze right from the pod, salad rolled into a papery covering, and soup with a broth that vaguely reminded me of the Milky Way. The food was very different, but not bad. Just... Peculiar.

"Who's ready for cake?" asked Rachel.

Claire and I looked at each other and smiled. We went into the kitchen and lit a bunch of candles. I turned off the lights and Claire brought the blazing cake to her sister. We all sang her happy birthday in French and then in English.

Rachel blew out the candles.

"What did you wish for?" asked Adil as he leaned closer to her. She winked at him.

"You do the honour," said Claire as she gave Rachel a long, thin knife.

"Just to be sure," said a voice from behind, "this cake is egg-free, right?"

"What?" Both Claire and I asked at the same time.

"Mom!" said Rachel, her voice low so that only I could hear her, "I called you last weekend to say that Sarah has a really serious egg allergy... Don't you remember? We talked about it for, like, half an hour!"

I *did* remember. But I *had* forgotten.

"I'm sorry," I said. I felt so stupid.

"It's fine, Mom..." she said. She served the cake everyone but Sarah. The empty space on the table was a glaring reminder of my decomposing brain.

"No worries, Mrs. O'Connor," said Sarah. "I'm not really hungry for dessert."

"Sorry," I mumbled.

The cake tasted dry, and I took no pleasure in eating it. I had lost my appetite.

The party died down not long after the cake was served. The mood had turned somewhat glum. The sun had set. Soon, there were only four of us left at the table.

"Young people these days have so many food-based restrictions... Have you heard of the raw foo —"

"Why are you so judgmental of my friends?" said Rachel.

"I'll go now," said Adil before I had a chance to respond.

"Okay, I'll call you later," she said.

The door hadn't even closed when Rachel was back at it. "You've always been so judgemental!" she said. "My friends are never good—"

"Mom, really, you are—"

"Claire, stay out of this!" I shouted. I was being attacked on both fronts. It made me angrier.

"I told you to write it down, Mom."

"So what?" I shouted. "I forgot. It happens to everyone. No one died or anything."

"Mom," said Claire, "you're wrong and you're just making it worse."

"It's my fault," said Rachel. The room became very quiet and we both looked at her. Such words were not commonly produced by Rachel's lips. "I should have told Claire instead. I'm just not used to..."

"Used to what?" I barked.

Not used to the fact that my mother is losing her mind.

January 26, 2016

Zandra gave birth to a perfect little baby girl last week. Thomas called me to say that Zandra was in labour and told me to drive down to Ottawa. That is what it took to make me excited about being a grandmother.

When I go to the hospital, Thomas was in the room with Zandra. I waited patiently. The hallway was ful of pleasant, distracting movement. The maternity ward is, for most people, a happy place. Less than an hour later, Tom came out.

"So? Is she here?" I asked, my voice getting caught in my throat.

Thomas fell into my arms, shaking. Like when he was a little boy. I stroked his thick blond hair.

"No, Mom. Still not here. I just came to see you..."

"Okay, Tom." I kissed his cheek. "Thanks for the update."

He took a deep breath and went back down a long, green corridor.

I knew that Zandra's parents could not afford to fly in from Brazil. She needed Thomas more than I did.

I watched the television set on the corner of the room. The news was scrolling back and forth, back and forth. Always the same information: the Flint email fiasco, Detroit teacher sick-outs, Putin's spy murder, a new planet on the edge of the solar system... As time went on, I got very hungry, but I didn't dare leaving the waiting room to go find food.

Thomas came to get me three hours later.

"She's here," he whispered.

I followed him to Zandra's hospital room.

When I walked in, Zandra was sitting in bed, propped up against a high pillow, huge tears in her eyes. She was holding tiny baby Laci in her arms.

I was overcome with emoton. When I became a mother with Thomas, I thought that it was the happiest moment in my life. His little pink face, his tiny fingers, his big, curious blue eyes... But there is something even more special about being a grandparent, knowing that your creation now has his own creation to love.

"Oh, Zandra," I said. I covered my mouth with my hand. "Oh... She is so precious."

"Thank you for being here," said Zandra. "It means a lot to me. Do you want to hold her?"

I nodded. I dropped my heavy winter coat and bag onto the chair in the corner and went back to Zandra's side. She handed Laci to me.

"What a tiny baby," I said. She had thick, dark hair, like her mother's. Laci's eyes were closed. I put my finger into her tiny hand. She held on. "I'll hold on to you too," I said to her. "Always. Sweet baby."

I looked over at Tom. He had tears in his eyes.

"Mom. I'm glad that you're here." I could red it in his eyes. *But I wish Dad were here too.*

"Thanks for having invited me, Tom. And Zandra." I looked over at her. She nodded.

"How did it go?" I asked.

"We came close to an emergency C-section," said Zandra. "But in the end, it all worked out."

"You should rest now," I said. "Can I get you anything?"

"No, I've got plenty of food from the hospital," said Zandra.

"Any good?" I asked.

"Actually, it is just fine. I don't see what all of the fuss is about!" She said fuss like *fuzz.* "Would you mind taking a few photos of us?"

"Of course!" I said. "With my phone?"

"Sure," said Tom. "We'd like to send out a couple of pictures to Zandra's family, and to Claire and Rachel."

I handed the baby to Tom and took out my cellphone. He went over to Zandra's bedside and they posed for me.

I took a few pictures and showed them to Zandra.

"Can you send me this one," she said. "And the last one?"

"No," said Tom. "My eyes are closed!"

"Okay, then this one," she said, flipping through the photos.

I sent them to Zandra and Tom, then to Rachel and Claire.

"Are you staying here for the night?" I asked Tom.

"I have no idea what time is even is!" he said.

"Quarter passed 11," I said.

"Oh!" said Zandra. "So late!"

"The nurse said that I can grab a cot and stay here overnight. Did you want the keys to our place?" he asked. "Or will you get a room here?"

"Do you mind if I stay the night at your place?" I asked.

"No!" they both said.

Tom handed me his set of keys. "Just leave them in the mailbox when you leave tomorrow."

Tom went out to fetch a cot for himself.

"Can you put her back in her bed?" asked Zandra. "Unless you want to take her for a while?"

"No problem," I said. When Tom came back in, I put Laci in the glass bowl of a bed.

I turned back and saw the two proud parents smiling at each other, eyes full of wonder and hope for the future. It was a private moment, my cue to leave.

January 29

Elvis and I got married just before Thomas' birth.

"Should we do it?" he asked. We were sitting in the booth of a fast-food diner. The place was old and crumby, decked in bright colours and photographs of the food. Perhaps it was because I was pregnant, but seeing up-close photographs of a hamburger made me want to do everything but order it. The windowsills were lined with pickled vegetables. Hopefully, they were placed there more as a decoration that a food source, as they were covered in a thick blanket of dust.

I was eating a hot chicken sandwich and he was eating three hotdogs and a plateful of fries. "Now that the divorce is legalized? Should we just get married then?"

"Elvis," I said, rubbing my greasy fingers on the cheap white napkin, "that is not exactly the kind of proposal that a girl wishes for. And anyways. I'm far too fat to shop for a wedding dress." I waved at the waitress — an elderly gal with bright red lipstick and yellowed teeth — asking for my side of onion rings. She nodded and was off to the kitchen.

"I mean like elope or something." He took a huge bite of his all-dressed hotdog.

"Of course we'd elope. Who the hell would come to our wedding anyways?" I asked.

"My parents might—"

"Elvis, come now. They're devout Catholics. They don't believe in divorce. Or premarital sex for that matter..." I rubbed my round belly.

"I guess... But what if we just get married, Nina?"

"What is the big deal? It's not like you live by the laws of the sanctity of marriage, do you?" I asked. I took a long sip from my soda. The contrast between the sweet drink and the salty food was exactly what I had been craving.

"I want to be with you for the rest of my life. There is no other human being out there that fits with me as well as you do, Nina."

"Oh, shut up, Elvis," I said.

Elvis' face became red. "You're such a cynic. Really. I love you so much that I could blow your brain to pieces sometimes."

"I'll come back at a better time," said the waitress from just over my shoulder. She continued to walk by our table with my basket of onion rings on her tray.

"No!" I shouted, a little louder than anticipated. She turned back. "I'll take the onion rings now. He's only joking..."

The waitress smiled — at least she tried to place her mouth into a curved shape, sides higher than the middle part, but there really is more to a smile, is there not? — and dropped the basket on the corner of the table.

"Shit," said Elvis. He really hated making bad impressions on people that he did not know. "But that is the best example of what I mean. You know I wasn't actually saying that I would shoot you—"

"Of course, Elvis. But because you won't shoot me doesn't mean that we should hop off and get married..."

"What are you afraid of, Nina?"

I dipped half an onion ring into a sticky pack of honey. "I don't know."

"You mean you admit that you're scared?" he asked. His round mustachioed face started at me, incredulous.

"What?"

"Do you admit you're scared?"

"Elvis, you just dumped your last wife to be with me a few weeks ago. Don't blame me if I'm a little reticent to believe that—"

"This is different. Very different. I had been with Ottavia since right after high school. Our parents basically set us up... But you're the woman I choose."

"Would you have stayed with her if you had been able to have children together?"

"What is wrong with you, Nina? I just proposed to you and you just keep going on about my ex-wife?" His face was reddening again. "Can't you just accept that you're in a good place, that you're happy, that everything will be okay?"

He had me there. Even in such a short time... He knew me well. "No. Not really."

"Let go, Nina. Let go of it all and you'll finally be free."

"Do you want to catch a movie?" I asked as I shoved an unreasonably large bit of sandwich into my mouth. "Or we can go walk along the Canal. Would you—"

Elvis stood up abruptly. Before I knew what was happening, he was on his knee on the side of the booth.

"Nina Wren O'Connor. You are the most stunning, smart, tall, graceful, kind, secretive, and difficult woman I have ever met," he said. Everyone around us was looking our way. I could feel my face burning. "You are a terrible cook, you don't listen to half of the things I say and you're rude with my mother. And I love you just the same. What do you say, Nina? Will you be my wife?"

I turned towards him as best I could, which was a difficult task indeed, because of my pregnant belly. Elvis took my hand into his and lightly kissed my knuckles. I could feel the energy in the room become tense.

"What did she say?" I heard someone whisper.

"If you think that—"

"Oh bloody hell, Nina. I don't want a speech. Just tell me: yes or no?" He was out of breath from being in a crouched position for too long.

"Okay. Yes."

Exaltation bubbled forward, not just from Elvis, but from the entire restaurant.

"Can you get up now?" I asked, pulling at his arm.

He kissed me on the forehead and then eased himself back into his side of the booth.

"This will be great," he was saying. "I am so excited! Where do you want to get married?"

"City Hall? It's not like you can get married in a church, can you?" I asked.

He gave me the finger.

"Who do you want to invite?" he asked.

"Elvis, can we talk about this another time? Your hotdogs are getting cold."

He stuffed a few fries into his mouth.

"Can you close your mouth when you chew?" I said. "You're making me lose my appetite."

"Nina," he said, mouth covered in a white potato paste, "isn't it nice that we don't have to creep around together anymore? That we can talk about marriage and a happy family?"

"Come to think of it..." I said. Suddenly, it was clear as day: there was nothing attractive about that prospect. Not in the slightest.

I was in a different mindspace, back then. It was not his fault. Only mine.

"What?" he asked, finishing his first hotdog.

"Oh, nothing," I said.

We ate the rest of the meal in silence, watching the people and the food move around us.

I waited at the door with my coat on as Elvis went to the washroom.

"Good luck with that one, sweetheart," said the waitress as she rushed by me. "I do not envy you."

February 5, 2016

"Mom, what are you doing?"

I spun around careful not to fall over. "Rachel? How long have you been standing there?"

She leaned against the doorway. "Did you forget that we had plans this morning?" A question with the sharpest of edges.

"No, Rachel. Of course not!"

She held out a small white box. "I brought snacks. You should get the kettle on."

I stepped down from my folding ladder. *How long have I been standing up there? And what on earth was I doing up there in the first place?* As I prepared the water, I scanned through my mind to a moment in which I vaguely remembered that Rachel and I had agreed to come take some tea before her class. I poured some tap water into the kettle and put it on the stove.

"So, Mom, what's new with you?" she asked. "How are things?"

Things.

"I'm fine, Rachel. Thanks. What about you?" Herself. Her most favourite subject.

"I am surprised to find in your pajamas, Mom." Her gaze was cold and analytical. "You look... You look at little..." She signed. "Just never mind, I guess."

"Oh, bloody hell, Rachel. Just spit it out."

"You've always been so put-together. Even when we were little, you never left your bedroom without having done your makeup and hair."

I looked at myself in the reflection of the window. I took the inventory: shabby pajamas, tattered bathrobe, disheveled hair that desperately needed a dyeing, plain face...

"It's not important, Mom. Sorry I mentioned it."

I looked at Rachel, really seeing her for the first time in a long time. She really looked exactly as I did at her age, only somehow more poised and commanding.

"I just got out of bed, Rachel. I didn't know that receiving you required the same protocol as seeing the Queen..."

"Maybe Claire and I can dye it for you," she said.

"Dye?" I asked, taking the seat opposite her.

"Your hair! It can't be that complicated..."

"It's fine, dear. I'll get it done sooner or later."

The kettle went off and I stood up to take care of making the tea. Neither of us said anything for a long while.

"I bought three kinds of croissants," she finally said, breaking the sticker along the corner of the box. "Almond, chocolate, and Gruyere. Which do you want?"

"I'll take the almond one," I said, putting two small blue and gold plates on the table. "Thanks, Rachel."

"So I can't be leaving too late, I am giving a lecture at noon," said Rachel.

"Of course. I understand." I took a bite of the fresh croissant. It was delicious, just the right combination of flaky pastry crust and the buttery greasiness.

"I'm excited about the class I'm giving, I just hope that the undergrads will be a little brighter than last time. Because last time, the questions they asked... I tell you, they came off as halfwits, seriously—"

"Sure," I said. I could feel my mind become more and more distracted. "I guess I should take care of my skunk 'do," I said, looking once again at the reflection of my hair in the window.

"What?" I realized that I had cut Rachel off midsentence.

"Oh, I was just thinking about what you said about preserving my dignity."

"What do skunks and dignity—"

"My hair," I answered. "I mean my hair kind of looks like a skunk. With the thick white part in the middle? Have you never heard that expression?"

"It's just that you're jumping from one subject to another," said Rachel, "and I was saying how—"

"Sorry. You go ahead. What were you saying about your apartment?" Rachel's face became red.

"What?" I asked again. "Sorry, what were we talking about?"

Rachel took a deep breath and looked down at her chocolate croissant. She tore a small piece off and put it into her mouth, never taking her eyes off of me. She chewed and the strained silence persisted. She wiped the tips of her fingers on her napkin and cleared her throat.

"Sometimes it's hard to know if it's the disease, or if you're just not listening, as always..."

"Rachel!" I didn't know what to say. She was always such an unpleasant person to be around... I know that a mother is not supposed to say that about her own daughter... But honestly, Rachel is an exception to that rule. Even as a child, Elvis and I used to talk about how diferent and dificult she was. Thomas was not always easy, but it was because he was so sensitive. And then there was the happy-go-lucky Claire. She may not have been the best in school, she may not have picked up after herself as a teenager... But at least she was nice to be around. Rachel, on the other hand...

"Sorry, Mom. I have to learn to be more patient... I'll get used to it."

Rachel went off to her class pretty soon after the argument. I was so frustrated — and hurt, in all honesty — that I wrote a text message about it to Claire. Usually, I tried not to drag my children into arguments with their siblings, but this time, I just needed to vent.

February 7, 2016

Random fact: on year ago today, the Canadian Supreme Court ruled that doctors can assist patients in suicide if their medical condition causes inhumane suffering and if the condition is permanent and worsening.

It means a lot more to me right now, but when I heard the news I remember thinking that it was a good thing. Dying in dignity, on your own terms, if you so choose to end it. The ultimate final decision. We're not talking about a suicidal rock star here: we're talking about people who know that their quality of life will not, can not, ever get better.

"I'm not so sure that is a good thing," said Thomas when we spoke about it later that week. "Think about it. What if sick old people begin to feel pressured to just end it? to stop their family's suffering?"

Thomas was always such a sensitive boy. It became most obvious when he was almost four years old, because that is when Rachel was born.

"But why did you need a new baby?" he asked when Elvis and I told him that he was going to be a big brother. "I'm still your baby." *I'm not good enough?*

It was a calmer time, just before Rachel was born. Elvis had decided to take some time off from his job, an agreement that was made on both fronts, and to stay at home when the baby came. Many people judged him, laughing and calling him all sorts of shameful names, but Elvis couldn't care less. He was excited about being a stay at home dad, to walk Tom to school and to take care of Rachel. Unfortunately, the peace was short-lived. His boss called him to return to work, or threated to give his well-paying construction job to someone else.

We were in the sitting room. I was on the couch and Elvis was sitting on the floor to be on the same eyelevel as Tom. We had read that it was important to do that when saying something serious to a small child.

"Tom, you're not a baby," said Elvis. "You're a big boy. You sleep in a big boy bed, and you go to preschool three days a week, and your room is full of big boy toys. Don't you like being a big boy?"

"Yeah. But I don't want to be anymore..."

Tom sucked his thumb.

Elvis and I looked at each other. We were not prepared for such a reaction.

"Okay," said Elvis. "Let's go clean out your room then."

"Okay!" shouted Tom. We went upstairs and I watched as he helped his father put all of his *big boy toys* into a large black garbage bag.

"Is this for big boys?" asked Tom, turning to his father with a yellow metal dup truck.

"Yep."

Tom threw it in the bag.

"And this?" he asked, holding onto the piggy bank that Santa Claus had given him.

"Sure," said Elvis.

"Are we all done?" shouted Tom, gleefully, after about half an hour of work. "Can I have my pacifier back too?"

"I guess I'll go throw these away now," said Elvis as he turned to leave the room with the garbage bag.

We both looked at Tom, who did not react.

"Mom, can I get my baby bed back? And will I wear diapers again?"

I was starting to feel that we had gone too far.

"No, Tom. That is enough for today."

"Well, are you going to give the baby back to the store then?" he asked. "Now that you don't need it?"

"That is not how it works, sweetheart."

Tom let out a yelp in protest.

"Enough," I said, my tone stern. I was not quite as patient as Elvis.

"You can act like a baby until your sister comes. But when she arrives, that's it. Your time is up, buddy."

"Sister!" he shouted. "This is the worst day of my life."

I truly hope that it is, I said to myself.

I hoped that by the time Rachel would arrive, Thomas would have had a change of heart. We tried to get him excited about being a big brother, getting him involved in picking out her name and painting her nursery, but Tom held his position. We bought him a doll – a present! just like that! – so that he could practice being a big brother. It becamse instead a game of trying to get rid of her.

I fell down an entire staircase once just tripping over the damn doll in the middle of the night. How worried I was for the baby! I called Elvis, who was already running down the stairs for all of the noise that I had made. Had Rachel not been busy kicking at my ribs – I was positive that she was alive and kicking, literally! – we would have called an ambulance.

Thomas kept himself busy by stuffing the doll into the microwave, into the garbage can, out the window, into the washing machine...

When we brought Rachel home, Tom refused to be in the same room as her. This went on for a whole week. He would scream so much that we actually let him win, myself and Elvis being exhausted by Rachel and her sleepless nights.

Thomas started wetting the bed again. I suspected that it was a ruse for attention, but part of my was worried that something more serious could be going on. I took him to his pediatrician.

"It is probably just a cry for attention," said the doctor, "but we'll carry out a few tests just in case." He gave me a cup with a screw-on lid, and a paper bag, and instructed me to get a urine sample.

I took Tom to the washroom.

"Okay, Tom. Take this cup and go in there and pee in it, okay?" I said.

"But why do I have to pee in a cup?" he asked. He backed away from me.

"The doctor is worried because you're wetting the bed again, Tom."

"But the cup..."

"Yes. You need to pee in this cup, this plastic cup, and then you have to give it back to me and I'll—"

He grimaced. "But if I pee in the cup, who will drink it?"

I tried to hold back a laugh.

"It is not that kind of cup, Tom. It is a kind that the doctor will use to take a sample and do some tests on it..."

He eye me suspiciously.

"What if I don't have to pee?"

"We'll wait right here until you do," I said, my patience wearing thin.

"What if I wet my pants instead?" he asked.

"Thomas Rossi O'Connor. You are grating on my last nerve. Get in there and pee!"

The people from the waiting room nearby glanced our way with very little subtlety.

Tom grabbed the cup and went into the bathroom, slamming the door behind him.

"You might want to be a little more calm with him," said an older woman who was standing in line for the ladies' washroom. "Or just wait until he becomes a teenager."

"Yeah. Thanks." Unsolicited parenting advice from an stranger. The best kind.

February 14, 2016

My first Valentine's Day without Elvis. Elvis was always so excited about Valentine's Day. I was always pretty cynical. About everything. Valentine's Day included.

Zandra and Tom were over with Laci from Friday to just before noon today. They played it off like they just happened to drive down from Ottawa. But I think they're worried about me. Being alone. On Valentine's Day weekend.

I am trying to remember the last Valentine's Day that I spent with Elvis. He was such a romantic.

There was one Valentine's Day when he built a playhouse in the backyard with the kids. Claire was three at the time, which means that Rachel was eight, and Thomas was 11.

"Oh, Dad!" shouted little Rachel. "It is perfect! It just needs some curtains..."

"Wow," mused Claire as she walked around the wooden structure. It was a perfect little cube with a slanted roof. The front door and window were all kid-sized. Elvis had dug up half of the snow from the backyard to be able to fit it on the ground.

"What do you think, Tommy Boy?" asked Elvis.

Thomas shrugged. He was out without a coat. It was cold, but the sun was warm and inviting. "It's fine," he finally said. He was at an age where he still like little kid things, but no longer wanted to admit it. "The girls will like it."

"What girls?" teased Elvis.

"'My sisters, that's what girls." Tom turned on his booted heel and walked back into the house.

I was standing in the doorway, arms crossed. I moved to the side to let him in. Looking over my shoulder, I watched him kick off his boots and stand on the rug near the door. He looked back outside through the glass. Claire and Rachel had gone inside the house and Elvis was squatting down, looking inside, laughing with them.

"You know, buddy," I said, "your dad spent a lot of time making that thing. Maybe you can use it as a fort with your friends?"

"No way. Rachel is putting up curtains." He stormed up the stairs and to his room.

"Nina!" shouted Elvis. "Can you grab the girl's coats? They want to stay out here a while."

I whispered some nasty things under my breath, then went to the front closet.

"Come in here, girls," I called from the patio door. "You're going to freeze. It is February in Montreal..."

They ran over to me.

"Mommy, did you see..."

"... so cool!"

"All my friends, and..."

"Thanks, Dad!"

I gave Rachel her coat, then bent over to put on Claire's. I'll always remember the look on her face. She was short, much shorter than her siblings had been at her age. She looked so much like Elvis.

"Mommy! A house!" shouted Claire. "For me!" she was fidgeting so much that it took me twice as long as usual to zip up her coat.

"Yes Claire, for you."

The girls ran into the playhouse and Elvis walked over to me.

They were tense times.

"Always the hero, aren't you, Elvis?"

"What do you mean?" he asked, making his way inside.

"You can be away for all of the time you like – golfing and conferences and weekend getaways – but when you come home, you pull a stunt like this, and bang!" I said as I followed him inside. "Theyre daddy's little girls."

"Nina, I really don't think that is—"

"That's accurate. You don't think. Who gets them up and ready in the morning, who cooks for them, who tucks them in? I do. But you spend one weekend building them a playhouse and suddenly I no longer exist."

"Nina, I—"

"Mommy!" cried Rachel as she ran back towards the house.

Yes, Rachel?

"Can you bake us some cookies please? To eat in our new house?"

I turned back to Elvis. "See all I'm good for? Stuffing their mouths."

I stormed into the living room.

"Nina," he said. I was sitting on the couch, pretending to be reading a magazine in front of the fireplace. In reality, I was just sitting there, hating him. "Nina, how can you be acting this way?"

"Elvis, you have no idea."

"Isn't that the whole point of being a team? Isn't that why there are two of us? So that we can be there when the other isn't?" He sat down on the couch next to me. "Are you sure you mad about the playhouse? Are you sure you're not just pushing me away again?"

"Elvis, if you bring that up every damn time we argue..."

"I am allowed to bring it up all I want. You're the one who made all of those stupid choices. But I'm still here. And you won't let me in."

We all build walls around ourselves to shield ourselves in times of sudden misfortune. The problems come when the walls become a cocoon instead, when we become centered only on ourselves. I see that now.

"Back off, Elvis."

"Nina..."

"No, seriously," I said, my throat full of poison. "Fuck off."

"Nina, relax!" said Elvis, standing up from the couch. "Let me make you some tea." He stood up and went into the kitchen. That is when I caught a sight of Tom peeking his head down the stairs. When he realized that I could see him, he jumped.

"Come down here, Thomas," I said. "Immediately."

He nodded and walked over, very slowly. He looked so small, standing before me in his red jogging pants and Teenage Mutant Ninja Turtle t-shirt.

"How long have you been standing there eavesdropping?"

He was shaking his head as Elvis came back into the room.

"I'm sorry, Tommy," he said. "I shouldn't have been so angry."

Tom shrugged. "I'm used to it."

Elvis and I exchanged looks.

"What do you mean?" asked Elvis.

"You are going to get unmarried, aren't you?" asked Tom. "Like Sean's parents?"

"No, Tom," said Elvis. "Your mom and I fight together sometimes. But it is how we find solutions to problems. But we still love each other as the day we met," he said. "Right, Nina?"

I nodded, smiled, pat Tom on the head.

"Come help me make some tea for you Mom," said Elvis.

Tom shrugged. "She yells and swears the f-word at you, and you make her tea? That is messed up."

February 15, 2016

Yesterday night, after Tom and his family left, I went for tea with Harvey. That is how we celebrated Valentine's Day together.

Harvey is a neighbour with whom I struck up a friendship since Elvis's death. We have been neighbours for nearly 20 years. His wife, Colette, passed away five years ago from a very aggressive form of breast cancer. She was a very handsome woman, exactly the lady that you would expect to see on Harvey's arm. She had high, dignified eyebrows, large eyes and thin wrists. Even with a headscarf, she walked about with as much pride as the Queen of England.

When Harvey actually made a move to ask me to go out, I was really apprehensive about it. Was it a date? What it a friendly thing? Was it a booty call? What the hell is a booty call? Being a fresh widow of 65 years of age, I had no prior experience in such matters.

It was early fall. Harvey came over and knocked on my door. I was surprised: these days, doors do not get knocked on as much as they used to.

I saw a very well-dressed gentleman through the glass of the front door.

"Hello?" I said as I opened it, only a crack. "Oh, Harvey!"

He stood there with a big smile on his face, his hair perfectly combed – as always – his facial hair groomed yet rugged – as always – his clothes expensive-looking yet understated – as always – and his eyes sparkling.

"Nina, how are you?" He was holding a bouquet of fresh-cut flowers, including a few roses.

"I'm well, Harvey. How are you? Would you like to come inside?"

"Sure. I was cutting the last of the flowers in the yard and I thought you may appreciate them."

"Oh yes," I said, gesturing for him to hand them to me. "Come, come in."

He followed me into the kitchen. I took a crystal vase from the cupboard above the refrigerator and filled it with water. I dropped the flowers in, rearranging them so that they stood up straight in the vase. I took a step back to admire my work.

"You have quite the eye for aesthetics," said Harvey.

"Oh." I felt myself blushing. When was the last time that a man made me blush?

"Sorry, I didn't mean—"

"No, don't apologize," I said. "Take a seat."

Harvey nodded and pulled up a chair.

"Can I get you a coffee?" I asked.

"I am more of a tea drinker, if you don't mind. I know that not everyone has got tea on hand..."

"Actually, I also am a tea-drinker. I always ask people if they want coffee, and i dont even know why. Funny, the unconscious, sometimes... Let me get the kettle on." I turned around and pulled the kettle out of the cupboard, then filled it with water.

"This is a really nice place. I love the countertops, are they real marble?"

"Yes," I said, turning back to Harvey. I went over and took my place at the table. "Being a real estate agent for so many years has its perks. With all of the connections I made working, I've been able to make a lot of renovations of this place for just pennies."

"Don't be modest. A lot of work has gone into this house. It's obvious. Every detail taken into account... I do not know much about design myself, but I can see that this place is very put together. The colours, the paintings, the lighting, the plants and rugs at just the right angles... It's beautiful."

"Well, thank you."

"I like to think that our homes are an honest reflection of ourselves."

"Well, then you must be a very opulent man indeed," I said. "Every time I look across the street, I am mesmerized by the façade of your house. The garden is perfect. Just wild enough, yet manicured too. And in the fall, like today... All of those coloured leaves across the grass... It's a home with character."

"I will take that as a compliment then," said Harvey. "Especially coming from you. You have seen many houses and you're an excellent judge of style."

The kettle whistled loudly.

"Sugar or milk?" I asked.

"What kind of tea are you serving me?"

"I was thinking a peony? It is a w—"

"White tea. White peony. Plush, floral, mellow. Sugar and milk would certainly ruin it."

I smiled. "Tell me more."

"Well, that is about as far as my knowledge base goes. I had done a tea plantation visit and tasting in China with Collette." He looked up at me, then looked away. "I don't think it ever gets easier, saying their name once they're gone..."

I poured the water into the clear glass teapot and put the lid on. I looked at the time. 2:53 PM.

"I'm not sure," I said. I brought the teapot and a pair of saucers and cups to the table. "I'm not sure if it gets easier. Maybe. Elvis has not been gone for so long, just yet. Maybe it gets easier. Or maybe we learn better how to mask our feelings from ourselves."

Harvey stared off through the back window. It was a quiet, comfortable moment. "Collette passed away on New Year's Eve, 2012. Did you know that?" he finally asked.

I shook my head.

"II wish the two of you had been friends. She was a wonderful woman..."

2:55. I poured out enough tea to fill the bottom of Harvey's cup. The steam rose and licked at the air and I could smell the tinniest hint of roses and melon.

"Is that steeped enough for you?" I asked.

He took a sip. He savoured it. "Yes. Thank you."

I poured us each a full cup. "I wish I had something to offer you," I said. Harvey looked up at me. "To eat, I mean... To go with the tea. But living alone, I don't really bake very much anymore. Except for maybe when Claire is over."

"Tell me how Claire is doing," he said. His light eyes were soft and kind, with wrinkles just at the right place to show that he smiled often.

"Oh, Claire. She is a wild one. She is – or at least tries to be – a professional painter." I wrapped my fingers around the mug. The sensation of warm liquid through the bone-thin china was my favourite part of drinking tea, even more than the taste itself. "She's engaged, too."

"When will she be getting married?" He asked.

I could not remember. Claire had told me so many times... But the date just would not stick in my head. "2017," I finally answered. "Sometime in 2017 probably."

"What type of painting does she do?" asked Harvey.

"You know, that terribly modern stuff," I said. He laughed. "To be fair, she did get a bachelor in fine arts at Mc Gill. She did well, too. Then she opened an art gallery in the Old Port with a few of her friends from school."

"That is rare, a sensitive, artistic type who also wants to go into business. She sounds like quite the woman."

"She is," I said. I could not help but smile. "She is wonderful, if not a bit immature at times..."

"That is how the youngest child is, wouldn't you say?" he asked.

"Yes, that's true. But it also cost her her business."

"That is unfortunate," said Harvey. "Did she take it too hard?"

"Not really," I said. "She has a way of bouncing back from things like that..."

"That's good," said Harvey.

"Sometimes. But at the same time, she doesn't take a whole lot very seriously..."

"Impulsive? Naïve?"

"It's like you've already met her," I said. "Interestingly, Tom is a lot like that too. Impulsive, naïve, very emotional... But he met a wonderful girl. They complement each other so well. She is very down-to-earth, she's a planner... She runs him well. And he needs that."

"It's a special time in life when we get to see our children making such good choices for themselves. It attests to how well they were raised, I think," said Harvey.

"How are the boys doing?" I asked.

He smiled. "Alexandre is running the world, as we always knew he would. He's the manager of a bank and does this educational-blogging thing on the side. He makes videos about how to save money, different accounts and things like that. I don't know much about it... I just share his videos each time he posts one."

"And how is Cedric?" I asked.

"That is a trickier question. I'd love to know the answer to that one, but I don't know..."

"Sorry," I said. "I didn't know—"

"Let's say that the last time I saw Cedric was at his mother's funeral. He took it really hard. They were close. She understood him in ways that I simply could not... He was brooding and moody, very emotional, but she always knew just how to talk to him, just how to bring him back down on earth."

"Typical younger child?" I asked.

"You could say that. Certainly impulsive. Last I heard, he was off to B.C. to plant trees. Said he needed to clear his mind... Planting trees for five years, he must have created a whole new forest by now..."

"Do you ever hear from him?" I asked.

"Only through Alex. He calls his brother every month or so..." said Harvey. He took a sip from his cup. It was probably lukewarm at this point, the temperature of mud.

"Well, I'm sorry that it seems like his reaction was to flee. But he probably needed it. If it means anything to you, I didnt the same thing when my mother was put into an institution. I was only 27 and I didn't know how to cope. I bought a one-way ticket to New Delhi."

"British Columbia is in our backyard compared to India!" said Harvey. "That must have been terribly difficult for your father."

"Sure," I said. *What father?* "But I needed to go. I needed to see something different, to get lost, to redefine myself. It was the best choice I've ever made." We sat quietly, each of us in our own world. It was comfortable.

"How long were you gone for?" he asked, breaking the silence.

"Oh," I laughed. "I was completely overwhelmed. The culture shock was too much. I wallowed in self-pity in a dump of a hotel in Delhi and was back home within a week."

Harvey laughed. When he laughed there was an amazing sparkle in his eye. I was taken.

"So much for an adventure, then," he said. "Did you ever go back?"

"Are you kidding?" I laughed. "No! I've never had the guts to do that again. I travelled a lot, especially before I met Elvis... But I keep to much more – how should I put this? – much more *comfortable* locations now."

"I'd love to go to India. There is something about the subcontinent that has attracted me all of my life. The colours, the smells, the sounds... I want to live it all, from the crisp Kashmiri mountains to the steamy backwaters of Goa."

"Well, don't wait then," I said.

Harvey looked at me with a questioning eyebrow.

"Are you calling me old, Nina?" he asked. He cleared his throat. "I am only a few years older than you, after all."

"No of course not, Harvey," I said. I felt sheepish. "Take Elvis. His biggest dream was to visit Japan. He talked about it all of the time, like you talk about India. I wouldn't want you to miss out. Since it means so much to you. Life is precious, I'm sure you recognise that."

"Isn't it?" he asked. "Isn't that true. And without the prospect of dying, it wouldn't mean a thing, would it?"

"You've gotten a bit too philosophical for me, Harvey." I was not entirely comfortable with the idea of discussing death. It was far too real, far too fresh to me.

"Would you come back to India?" he asked. "With me?"

I laughed. "I really don't think so, Harvey. It nearly killed me the first time, I am afraid that it would finish me off for good." So much for avoiding talking about death.

"I understand. And maybe this is something that I have to do on my own. Do you know what I mean?" he asked. I nodded. "There have been a few times in my life," he continued, "a few times when I have felt the call to do something really crazy. My first instinct is always to look for a co-conspirator... But it is always more meaningful when I just did it on my own. I've walked away from a few situation, from some very important people, to... To live. To experience life. To be on my own."

"That is better than a Corvette-style midlife crisis," I said. He laughed. "Did you always find your way back to where it all began?" I asked.

He smiled. "I guess you could say that I always did."

"Then I wouldn't worry too much about Cedric," I said. "If he is anything like his father, he will find his way back too."

"That is very kind. The only thing that I can't understand is why I didn't come over here sooner. But I was pruning the roses, and they looked so beautiful. And I realized that if I put them in my house, well, I wouldn't really appreciate them. And I'd probably forget them in a dark room or something, and then they would have wilted, never having been really appreciated. Anyways, I'm probly getting too philosophical again. Let's just say that I saw the flowers and thought that you would give them the respect that they deserve."

I looked over at the vase. The flowers were beautiful, as if taken from a Manet still life... But I loved the wildflowers even more.

"It was really thoughtful of you to come by," I said.

"What time is it?" he asked, looking at his wristwatch. "What? 4:30? Have I really been here for that long?"

I looked outside, the setting autumn sun confirming just how late it had gotten. I stood up, turning on the kitchen light. The brightness surprised us both.

"Well, next time, I'd like to have you over. If you want to come, that is. Just come by whenever."

He stood up and I walked him to the door. I turned on the light in the entryway.

"This carpet," he said as he bent over to pick up a shoe. "It's beautiful. Where is it from?"

"Special order from Udaipur. It's a small city in Rajasthan. There is a huge hub of artistic activity there."

"Well I'll be," he said. He stood up straight. "How long have you had this rug?"

"I'm not sure. But it has been a while. 10 years maybe?"

Harvey chuckled. "See, you've been trampling all over India for the last 10 years without even noticing. Maybe I'll convince you yet."

He kissed me on the cheek. I smelled his cologne. Then he was gone.

So that is how Harvey and I became friends. In my mind, that afternoon will always be tinged with gold. I really hope that I can hold onto this one to this memory.

It began to snow that very week, which was early, even by Montreal standards. That was also the week that I brought my casserole out to the car.

February 24

Today is Wednesday, the day of the week with the least personality. Not the dreaded beginning of the week, not the glimmering end of the week. Just... the middle of the week. Stable. Reliable. Commonplace. Overlooked.

Sometimes I feel like a Wednesday.

Last night I had a nightmare. I could not get back to sleep afterwards. I am exhausted.

I dreamt that I was walking down a dark laneway. All of the lights were out, and I knew in my heart that it was done intentionally and for malevolent reasons... I tightened the belt of my trench coat and folded my arms across my chest. The sound of my heels clicked loudly, unnaturally. I picked up my pace when I suddenly felt a tug at the back of my coat. I was too afraid to look back. I walked even faster.

I could see the end of the alley, but whatever had been pulling at my coat became too strong. I struggled forward trying to take off the coat. But I could not take off the coat. It was wrapped around me so many times that I was stuck. I could not move at all anymore. I could hardly breathe. I turned to face the demon that had been following me. It was a very small person – perhaps a child? – covered in a black robe.

"What do you want?" I asked. My voice was raspy and hardly carried far enough for the figure to hear me.

"Don't you love me?" came the voice of a child.

"Who are you?"

"Don't you love me?" it asked again, still holding my coat tightly. All I could see were its tiny white fingers.

"I don't know you. I'm the wrong person... I don't know who you are..." I tried to pull at my coat but it would not come free from the child's deadbolt grip.

The child pulled something out of its pocket. It was a match.

"Take this," said the child.

I reached out for the match and when I took it, it lit itself immediately. The only thing that was illuminated by the thin flame was the child's face. I could not make out whether it was a girl or a boy... Its face looked pale, gaunt, worn-out.

"Sleep is bad, you know," said the child. "I don't want to sleep. Nobody loves me and bad things happen when I sleep."

"I'm sorry..."

The child reached into its pocket again. This time, it produced a long, thin knife.

"I won't sleep anymore," the child said. It reached into its own face with the knife. I tried to understand what it was doing, but it all happened so fast...

A single moment later, the child pulled its hand away. Half of its face was covered in blood.

"Look," it said as it lifted its hand towards me.

I did not want to see... But I could not look away.

There, in the child's palm, was an eyelid.

"You do the other," it said. "That way, I can't sleep."

I stood there, staring, horrified.

"Won't you help me?" it asked. Blood dripped down its face.

"No," I said.

"Please?"

I shook my head. The child shrugged and then lifted the knife to its face again.

"No," I tried to say, but no sound came.

I felt the fire from the match catch my finger, then burn out.

Darkness.

March 5, 2016

I got up early this morning to go to a breakfast-art-gallery-event with Claire. How she manages to convince me to go with her to these things, I will never understand. I asked her about the text message that she never answered: she said that she never received it.

It has been almost four months since my diagnosis.

It is really a strange universe, that of the person who knows how she or he will die. It is hard enough to cope with the information, but then you have to watch your loved ones digest it too...

I find myself constantly apologizing, as though I am worried that I have somehow offended them.

"Yes, Thomas. Alzheimer's. But it isn't so bad... I may even have a whole decade ahead of me before I slip into a deep dementia from which I will never return. It's okay, Tom. By the time that happens, I won't even know what is going on anymore."

"Rachel, sweetheart. You don't need to feel bad. At the end, I won't even recognise you. So you won't need to come visit me anymore, because even if you do, I won't know that you did. No, Rachel. You will not be able to carry out your research quickly enough to save me. But it's okay..."

"No, no thank you Claire. I don't want to see your sorcerer friend. I am sure that she is wonderful, but I just can't see myself drinking bat blood or sleeping with a dozen spools of thread in my hair. I'll stick with the treatments suggested by Dr. Lee, okay, Claire?"

The only person who I cannot bring myself to tell is Harvey. With

Harvey, I feel warm and comfortable and safe. It is like I had never gotten the diagnosis at all, because he does not look at me with those eyes, those same eyes as everyone who knows: constantly analysing my every movement, my every word, sifting through it all for evidence of the disease's progression. I want to stay normal to him. With Harvey I feel like myself, not a giant disease incubator.

I am trying to get myself into a new mindset, to take advantage of every moment instead of watching it pass, sadly, trying to hold on. what fun is there watching a show when you're constantly distracted by how soon it will end?

Anyways, the event at the art gallery was organized by her boss Emma and her husband, Chris. It was a fund-raiser for a kid in their family who was suffering some sort of disease.

"What are you wearing?" asked Claire as she came into my house. She had on a black dress with a very low neckline – especially for a Saturday morning! – and a pair of purple stilettos.

"What did you do to your hair?" I asked. "I hope you didn't pay for that! It's shorter on one side than the other! Is that intentional?"

"Welcome to 2016, Mom," she said as she ran her hand through her hair. "We have to leave really soon. What are you wearing?"

I looked down at my long-sleeved floral nightdress. "Not this, I guess," I said. "Maybe my blue one?"

Claire frowned but said nothing.

"Joking," I said, "it's just a joke, Claire."

She pushed my arm and went upstairs to my bedroom. I followed her into my walk-in closet. She made a mess going through my dresses, hangers getting stuck and shoulder straps stuck with the buttons and zippers of other dresses.

"What about this one?" she said, holding out a red dress with lace arms.

"Isnt that more of an evening dress?" I asked.

Claire threw it on a shelf and kept going through my clothes. "This one?" she asked, holding up a black dress this time.

"I'll see if it still fits," I said. I took it into the bathroom and tried the dress on. Even before I zippered it up, I could tell that it was far too big.

"Look," I said to Claire, grabbing the fabric under my arm. "I could fit in here twice."

"Wow," said Claire, "isn't that the one you wore to Dad's funeral?"

It was.

"I knew you were looking thin, but I didn't realize..." said Claire.

"Can I just do a pant suit?" I asked.

"Sure."

I got dressed and joined Claire downstairs.

"Let me do your makeup," said Claire. I handt been planning on wearing any makeup, but I knew that resistance was futile.

I sat on the chair in the kitchen as she plucked my eyebrows, curled my lashes, applied my lipstick.

"Voilà," she said leaning away from me.

I went to look at myself in the mirror and was surprised by the lady who stared back at me. "When did I get so old?"

We got to the art gallery at the exact right moment, when the fun was picking up and everyone was in a good mood.

We left early, probably much earlier than Claire would have liked, but it was a lot for me.

Anyways, I always beliebed in the philosophy: leave while you're still enjoying yourself, that way, your memories will remain sweet

March 15, 2016

When I was a little girl, I kept a diary. I penned daily observations, dreams for my future, and sickly sweet poetry. I always felt the need to do things either all the way, or not at all. And so, at the age of 11, I made a promise to myself that I would write in my diary every single day for the rest of my life. Or at least until I turned 18, which seemed like a very symbolic and mature choice to me.

My mother had moved us off the Island, into this little shack of a house somewhere in the Eastern Townships, in a village called Gould, to live closer to her boyfriend of the time. It had running water, but not on a regular basis. The place was heated by an old, rusted, wood-burning stove. We lived there for a few months, but when my mother and her boyfriend broke up, and the winter was becoming unbearably cold, we made the move back to Montreal.

The former owner of the shabby cabin in the Townships had left all of her belongings behind, and so there was a dusty little bookshelf in the corner of the living room full of books just begging to be read.

I came across *The Diary of a Young Girl* by Anne Frank. That was the catalyst for my own diary writing. I loved that book so much that I must have read it a dozen times that year alone. I would hide in bed for as long as I could, reading about Anne's day to day life, about her thoughts of the war, and on her own personal feeling of isolation and deprivation... She seemed so adult to me at the time, writing about her identity and allegiances, things I had never myself considered. It broke my heart, the suffering that she described. What I loved the most about the novel were the parts about Peter. I was mesmerized by how Anne seemed to love him so deeply, and then on the next page, she was utterly disappointed with him. She cherished him, asking in return from him to be kind... And Peter acquiesced. But why? Did he love her too, or was he altogether lazy and uninterested, not even bothered enough to say anything at all?

Looking back, as an adult, I even wonder if Peter was not merely playing along with Anne's childish requests to keep the piece in their tiny shoebox of a home.

It was the ending of the novel that spoke to me above all. I was haunted. Each time I would read it, I would get to the last page and then turn it, always expecting more... How could such a grand book end so plainly? I knew that in the world-after-the-novel-time, Anne was found and sent away. I knew that her father lived through the war, while she did not. I understood that Anne's life ended suddenly, much like that of her favourite fountain pen. It all made me think that my time could be near and that I would not even know it. That felt very romantic to me. I did not understand how permanent death feels once you really understand what it means.

So I was 11, and I decided to pick up diary writing in honour of none other than Anne Frank. I felt a kinship with her: I saw myself as a young, tortured soul. I also lived in a cold, broken house. I too was very lonely, and often quite sad. I too was convinced that my mother cared very little for me. Perhaps it would be an insult to her that I saw myself in her words, because she was in hiding for her life and I was just a stupid lonely kid. In my defense, if it makes any difference, I my feelings were as sincere as they come.

My mother was drinking heavily and her boyfriend was coming around less and less often. That was tough, because not seeing him made her irritable, but then when she saw him, and they didn't get along, she was even worse. His name was Dave or David or Daniel, and if I remember correctly, he actually had a whole other secret family living in nearby Weedon. Well, technically, they were his real family, and we were the secret.

One cold and metallic night, I had a particularly difficult argument with my mother, who, incidentally, had come across my diary and who had read the terrible things that had to say about her... Since she could do nothing to change the words which had been given a permanent home upon the pages, she did the next best thing: she threw it into the wood stove.

I screamed and cried as my mother stormed out of the room. She smelled of vomit and greasy cigarette smoke.

I watched my diary burn and thought of Anne's fountain pen. An uncomfortable feeling sat in the back of my mind as I watched the destructive flames go to work. Today, I recognize that feeling as irony.

March 20, 2016

Dr. Lee suggested that I meet up with a support group. The idea is both terrifying and absolutely insulting. Support for what? I may have Alzheimer's, but I still have a few golden years ahead of me, do I not?

I think that she suggested it because I told her that I have been having trouble sleeping. She also wanted to give me medication to help me sleep.

"Dr. Lee," I said, "it this really necessary? It has only been a week or so of bad nights. I'll figure it out."

"Have you ever had trouble sleeping before?" she asked.

"No, not really. Not since I was pregnant..."

"Are you still seeing your psychologist?" she asked.

"No," I said, sheepishly. "Our schedules are hard to align..."

"Aren't you retired?" asked Dr. Lee.

"I'm very busy with my family," I said. "Did you know I'm a grandmother now?"

"That is wonderful, Mrs. O'Connor. Congratulations. But for your grandchild's sake, if not for your own, you must keep yourself healthy. Either you go to the support group or you go to the psychologist. Both would be best, but I know you—"

"It's really not necessary though."

"I know that you *feel* that way, but you're being stubborn about the wrong things."

I thanked Dr. Lee and as I walked out of her office, I was surprised to see Claire sitting in the waiting room. Then I remembered that she was the one who had brought me to the clinic in the first place.

"You okay, Mom?" she asked.

"Yes, Claire. Do you want to grab a drink?" I asked.

She agreed and we walked over to the small teahouse a few blocks away. The sky was grey and threatened us with unseasonable rain.

"It is a warm day," Claire said, "but it is just so windy and... miserable. What gloom."

We walked into the small shop and closed the door behind us, moving from a blustery world to one of balmy humidity.

The waiter showed us to a booth at the back of the room dimly lit room. The décor was subdued, with a certain Asian undertone. Blue and white china hung on the walls and there were a few bamboo plants scattered around the place.

"Have you heard from Rachel lately?" I asked as I sat down. "I just realized that she hasn't spoken to me once all month. It's weird."

"That is weird. How often to you speak, usually?"

"Usually she calls at least once a week. She said would get into the habit of coming by for tea before the class she gives. Last time she came over, we argued. I wonder if she's still mad at me."

"Rachel is... well, Rachel..." said Claire. "But she has never been the type to hold a grudge."

"I know. I guess I should have called her. I have just been busy these last few weeks with Laci and Harvey."

"So, how is Harvey?" asked Claire.

"He is well," I said. "Did I tell you that he wants to spend a few days in Prague this spring?"

"That sounds wonderful!" she exclaimed. "Would you go with him?"

"I'm not sure that he really invited me," I said.

"How is he taking all of this? Is it hard for him, you know, about your... disease?"

"He is... he is strong. Don't worry about Harvey." I wanted desperately to change the subject. "How's Robin?"

"She's good. He must find it hard to know that you're facing this disease when he just lost his wife—was it three years ago?"

"Five years. What is Robin up to? Why don't you invite her to join us?"

"She's working. Anyways, how did he react when you told him about it?"

"What kind of contract does she have now?" I asked.

"What?"

"Robin. What kind of work is she doing?"

The waiter arrived to take our orders.

"Mom," said Claire as soon as the waiter turned away, "I get the feeling that you're trying to change the subject."

"It is strange for a mother to ask about her daughter's fiancée?" I asked.

"Well, no... But—"

"I like her very much," I said. "You really must have her come by the house with you more often."

"Robin feels the same way about you," said Claire. "But why do you keep changing the subject?"

"He doesn't know, Claire," I said. "I haven't told Harvey about my diagnosis. So far, he thinks I'm a bit loopy, but as far has he knows, it has nothing to do with Alzheimer's."

"Oh."

"Is it wrong?" I asked.

"I can't really tell you what to do, Mom... But put yourself in his place. He already lost his first wife and now his girlfriend is... sick... and she hasn't told him? He probably won't just leave you, Mom. But at least he deserves to know what kind of situation he's getting himself into. Don't you agree?"

"I am not a *situation*, Claire."

"You know what I mean, don't be so dramatic..."

"When *do I* get to be dramatic then? Huh? When *is it* my turn to feel sorry for myself?"

"It won't get you anywhere, Mom. Maybe you should see the psychologist to talk about this? I don't know what to say."

I could feel my eyes fill with tears as I tried desperately to hold them back. I could not allow myself to cry: that would be too obvious a sign of weakness. Weakness? No. Thinking back, I realize that to allow myself to cry would have been an indication of strength, not weakness.

"I don't need a brainshrinker, Claire. I'm fine."

"A what?"

"I'm fine!" I shouted.

"You don't look fine, Mom. Not since you walked out of the doctor's office. You look very... tired."

The waiter arrived with the tea and two plates. The little dessert bites looked more like art than like food. There was one green cube with a little purple flower on it, one mini crepe with what looked like raspberry caviar, and one circle of pink sponge-like cake with fresh grated ginger.

"You're right. I haven't slept much these last few days... I have been having nightmares." Defeat. I am not in control.

"Is that a symptom of the disease?" she asked.

I nodded. "Apparently."

"Can't you take some medication for that or something?"

"The deterioration starts."

"Mom," said Claire. She reached across the small table and took my hand. "Taking medication to help you sleep – even just temporarily – is not *deterioration*. It's the opposite... It will help with your quality of life, not—"

"Claire I am just nervous. I need to relax is all. Get a massage, or go to the beach for a week or two... Then it will be fine. I'm just stressed." I took a bite of the crepe. It was sweet yet tangy.

"Okay. But until then, don't you want to sleep?"

I felt my impatience rise. I knew that my diagnosis would cause me to progressively lose my autonomy... But I did not realize that it would happen so quickly. Since when did my personal choices become everyone else's business?

"What if I just want to make my own damn decisions in my own damn time without being treated like a child?" I had raised my voice above the admissible level: the couple sitting in the booth across from us looked over disapprovingly.

"Mom, you don't have to take it that way."

"Well, maybe if you didn't... If you didn't..." I could not remember what I was going to say. That only flustered me further.

Claire took a deep breath, then picked up the pink cake with ginger. She closed her eyes and smiled, reminding me of when she was just a little girl. How precious she was, so different from her siblings, so much like her father.

"What are you smiling about?" she asked, her mouth full of cake.

"You. You make me smile."

"Oh, Mother," she said as she rolled her eyes.

"Do you think that you and Robin will have children?" I asked. I picked up the pink cake and took a small bite. It was light and had a soft hint of almonds and roses. The ginger lingered after each bite.

"I think so," she said. One more bite and she was finished eating the dessert. She was always the one in the family who loved food the most, who did not discriminate against any types of food, especially not sweet treats. "I think that we may adopt, but it's kind of hard, being a homo couple. If it gets too complicated, I think that Robin wants to be the one to get pregnant. And that's fine with me. I certainly don't need to put on any more weight." She licked the crumbs off of her fingers. "Do you think that Rachel and Adil are an item?" she asked. We slipped into comfortable, familiar gossip.

March 21

Yesterday Harvey and I went out to the Saint Patrick's Day parade. He insisted.

"As an O'Connor," he said, "you should be ashamed to have even considered missing the parade."

We got bundled up – winter in Montreal is never quite over until May! – and made our way to Sainte Catherine Street. It was cold day, but with a big, bright sun and open blue skies.

We stood a ways away from the street to escape the densest parts of the crowdes. A group of young girls doing traditional Irish dances came by dressed in bright pink dresses. The crowd reacted, clapping and dancing along, laughing.

I looked at Harvey to catch his reaction. He stood there, smiling his perfect smile. Everything about the way Harvey looked... He was wearing the perfect felt coat, hat and matching gloves. He was also wearing cologn, the scent that gave me a bit of shiver each time he came near me. Although we were surrounded in an ocean of people the smell of Harvey's cologne stood out to me.

"It is nice, being outside, isn't it?" he asked.

I smiled, looked up to the sun. "Sure is, on a day like today."

"Aren't your feet cold though?"

I looked down. I had put on a pair of light canvas lace-up shoes without socks.

"Well, I figured that the streets and sidewalks would be clear," I said.

"I hope they're warmer than they look," he said.

"Oh," I said as I tried to remember why I had slipped into a pair of summer shoes at this time of the year... "I must have been distracted, knowing that you were waiting for me. I was too excited!"

Harvey smiled, but for the first time, it was not his usual smile. There was a hint – just the tiniest of indicaitons – of the concern that I saw in my children's eyes.

We watched a group of people walk by with a pack of Irish Setters wearing green vests.

"Dogs," said Harvey. "How I dislike dogs."

"Really?" I said. I did not know that it was possible not to like dogs. "Did you get bitten as a kid or something?" I asked.

"Bit? No, never. It's just... I think that dogs are much smarter than we give them credit for."

I laughed. "So you're afraid of dogs because of their acumen?"

"I think that they watch us. Quietly, subtly... They are always there, right? We talk freely around them. And there they are, watching us. It horrifies me. Did you know that some people even go to the toilet in front of ther dog?"

"Oh, Harvey!" I exclaimed. "You're too funny. The dog couldn't care less about you doing your business!"

"Well," said Harvey, his voice playful, "it's all very strange to me."

Next came a group of firemen carrying a banner for the Catholic Church. They were handing out slips of yellow paper.

"Are you religious?" asked Harvey.

I was surprised by his question. We had talked in detail about ourselves in our three month relationship – family, friends, travels, work – but we had not really touchd upon any subjects that could be considered controversial. I just thought that it was safer that way.

"Well, not really," I said. "I prefer to see life differently. I can't bring myself to even consider that we may be ruled by some humanoid up above the clouds and swirling storms in the stars."

Harvey chuckled. "Never one to mince your words, are you, Nina?"

"Have I offended you?" I asked.

"Oh, that is highly unlikely," said Harvey. "I would say that I am not religious either. There is nothing more ridiculous to me than organized religion. But..."

"There is more?"

"Yes. There is more. That's exactly my point. I don't believe in god or anything like that... But when Collette died. It took me a while to... To really accept that she was gone. And I just could not believe that she was really, completely, *gone*. Do you know what I mean?" he asked.

"No, I don't think so," I said.

"She was so important to me," he continued. "She still is. and I cant bring myself to believe that she is just dead. Gone forever. I think that she is there, out there, somewhere, if only in spirit. And she is really happy."

"A happy dead woman watching over you..." I said. Well that is bloody creepy. I watched the parade as a giant inflatable man with a gold and green cape floated by.

"You don't think that Elvis is somewhere up above, watching out for you when you need him?" asked Harvey.

I shook my head. "Elvis' ashes are scatered around a tree in the back-yard. He is as dead as they get. Not much more to it..."

Harvey said nothing, only buttoned up his felt jacket up to right under his chin.

"It must make things unbearable sometimes," he said after a few more floats had gone by. "To think that you are so very alone in this world."

"I am not alone, Harvey. You are standing right beside me," I said. My mouth tasted sickly, like I had let a mouthful of apple juice ferment against my teeth.

"It is not a question of the body, but a question of the soul," he said.

Well. Fuck you, Harvey the mystic.

He looked over at me. "Don't murder me with your eyes, Nina," he said.

Touché.

"Maybe I'm the one who is wrong. Maybe Colette is dead, cold, in the ground. In that case, it is my job to keep her alive in my heart," said Harvey.

"I'm sure that your sons will do the same," I said.

"Do you want to go grab a bite to eat?" he asked. "I'm feeling rather cold all of a sudden."

"Sure, I said. Where to?"

"Irish pub? To go along with the theme of the day?" he asked.

"Sure," I said. "So have you heard anything from Cedric recently?" I asked as we walked in the direction of Bishop Street.

"I was sure that I had told you," said Harvey. "Didn't I tell you about the letter that he sent me?"

"No, I don't think so..." I said. But what does it matter what I *think* that I think?

"He wrote me a letter about two weeks ago," said Harvey. "From the States."

"He lives in the US now?" I asked. "Legally?"

Harvey chuckled. "That much is unclear. He said that he is feeling better, that he met a girl and that he wants to bring her back to Canada."

"That is nice. Maybe he is finally ready to turn a new page," I said.

"What I have learnt through Cedric – with much pain and difficulty, I may add – is that people need their space."

"Grieving is different for everyone," I said, thinking of my own three children when they lost their father, or when they found out about the slow draining away of their mother.

"Not just about grieving though," he said. "Some people need a corner of a room to themselves, others an entire house, and people like Cedric... a few thousand kilometres?"

So very true, I thought to myself. We arrived at Fiddler's Green and Harvey opened the door for me.

We exchanged *bonjours* with the waitress and were told to take which ever seat we pleased.

"Is Cedric working out there?" I asked as we went to the booth closest to the front window.

"He seems to have found work picking melons in Arizona," said Harvey. "Speaking of which, did you see what happened in Tucson yesterday?" he asked and he let himself fall onto the wooden bench.

"Tucson?" What the hell is a Tucson?

"At the Trump rally?" said Harvey. "There were a few protestors who were roughed up but the security guards."

"Seriously?" I asked as I took of my coat. "What scum."

Harvey said nothing.

"What, are you a Trump supporter?" I asked.

"Oh, no," he said. "Certainly not. I was just thinking about what you said about Cedric being an illegal worker."

"I wonder too, would he be the type that Trump would deport?" I asked.

Harvey shook his head. "No. That's not it. I remember now. I told you about Cedric, and you asked the very same question last time."

"Me," I said brightly, "no! You must be talking about your other girl-friend!"

He continued to shake his head.

March 28

So obviously, Harvey and I have gotten closer since he rang on my doorbell in October. I had developed feelings for him, but at the same time, I felt so guilty...

It was the end of December when things between us became more serious. Elvis had only been gone for five months.

We were standing on my doorstep, a soft white snow falling. Yes, I know, it was a very Gatsby-kissing-Daisy-before-the-war type scene... But this time, it was real.

Harvey stepped closer to me. I put my hand on the doorknob.

"So how often do you look across the street, Nina?" he asked.

"I don't understand what you mean," I said.

"The first time we met. Remember, when we first had tea in your kitchen?" I nodded. "Well, you said that you loved to look at my house, that you were charmed by it. But do you look often?"

"Harvey, you know that I don't do these riddles and trick questions..." I said.

Okay, I'll be frank. Am I on your mind as often as you are on mine, Nina?"

"Harvey, we're neighbours. And friends..." I could feel my face getting very warm. The wind swirled the snow around us, wrapping itself around the streetlights.

"I'd like to think of you as more than a friend." He looked into my eyes and I looked away. I leaned back against the door.

"Harvey..." I could not bring myself to look at him.

"I've gone too far..." he said, taking a step back. I was vaguely aware of the smell of his cologne fading away. The wind continued to spin.

"Harvey, I was married to Elvis for 36 years..."

"Nina," he said, "it is not your fault that Elvis passed away. And it's not my fault that Collette is gone either. We are not responsible for that. We loved them. Truly." He took a step towards me. "But Collette and Elvis... They are gone, but we are still here. And they would want us to be happy. I know in my heart that they would. You deserve to feel loved, Nina."

"Of course I feel loved, Harvey. I have my children and my—"

"You know very well that that is not what I mean."

The wind picked up.

"Harvey," I said, "what you are asking of me... It isn't fair. How can I put up any defenses against you?"

"You don't need to, Nina. Why do you need to defend yourself from me? Listn. We don't need to get married. We don't need to move in together. We don't need to vacation in the same hotel room. We don't even need to tell anyone else about it. I just need to know if... If you think about me too."

"Harvey," I said. I took his gloved hands into my own. "Aren't we too old for this? Dating and stealing kisses and sneaking about... Aren't we at a different stage of life now?" I asked.

"No. I want to sneak about with you, Nina."

"Don't be angry, Harvey," I said, taking my hand away. "You're just asking for more than I have to give."

"Nina, being with you is the brightest part of my day."

"I feel the same way," I said. "But I'm just not ready."

"I can wait," he said.

The wind tore at my face. My eyes watered. "I don't want you to wait," I said. "Find someone who is worthy of your affection, Harvey."

"No," he said. "No, there is no one else. I will continue to pursue you, Nina. Unless you tell me not to. Unless you say that you're done with me."

"Why does it have to be this way?" I asked. I could feel myself geting angry. "So either I say that we can be friends, and you continue with your romantic advances... Or we are through. Goodbye? Just like that?"

"I am too much in love with you to be a good friend to you, Nina. But I understand if you don't see me that way."

"You're being unfair, Harvey."

"I can't help it," he said. "You're right, but I can't help it."

I leaned back against the door. "What are you really asking me, Harvey?"

"Am I on your mind?" he asked.

"Of course," I said.

"Do love me? Like I love you? If you weren't worried about people's reaction to our relationship, if we were in a world of our own, would you want to be with me, Nina?"

The answer was burning my lips but I could not bring myself to say it.

"Nina?" he leaned closer to me again, so close that I could feel the warmth of his body. "Can we see each other again? Or should I stop coming to your door?"

I stood there, still silent. The wind finally died down.

"Nina?" He took off a glove and put his warm hand on my cheek. "Can we go for tea tomorrow?"

I lifted my hand with the intention of taking his away, but instead, I just held it.

"Okay," I said. "Okay. We can go for tea."

"That will do for now," said Harvey. He leaned forward and kissed my forehead.

"Goodnight, Nina," he said as he turnd away.

"Goodnight."

The smell of his cologne lingered on me long into the night.

April 3, 2016

"I know about him" said Elvis.

"Who?" I asked, taking off my earrings and dropping them into my jewellery box.

"Where were you tonight?" he asked.

I turned to Elvis and unzipped my dress from under my arm to the top of my hip. "What are you talking about, dear?" I asked,

"I saw you outside the restaurant."

"You knew that I was going out with a couple other associates," I said, stepping out of my dress. "Are you joining me in the shower?"

"I'm serious, Nina..." he said.

I walked into the ensuite bathroom and he followed me.

"Who was he?"

"A colleague, Elvis." I leaned in and turned on the shower. Elvis reached in and turned off the shower. It was a surprising, brusque movement, especially coming from him.

"You said that this would stop, Nina."

"Stop what? Elvis, you're acting like this because I went to the restaurant with a few colleagues?"

He shook his head. "Nina. Stop it! I followed you!"

I blinked. Shit.

"What did you do with Tom?" I asked, "while you were creeping around?"

"I brought him with me."

"Elvis," I said, crossing my arms over my bare chest. "That is irresponsible... This has nothing to do with him! Poor baby. This may have an impact on him... psychologically, when he grows up. Sneaking about in the bushed, spying on his Mom. Really, Elvis?"

"Sorry," he said, shaking his head. "I didn't think of that. But that is not the point!"

"What is your point?"

"You admit it then? Just like that?"

"Okay," I said, impatient. Inconvenienced. "What is your point?"

Elvis started crying. We were standing there, him fully clothed and sobbing into his hands, me totally naked, arms crossed, indifferent.

"Nina... You're breaking my heart."

"Elvis... It is not what you think."

He shook his head. "I don't deserve this."

I shrugged.

"Who is he?" he asked.

"No one... You're just making this worse. Leave it alone, Elvis," I said.

"Nina, you're poisoning me. Why? I love you so much..." he crumbled to the ground next to the sink.

"If you knew that you would feel this way, why did you follow me?"

He did not answer.

"Elvis. You're doing this to yourself," I said.

He shook his head. "This was not how it was supposed to be."

"Sorry to disappoint..." I said.

"Why do you do it, Nina? Why?"

"I don't know, Elvis," I said, sinking to the floor in front of him, my back against the cold bathtub. "What do you want me to say?"

"How long has it been?" asked Elvis.

"Once. Only once..."I said.

Elvis looked up and shook his head. "Who is he?" he asked. "Not another client..."

"Yes..."

He wiped his face. "Nina... Why?"

I shook my head. "I don't know."

"I think I'm going to be sick," he said as he got to his feet. I went into the bedroom and closed the door behind me. Elvis followed, a few minutes later, eyes shiny, face red, the front of his shirt soaked in tears, hairy belly fat sticking out at the bottom.

"Why don't you just leave me?" he asked. "Wouldn't that make it easier for all of us?"

"I can't leave you, Elvis."

"You won't leave me, because you're afraid to hurt me?" he asked.

"No, I—"

"You've hurt me enough, Nina. except this doing it this way is a slow torture."

"I don't mean to torture you, Elvis..." I said. And I meant it. I had no intention to cause him any pain... If only he stayed out of it!

"Is there something wrong with me? Is it my fault? I can change, Nina... For you, I can change. I would do anything..." he began crying again.

"You haven't done anything. Its me, Elvis. Not you."

"Me not you. You not me. It doesn't even mean anything anymore," he whispered. "We don't mean anything anymore."

"You do mean something to me, Elvis," I said. "This stuff... It's all stupid. I'm stupid. I don't deserve a good man like you."

"I am not afraid of being alone, you know," he said. "And I'm not staying because of Thomas. I want you, Nina. *You*. You are the love of my life. But I can't take what you're doing to my heart anymore. I don't know how much longer I can survive like this..."

"I said its stupid. It didn't mean anything. What more can I say?"

"How did we get to be this way, Nina?"

I had no idea what to answer, seeing as I had no idea what the answer could be. Looking back at my behaviour – now that I am older, happier, now that Elvis died of a heart attack – I am ashamed of myself. But I still don't know why I acted that way. More than anything, I new that he deserved better. But even more than that, I wanted to have a good time.

"We didn't get this way, Elvis."

"What did I do wrong? What can I change? How can I make you happy?" he asked. He begged.

"If it means so much to you, I will stop seeing him right away," I said.

Elvis nodded. "Okay."

I went to hug him, but he pushed me away.

"You smell like him."

"Sorry," I said. "I'll go shower."

As I stood under the scalding hot water, I tried to decide how I would handle this latest incident. Poor Elvis. Had he been angry, or hostile, or at least something other than sad... I may have been able to respect him. But this big, crying, snotty, self-pitying man? Not my concern.

When I got out of the shower, Elvis was lying on his side of the bed, his back towards me.

"Goodnight," I said as I got into bed. No response. "I will be home late tomorrow. I have a training session on the South Shore." No response.

April 12, 2016

I called Rachel yesterday morning to ask if she wanted to come visit before the class that she was giving.

She said "Why, so you can write to Claire and bitch me out? Are you out of material now?"

"Rachel, what are you talking about?" I asked. I felt very small. I had a bad feeling about the last visit but I could not quite place why. "What did Claire tell you?"

"You're an idiot. You're the one who is fucking difficult to be around. And your house was smelly and dirty. Just like you. You may want to remember to text the right person next time, Mom."

"Rachel, I'm not—"

"You never could admit your mistakes in the past, only god knows why I would expect it from you now," she said.

"Rachel—"

The line was dead. My stomach felt heavy and watery.

I went into my bedroom to fetch my cellphone only to realize that I had not connected the wire properly, so the battery was uncharged. I plugged my cellphone into the wall – on a wire far too short – and stood there awkwardly waiting for the screen to flash on so that I could check my text messages.

Finally, it turned back on. I waited for several moments while the whole thing loaded. I checked my past messages to Claire, scrolling back one, two, even three months. Nothing. There was nothing about Rachel at all... So if I had not sent the message to Claire... I sank down to the ground, my back to the wall. Then it hit me. I checked in my text conversation with Rachel. And there it was.

Rachel came over today. She really pissed me off. She made a bunch of coments about my hair and the house and things. She is so fucking difficult to be around. Anyways. Just needed to vent. Good luck with your gallery event tonigh. X

I felt terrible. It was one thing to be angry about Rachel's comments, it was another thing to need to get it off my chest, but I certainly did not need to be so so rude... I decided that the best thing I could do was to write her back. To apologize for everything.

Rachel, you are right. I sent that mssage to the wrong person. I feel terrible about the whole thing. I dont expect you to forgive me right away... I understand if you need time. Ill try to call you again in a few days to talk about all this.

Her response?

Typical. How can I forgive you if you havent even asked for forgiveness? Im tired of trying to teach an old dog new tricks. I'm done.

April 15, 2016

I was reading a newspaper article today, boy was it depressing as hell.

so this young girl, Claire's age or so, living in the UK, was diagnosed with a terminal cancer. Six months to one year.

And what did she do?

Well, she decided to live.

Isn't that the most glorious thing that you have ever heard?

"What use is there to fold in on myself and just wait for death,' – I paraphrase, "– when we all know that it is coming? The only difference is that my clock is ticking a little faster. So beit!"

She went on describing how she worked, dated, went to the movies and saved up for... a rainy day?

"Will you be starting a family?"

"Oh," she said, "I don't think so. I'm not quite ready for that!"

"Do you tell people around you that you are dying?"

"Oh," she said, "no, not generally. People seem to get really freaked out by that kind of thing. At the end of the day, I'm not looking to make anyone depressed or anything!"

"How is your family taking it?"

The girl broke eye contact for the first time, wrote the journalist. "They wish that I would slow down. They wish that I would prioritize my medical appointments, not my social life. They wish that I would get nine hours of sleep a night, eat my vegetables, drink only water. Well. May I ask? What the hell is the point of prolonging a life that I don't want to live?"

The journalist added, on last line, that girl died before the article made it to publication.

April 18, 2016

I've been sleeping like shit.

I had Claire over today. I wanted to ask her about what I should do with Rachel.

Claire was distant. I thnk that she sidded with her sister.

Thank goodness I have Harvey. He is the only person who isn't brining me down.

I am so tired. The child is back. She has a younger brother. Only he has eyelids. Only, no eyes.

I think it is all a subliminal message coming from my brain.

Why am I so blind?

Is it possible at my age to only need two hours of sleep a night?

Being painfully awake as the whole world sleeps was hard enough, but add a bunch of fucked up nightmares during the few moments when you've FINALLY drifted off...

April 28, 2016

There is a house for sale across the street. It is being sold directly by the owners. It is incredible how much times have changed since I stopped selling houses.

I am not sure how I got into the real estate business. I think that what drew me in, more than anything else, are two main things:

1 – it was a respectable career that was reasitic for a woman

2 – it was all very superficial

My boss used to say that 50% of our job was to show up and look good. 49% was for the staging of the house. 1% was given to the actually place itself. An average buyer would make up his mind on whether or not he was taking the place before the front door closed behind him.

Back when I started, there was no alternative to the real estate agent. We were kings. Everyone had to come to us, unless they were inheriting a dead relative's property. Now, with all of those websites and applications, I think that the job of a real estate agent is not taken as seriously as it was.

When I graduated from high school, my mother expected me to move out on my own. A parent of one of my friends was a real estate broker. She showed up at school once to pick up Marie, her daughter, and I was taken.

"What does you dad do?" I asked Marie the next morning.

"He's a barber. Why?" she asked.

"He must be pretty good at his job, I said, if it means that your mom can dress like that."

"Actually, my mom has her own job."

"What does she do?" I asked, surprised.

Today, all of this talk sounds silly. But in the 1960s, there were only a handful of options: nurse, teacher, secretary. As far as I knew, there was no other way for a woman to have a career for herself. Well, unless you were willing to be a call girl.

"She is a real estate broker," said Marie. "She graduated from a real estate college in New York State called Sir Gallaher's or something."

"You have to go to college to sell real estate?" I asked.

"No. If you find an internship, you can work your way up like that."

I nodded.

"Why? Are you interested in real estate?" she asked.

"Not really. But I want her suit," I said.

Marie laughed. "I'll let her know."

By the end of the summer I had quit my job working in a Westmount flower shop – what a horrendously dull job! – and had begun a semi-paid internship with Marie's mom, Hélène.

I was the coffee girl, then the copy girl, and finally I was Hélène's personal secretary. She recognized my aptitude for anticipation, my creativity, my allure.

She let me do my first house showing some time in the new year. I was so nervous and it turned out horribly. I answered multiple questions with wrong answers, thank goodness Hélène was there to correct me. I wrapped up the visit with a door slammed on the client's thumb, which was visibly shattered. The thumb was shattered, not the door. So obviously, she left the house to go straight to the ER. I expected to be punished.

The next day when I showed up for work, Hélène went about as if nothing had happened. She handed me the files for another house, one further out in the suburbs.

"When will you be ready?" she asked. "Ring up the clients and give them a meeting time as soon as you're comfortable with the property."

"But why?" I asked.

"Don't you want to be a real estate agent?" she asked.

"Yes... But with what happened last weekend..."

Hélène squinted her eyes at me. That usually meant that she had something important to say.

"Nina, remember one thing," she said. "The best case scenario is that you come face to face with the worst case scenario the very first time that you try something. That way, you know what a bad feeling it is. you know what failure is, as true and hard as your own bones. It was a perfect showing," she said.

"No, it wasn't…"

"That is the point. You've gotten your ass kicked. You're a cocky little lady. You needed that. Stay humble, Nina. And read over that file."

She threw me into the fire, then let me roast ever so slowly. Hélène really took the time to mentor me, so that three years later, I was the top-performing agent.

A head-hunter from another company invited me out for drinks.

I met him in an upscale hotel bar. The whole place was dark and full of cigarette smoke. Men in tuxes and women in cocktail dresses and sky-high bangs leaned back and forth in their seats.

The recruiter was a younger gentleman, who seemed like an older man at the time, but who was probably about 35 years old. He led me to a table away from the crowd, against a back wall.

He ordered two martinis and excused himself to go to mensroom. When he came back, the drinks were already on the table.

"Tell me about yourself," he said as he took out a long, thin cigarette.

"There isn't much to tell," I said as I eyed him from above my martini glass. "And I'm not so much into small talk."

He nodded, took a drag from his cigarette. "Well. I am looking to hire you. Well, not myself. but a rather well-known client of mine." He blew out the smoke and it smelled of menthol.

I nodded.

"High end real-estate. Residential, but also commercial lots. The company is looking for qualified agents, but also for a girl who looks good in heels. No fat or ugly ones. Know what I mean?"

I nodded again.

"What is the old battle-axe paying you?"

I should have spoken in Hélène's defense, but I did not. Maybe I was too taken up by the compliments? Or maybe I have never had a soul, no sense of obligation, no personal attachment, no feeling of moral duty.

"What is your final offer?" I asked, trying to play it tough. I probably sounded like a moron.

An arrangement was made, and I left my little cocoon to blossom in another garden. The salary increase was quite drastic.

That is when my life really began: sun, snow, ski, sex, sand, surf... only the best S words for this little lady.

Point two, the superficiality of the domain.

I loved seeing a house, with two homely little owners – elderly couple looking to sell to downsize, frumpy middle-aged couple looking for more bedrooms, obnoxious first-time parents looking for a place near a park and a good public school – just begging to be told what to do. It was so much power (point #3?).

Fix your flowerbed, paint the doorframe, add a rug, buy a plant, polish that faucet, yellow in a kitchen? Never!... And they loved being told what to do! they begged for more!

I made myself a rule: never sleep with your clients. That rule quickly shifted to: never sleep with your married clients, which became: don't sleep with a client before the deal is sealed.

Retiring from real estate selling was tough. I hardly took any time off during my 40 something year career, save for the time my mother was institutionalized, and the birth of my children. So to leave it for good... I felt like I was giving up on life. It was Elvis who confinced me to quit, and I only accepted under two conditions:

1 – that I could still sell the houses of friends who asked

2 – that we would pick up and travel the world together

By then, my relationship with Elvis had shifted into something that I actually wanted for myself. I may even have though I deserved him.

May 6

POEM: MY LIFE WAS A TSUNAMI

Life is like a glass of water
When you are born, the glass is full
And slowly
Very slowly
It begins to tip
And to drip
And before you know it
Every screaming, futile, blurry moment has passed
And the glass is emty
My life was a tsunami
Now the wave has rolled away
Onto a different shore

May 11, 2016

I spent last weekend at Tom's place. It was a nice break.

Laci is doing well.

I asked Tom what he though about Rachel. It was Saturday morning and we were sitting around the circular chrome plated and fiberglass table in a kitchen so small that it had to be stuck to the wall.

"Mom, you cant take those things too seriously," he said. "It is Rachel. You know now she can get."

I explained about my text to the wrong person.

"I've done that once," said Zandra. "When I was a teen. I wrote this terrible email about a friend, meaning to send it to another friend. It was mean, but I just wanted to... You know, I needed to express myself. But since I was thinking of the frined that I wrote the email about... I accidentally sent it to her."

"Oh," I said, "what happened after?"

"Bad example," said Zandra. "Sorry. She never talked to me again."

"I think that Rachel just needs some time to digest what happened. Did you apologize to her?" asked Tom.

"Yes. I apologized, but she refuses to hear it. Can you talk to her, Tom?"

He and Zandra exchanged uncomfortable looks.

"Uh, we already did..." he said finally.

Zandra stood up. "I will go check on Laci, then take a shower..." She left the room.

"What do you mean, Tom?" I asked. "What do you mean, you already spoke to her?"

He stood up. "Would you like something to drink?" he asked. "I'm grabbing some orange juice. Do you want some orange juice?"

I picked at the egg on my plate with my fork. Suddenly, it was no longer appetizing: the yolk screamed at me like a little yellow guerilla soldier.

"Mom?" he asked, glass in one hand, carton of milk in the other. "Do you want a glass?"

"No. I want to know what is going on, Thomas. What did Rachel say?"

He sat down with his glass. "I called Claire the other day. Just to talk. It was not long after she had been over to your place. When you explained the misunderstanding?"

"What did she say?"

Tom leaned back, his 70's flower-print plastic and fake chrome chair giving slightly under his weight. "Basically. She said that you fucked up. She told me a bit about it, so I called Rachel."

"What exactly did *Claire* say?"

Tom let his chair fall back onto all four feet with a bang. "Claire said that you spent a morning with Rachel and then decided to text her to bitch about it. Only that you messed up and sent it to the wrong daughter."

"Did Claire... Did she sound upset with me?" I asked.

"Not really. Well. A little." Tom played around with his spoon in his empty cereal bowl. "She was sad because things were finally going better between her and Rachel. But you really set things back making it seem like you and Claire had a habit of talking about Rachel..."

"We did," I said. "I mean, we used to..."

"Mom, I'm not trying to act like your parent or anything... But I don't think that you should talk about Rachel that way anymore. And especially not with Claire."

"Well," I said. My heart was heavy. "I didn't know that Claire felt that way. She never told me."

"You shouldn't need your daughter to tell you not to say things like that, Mom."

I shrugged.

"Anyways, so I called Rachel after," said Tom. "She was really hurt. Especially because she felt like you and Claire were teaming up against her."

"Oh, Rachel has always felt like the odd one out," I said. "Doesn't she see that she most of the time, she is the one who exludes herself?"

"Mom," said Tom. "That may be true... But you just shouldn't say stuff like that."

"What is her problem?" I asked. I could feel my patience waning.

Tom took a deep breath, still staring at his bowl. "She blames you for having been gone so much... for the way you treated Dad."

"It is easy to blame someone else when things go wrong in your life... I don't mind playing to role of... play the... the person who takes the blame—"

"Scapegoat?"

"Yes," I said, "I don't mind being the scapegoat, so long as she doesn't corrupt the rest of you."

Tom rolled his eyes. I could not tell if the gesture was directed at me or at Rachel, but I let it slide.

The drive home the next day was very tiring. Tom said that he will pay for my bus ticket next time I visit, an offer which I may very wel take.

I stopped along the way home for a quick lunch in a casse croute.

I ate a plate of fish and chips with tartar sauce. The batter was perfectly greasy, and together with an ice-cold Coke, it was a little slice of paridise on the tongue.

There was a woman with three sons who came in as I was about to leave. She was clearly outnumbered and overwhelmed: she carried the smallest child in her arms – he was screaming bloody murder – she was holding one by the hand – he was also screaming bloody murder – and the third was walking along behind her, a shoelace dragging along the ground.

"Tie your shoe, Max," she said, her voice barely audible over the two smaller ones.

"I can't!" shouted the eldest of the pack. "Help me!"

She sighed and tried to get on her knees.

"I can do it," I said.

She looked up, at first surprised, but then she said "thank you!"

I got to my knee to help with Max's shoelace. He looked away, embarrassed. I took one lace in each hand. Then... I looked at them. "How does this go again?" I thought.

The mother got her youngest into a highchair and the second in a booster seat. I was still trying to tie the damn shoe.

"Mom..." said the boy when he saw that his mother's hands were free, "the old lady forgot how."

May 19

Rachel is so hard on me... I really do not believe that she realizes how hurtful words can be. She cannot possibly care about me, or my condition, to say and do the types of things that she does.

Dr. Lee convinced me to go back to the psychologist. She suggested that I bring Rachel. I do not understand why I accepted, even less why Rachel agreed to show up.

We sat in different corners of the waiting room. The receptionist was surprised when we both stood up together to go into the physiologist's office. I sat in the armchair and Rachel took the loveseat opposite the doctor.

"Tell me why you have brought your daughter today," he said. "Should I call you Ms. Rossi, Ms. O'Connor, or—"

"Call me Rachel."

I cleared my throat. "Rachel is very angry with me right now. We are not on speaking terms. You see, there was—"

"You just won't change, will you, Mom?"

I looked over at her. I shrugged. I could not see her point, could not understand her problem.

"Rachel," said the psychologist, "let your mother speak. You will have your turn, and she will give you the same respect."

Rachel crossed her arms tightly and looked away. "Doubtful..." she whispered under her breath. *And she thinks that I won't change?*

"Continue, Mrs. O'Connor."

"There was a misunderstanding between myself and Rachel. I wrote her something that I should not have. It was stupid of me, and I feel terrible. I was trying to vent, but I went about it in the wrong way. And now Rachel – and even Claire – won't talk to me."

"Would you care to elaborate on this minunderstanding, Rachel?" asked the psychologist.

"No."

"Rachel!" I shouted. The psychologist eyed me and I shut my mouth.

"I can tell that you are frustrated, Rachel. At it would seem that your mother admits to have done something in order for this frustration to be merited."

"I'm not frustrated," said Rachel, still not making eye contact with either of us. "To be frustrated would show that I care, it would mean that the words that come out of her mouth matter to me. It would mean that I feel an emotion towards her. Well, it is not the case. That time has long slid away."

"So it is not really about this most recent quarrel, is it?" asked the psychologist.

Rachel shrugged.

"Sometimes we fight ofer small events, when in reality, it is a much more important underlying problem that is really bothering us. Is there a history of this type of issue, Mrs. O'Connor?" he asked. "Have things always been this tense between the two of you?"

I took a deep breath. He was barging into dangerous territory. "Rachel has always been a mystery to me. She has always been difficult to understand. Her father and—"

"Don't you drag him into this," said Rachel. She finally looked me square in the eye. "You have no right." Each word was measured, its own small, threatening explosion.

"Explain your reaction," said the psychologist, his tone gentle.

Rachel stiffened up again and looked away. "He was always there for me. He was my hero. I miss him so much..."

I tried to reach over and put my hand on her knee to comfort her. She moved further away on the loveseat.

"I miss him too, Rachel."

"Yeah, right," she sneered. "That is why you were such a good wife to him."

"It is none of your busin—"

"Oh just stop it, Mom! You drove him away! Constantly! If he was on the road all of the time, if he chose to have jobs that took him out of the country, it was to get away from you. I know the truth, Mom." She wiped a tear that had freed itself and was rolling down her cheek. "I know about you affairs, Mom. I know about it all. Why do you think that I'm so fucked up? Why do you think that I paraded around like a fucking slut all through high school, when in reality, I was still a virgin until university? I have no self-respect. I have no idea how to have a *normal* relationship with a man. And how could I have learnt? Who was there to teach me?"

"Rachel—"

"The only way I have ever learnt how to gain respect is through my studies. I am so lucky that I met Adil..."

"Rachel, that is silly..."

"It is your fault," she said, shaking her head.

"I had no idea that you felt that way," I said. "You're such a smart girl, Rachel. You have so much going for you..."

"I'm not a girl. I'm a woman. A poor, sad, lost, broken woman. And I'm fatherless. And I am alone. Dear god, I am so alone right now..." Rachel bent over, hiding her face in her hands, her blond hair spilling almost to the floor.

"You're not alone, Rachel. I'm here for you."

"Of course you're not," she said, looking up. All of the life had seeped out of her voice. She was no longer animated, but subdued. Distant. She scared me. "You fucked me up and you can't fix me. And you will never be forgiven because you will never apologize for what you did."

"I was selfish, Rachel," I said. "You're right. I was so selfish. I thought that because you were so little... I thought that you would not remember. I was stupid."

"See what I mean?" said Rachel, looking at the psychologist for the frst time. "I swear," she chocked back a laugh, "I swear, this woman cannot apologize for her actions. It is physically impossible." She bent over, burying her face again. I had never seen Rachel look so vulnerable.

"Well, Mrs. O'Connor?" asked the psychologist. "Clearly, Rachel is hurt. And she needs for her feelings to be validated. She also needs to hear that you are sorry for the pain that you've caused her. What do you have to say to your daughter, Mrs. O'Connor?"

I turned to Rachel. "I swear, Rachel. I had no idea that you felt this way."

Rachel jumped to her feet. "Fuck you. To hell with you. I'm done." She left the room, slamming the door shut behind her.

"You may want to try to get to know her a little better," said the shrink.

"What?"

"She is no longer a child, no longer a teen," he said. "And she clearly feels as though the two of you are strangers. Have you tried having an open conversation with her, Mrs. O'Connor?"

"She gets offended no matter what I say," I said,

"What about letting her speak? And you just listening?" he asked.

Why? I thought. Because she bores me nearly to death. Because all she does it talk about university. About her fantastic achievements, her grants, her classes, and her grades. But never about... never about anything important.

"I strongly suggest, after she has had the time to calm her feelings, that you too come back together. This is a safe space, a neutral space," he said. "But until she is ready, keep you distance. Don't push her. And when she feels that she is prepared to talk to you again, we can certainly make some progress together. Just let me know when you'd like to meet again."

"Sure thing."

When I went out the waiting room, she was already long gone.

"Claire?" I said when she picked up the phone. "You will never guess what happened."

"I cant talk now Mom," she said. "I'm busy at work. I'll get back to you later."

I decided to drive right over to the Old Port to talk things over with

Claire. It hurt me that she had been avoiding me, that she wasn't taking my side on this issue.

As always, it was hell to find parking. When I finally did – and payed good money for it, of course – I rambled up and down a few cobble-stone streets until I came upon the right art gallery.

The door was propped open, as it was an unusally humid afternoon. I looked in, and who did I see standing at the cash talking to Claire?

None other than the detested Rachel. That kite.

May 26, 2016

Thomas was four. Rachel was four weeks old. I was getting ready to head back to the real estate business in a couple of weeks. Things between Elvis and I were rocky, at best.

"Oh, Nina!" he shouted one night as he walked in the door. I was in the living room, busy trying to breastfeed Rachel – an endeavour which I would quit only a few days later – and Tom was having a fit in his room.

"What." It was not a question. It was a statement. What. What the fuck. My life is a fuckstorm. What. Go to hell. Fuck off. What.

I heard the sound of scratching on the floor. "Can you come over here?"

"You come here," I shouted. Rachel began to whimpr. So did the something at the door. "What have you done, Elvis?"

Without warning, a golden-red puppy came scampering through the house. The first thing it did was pee on the carpet under the ottoman. Elvis' smiling face peeked around the corner of the living room doorway.

"Isn't she adorable?" he asked. The tiny dog-sized intruder looked up at him, long fiery locks flowing about. "What should we call her?" he asked.

Tom, sensing a change in energy in the house, had dropped the toys that he was busy hurling around his bedroom and came to sit in the stairs.

"Puppy?" he asked.

"What should we call her, Tommy Boy?" asked Elvis.

I was still sitting there on the couch, half of my blouse open, Rachel stirring uncomfortably, my mouth gaping.

"Puppy!" shouted Tom.

"Poppy it is," said Elvis.

"She pissed on the carpet," I said as I went into the kitchn.

"I'll take care of it!" shouted Elvis, struggling to follow me and to take off his boots all at the same time. He fell and caught himself on the doorframe.

A few minutes later, Tom and Elvis came into the kitchen all dressed in their winter clothes. They chatted back and forth to each other, thick as thieves. I watched them play in the backyard through the patio door. The puppy was running around in circles and Tom kept cracking up, bending over all letting himself fall into the snow. The dog would bark, jumping her front paws up and down, then run around in circles. I was still holding Rachel, who was dozing in my arms uneasily. She kept jumping up and scaring herself, her eyelids fluttering open each time.

Tom was busy digging a hole in the snow as the dog sat next to him, watching him. Elvis walked back to the door. "Do you want to come play outside with Poppy?" he asked. "I can take care of Rachel."

"What was the big idea getting a dog, without talking to me about it, when we have a four-year-old and a newborn? Are you mad?" I asked.

"I thought that it would make Tom feel less alone. Having a dog helps build character, helps to make kids responsible," he said.

"You didn't even ask me."

"Well, fuck! You're not my mother, are you?" he asked.

I shook my head. "No. But it sure feels like it." Anger welled up inside me. I could feel my face getting warm. "What will happen next time when you're out of town? Who will be stuck taking care of the dog then?"

Elvis did not answer me, instead sliding the patio door shut in my face. The desired effect was some sort of slam, but the loose screw in the bottom track made him struggle and have to pull the door back a forth a few times before it would shut completely. I stormed back into the living room.

The door reopened about 20 minutes later and the dog ran in. I watched as she went back over to the spot near the couch where she had peed. Tom and Elvis came into the room, their arms full of their sopping wet winter cloths.

"Don't you love her!" called Tom.

"Be pleasant, Nina," said Elvis, his lips hardly moving as he spoke.

"She's a fine dog," I said. "Did you clean up the piss, Elvis?"

"You left in there?" he said. "I'll take care of it..." he threw the outdoor clothes down the stairs into the basement.

"You know that they won't find their way into the dryer themselves!" I called after him.

Tom ran over to me, then noticed that I was holding Rachel. He pouted, turned around and ran back up to his room. The dog tried to follow him up the stairs, but was too little. She kept jumping on the first step, then falling onto her back. Giving up, she began to chew on the rug on front of the stairs. Elvis returned to the living room with a handful of papertowel. He wiped up the little puddle.

"There you go," he said. "Good as new. Where is Tom?"

"Ran back upstairs," I said. "Your dog is chewing on the carpet."

Elvis went to pick up the dog.

"Why is Tommy upstairs?" he asked.

"Because Rachel is in the room," I said.

"I will bring Poppy to his room" said Elvis. He stopped halfway up the stairs. "I love you, Nina."

"Don't forget about the clothes in the dryer."

June 16, 2016

Sleeping continues to be a struggle. One hour. Two hours. Just blinking at the ceiling. Ugh.

I saw the psychologist a few days ago. I harent written since, he pissed me off so much. God dammit. Treating me like a child.

So I walked into the office, and of course, the first thing he wants to know is how things are going with Rachel. So I tell him watever, no change, and he does not really like that answer.

I'm pissed because I don't want to be back there in the first place. Then he drops another bomb.

"I am a bit confused," he admitted. Finally something that I can agree with! "Mrs. O'Connor, let me be frank. In the last few appointments, I have begun to feel a very high level of agitation on your part, and a lot of hostility towards me. Since Mr. O'Connor—"

"His name is Elvis Rossi. I'm the O'Connor," I say, happy to have a reason to cut him off.

"His name *was* Elvis Rossi," said the psychologist, just as glad for a chance to correct me. Fuck. "So let me go on, please. Since the death of your husband, have you had any other very remarkable behavioural changes? What do your other two children think?"

I sat there, silent, immobile, brooding as he looked through is papers.

"Thomas and Claire," he read from my file. "Have they said anything about—"

"Oh, come off it!" I shouted, surprising both the psychologist and myself. "What does this matter?"

"Okay," he said, both hands in the air as a sign of a peace offering. "Let me change the subject for the timebeing. Have you been writing at all?" he asked. "Keeping some sort of journal or something of the like?"

"No," I lied. "I don't like to write."

"If you remember what we said before," he said, "I strongly suggest that you keep some sort of journal, Mrs. O'Connor. It would be useful for many reasons, including keeping your brain active."

"And what are the other reasons?" I asked.

"What do you think?" he asked.

"Well, shit," I said. "Now you're having me your job for you."

His eyes jumped up to meet mine, then went back to the paper in my patient folder as he took a few notes.

"What is the point? So that you can read how I slowly forget to spell my own name?" I asked.

"No," he said. "Of course not. It is a private journal. I would not read it, Mrs. O'Connor. Well. Unless you were to ask me to read it."

"And what is it that you would find?" I asked.

"You mean regarding your ability to write?" A question answered by another question.

"Yes?" Never two without three.

"Slowly, as we age, we begin losing some language skills. Even without Alzheimer's, it happens to us all with age. But your state... It may change a little more quickly. Already when you write, you have probably started to make some simple mistakes, especially when you're tired or when you're feeling emotionally distressed. Some studies of Agatha Christie's writing have come to the conclusion that she had Alzheimer, although she never received that diagnosis. She—"

"What happened to her writing?" I asked, curious, despite myself.

"There are some subtle changes that can take place before the evident mistakes begin to grip the pen. In Christie's case, researchers found that fewer words were used altogether, that the words she did use were less precise, that she wrote many more indefinite pronouns, that she became prone to repetition... That type of thing," said Detective Poirot. He took a deep breath. "Had she been able to continue to write, she would have made more and more spelling, grammar and punctuation mistakes. And then, the sentences which had grown gracelessly long would have become simplr, shorter, and less and less coherent. Eventually, she would have found it too strenuous to write at all."

Suddenly, my journal began to feel more like a ticking time bomb than a means of self-expression.

"I had no idea," I said, more to myself than to the psychologist.

"Did you get a chance to read any of the literature?" he asked. "I am sure that there is a section about language skills."

"Literature?" I echoed.

"Those pamphlets that I gave you? When you were first diagnosed?" he asked, jotting down a few more notes.

"Literature! That is not literature! There is nothing further from literature than those pamplets! The crap you gave me is... is..." I realized that I had been shouting. I took a deep breath, exhaled, got a hold of myself. "What you gave me is depressing as hell."

The psychologist eyed me with curiousity. "Are you having these angry outbursts more and more frequently?" he asked.

I got up and left, the question with a million implications left suspended, dangling about in the thick air.

June 21, 2016

"You haven't been yourself lately, Nina." Gianni moved closer. I was standing at a large metal filing cabinet with the top drawer pulled out.

"What do you mean?" I asked, turning all of my attention to him. I inhaled and held the air in my lungs for a few seconds, because I had read in some magazine that it makes your figure look even more attractive.

"Usually, you come to work so... So put together. Your hair, your makeup, everything..."

"What are you suggesting?" I crossed my arms over my chest.

"Like I said. You're not yourself..." he turned his head and looked out my office door. "You have always been the perfect woman to me," he said very quietly.

What? I am a married woman, Gianni. He was out of line, but I said nothing. I liked the attention. Truth be told, it was not the first time that he had spoken to me in this way...

"Really, Nina. I think that you need some time to relax. You should get away or something. Don't you think so?" he asked, looking back in my direction. "For yourself?"

"Get away where, Gianni?"

"I don't know. There must be a real estate conference going on sometime soon. Somewhere... else. Maybe we could go together?"

Butterflies stirred my stomach. I pushed the thought of Elvis, Thomas and Rachel to the back of my mind. *I want this. And I am not guilty. You are the initiator. What happens next is in your hands.*

"That might be tricky, Gianni. I don't know that I can just pick up and go for a week."

"What about just the weekend then?" He leaned back against my desk. He was so tall, his legs so long, his shoulders so broad...

"Gianni—"

"Just think about it. I'll call around to see what kind of events are happening next month."

"Okay. I'll think about it," I said.

Gianni did not smile, he only walked out my office. When he got to the door, he stopped. "I have always been infatuated with you, Nina," he said. He stood with his back towards me. "You have always been that... That unattainable woman. You're so damn cold. I love it..."

June 30, 2016

Claire sat in front of me at the table, hair a mess, makeup smeared across her face, her two hands embracing the warm mug between them. She sighed heavily.

"He is such a jackass," she said.

"I know. But you need him..."

"I don't *need* him. I just—"

"Claire. If Chris doesn't let you work at the reception of the art gallery... You have no job. And no connections. You really do *need* him."

"So I just let him take advantage of my vulnerable situation? Work one hour every four days? And shut my mouth, hoping that he will let me expose my work again soon?"

"Claire..." I put my hand on her forearm. "There must be more to the story than you're letting on. It just doesn't add up."

"Emma did it. She must have..."

"But why?" I asked. I stood up and went to the refrigerator.

"Mom. Remember a few months ago when I said that there was money missing from the safe?" she asked.

"I'm not sure that you told me about it," I said.

"Yes, it was just after the event in April. Remember?"

"No."

Claire sighed again. "Chris asked me to get him the extra money in the office so he could deposit it. Remember?"

I shrugged.

"His phone rang, so he told me to wait a minute. So I went to get the money while he was talking," Claire continued, "and brought it to him at the front." She took a sip of her tea. "He looked at me, frowning, and counted it twice. Then went back into the office, acting really strangely. Remember I told you about it? So when he came back, he was off the phone. I tried to ask him what was up, but he was totally evasive... Well I've been thinking about that day for a while now. Something felt wrong. Yes. I told you about it while we baked Rachel's birthday cake. You know when I mean now?"

"I'm not so sure, Claire. Go on," I said.

"Why are you standing there?" she asked. I realized that I had been standing with the fridge door open for a whole minute. I closed it – a little more loudly than anticipated – and returned to my place at the table.

"You were saying?"

"I was saying that it all started in the beginning of January. Chris went out with the money, came back a while later, and eyed me strangely. Well, I had a strange feeling about the whole thing. So I thought back. And not long after that day... I had been working with Emma."

"That doesn't make her guilty of anything, does it?" I asked.

"No, Mom. I'm not finished. So I was thinking back, and as it turns out, I was working with Emma a few days before. And then a bell went off... So she also had asked me to go into the safe. I had never been give the code before... So she wrote it out on a scrap of paper. But 69-69-69 is pretty easy to remember... Emma had me take about $200. Then, she had me go out and pick up a few things... Erands for the gallery, she said. She had written me a list. Only... Now that I think of it, none of those things every showed up in the gallery."

"What kinds of things did you buy?" I asked.

"House stuff. A rug, a ridiculously expensive plant... It all would have fit in the gallery. But it never ended up there."

"Didn't you bring it back to the gallery with you?" I asked.

"No. Emma had be send it to an address that she had written on the paper also."

"Jesus, Rachel..."

"What?" she asked.

"What?" I echoed.

"What Rachel?"

"Rachel?" I asked. It hit me that I had said Rachel instead of Claire. She was on my mind so often...

"Never mind..." she said. "So anyways, I think that Emma must have... She must have told him that she saw me buy those things?"

"It is surprising to me that they would do that kind of thing to each other. Is their marriage on the rocks?"

"Mom, they are brother and sister..." said Claire.

"Well then! Even more of a reason to expect them to be honest with each other," I said. "So what are you going to do now?"

She put her face in her palms. "Mom. What can I do?"

"Well, you could just ask him why he cut your hours and why he only has you work on days when you're working with someone else... That can't hurt."

"I should have said something to Chris right away. Now it looks stupid. At this point, it will be my word against Emma's."

I thought for a moment. "Is she really such an admirable foe?"

"Yes. Frankly. The world of art galleries here in Montreal is not immense... Everyone knows everyone else, and everyone especially knows Emma." Claire sighed. "If I end up on her bad side, there is no way that anyone will accept to show my work. So I shot myself in the foot twice..."

"Or in both feet."

"What?"

"Oh, it doesn't matter. I'm being stupid," I said.

"Mom." Claire straightened up. "Would you... consider... Letting me come back and live with you for a while? So that I can get myself organized, figure things out? Maybe go back to school or something?"

"Oh, Claire..." I said. I shook my head. "Claire..." A million ideas raced through my mind: the need for privacy, the desire to come and go with Harvey as a pleased, my love of my own autonomy... But Claire needed me. I sighed. "For a short while, sure. But I'm done raising you," I said. "Do your own groceries."

She nodded.

"Maybe you should talk to the police about the whole thing," I said.

Claire shook her head. "I can't! What proof do I have?"

"Isn't the art gallery under camera surveillance?"

"Sure, there are cameras," she said. "But even if they are plugged in – and I am not sure that they are – all it will show is that I took money from the safe and left with it, returning with nothing."

March 31, 2016

"You know, Nina... I had to fight to get you in the first place, I will fight to keep you."

"I don't need to be fought over," I said. "Fighting is for the battlefield."

He sighed, rolled his eyes. "You really revel in playing hard to get, don't you?"

"Playing? This isn't a game," I said.

Another sigh.

The truth, of course, is far below the surface.

What happens to a person when he or she opens himself to other people?

Vulnerability. There is nothing more scary that vulnerability.

So what to do in order to avoid such a condition?

Well, first of all, you make yourself closed. Not just your eyes, your body, but also your heart.

You let nothing in, that way, nothing can touch you. You remain safe, whole, intact.

Some people go through such difficult things in their life that they must be this way, closed to the world, in order to keep themselves safe... because one more strike would mean a guaranteed shattering of the heart.

Others do it in order to be able to function, to do their work or help their family or pass the time. They sacrifice their sense of feeling in order to do more good – or bad – to others. For example: the ER doctor who has to stay cold in order to better function under pressure. Or the parent who has to cut all strings with a drug-addicted child. Or the lighthouse keeper.

So why am I so cold?

July 9, 2016

It was Harvey's birthday last week. So I decided to go all out, to buy some wonderful tea for him. Because tea was what brought us together in the first place, our first common interest. How's that for romantic?

I went to a specialty shop and ordered some yellow tea. Huángchá. Flown in directly from China. It cost me more than I had spent on tea for myself in my entire lifetime, probably. But I knew that Harvey would just love it.

I bought a card but could not think of what to write inside it. What type of message does an old woman write to her old boyfriend? After a few drafts, this is what I came up with:

Dear Harvey,

Thank you for being in my life. I look forward to many more evenings with you, under the stars, sipping at a warm cup of shared happiness.

Love, Nina

I put the card into an envelope, then placed it all into a gift bag. The small tin was bright pink with white flowers and flowy Chinese characters. I dropped it into the bag gently. I fluffed up a few pieces of chiffon paper and placed them into the bag.

"Do you write something on the tag of the bag, even if there is a card inside?" I thought aloud.

"Probably," said Claire, who was busy buttering up her burnt toast.

I picked up the pen and took the small tag into my hand.

To Nina, with tea. I wrote. *Love... Love...* Love, who? What?

I put the pen down, took off my glasses, rubbed my eyes and put them back on.

Godammit.

To Nina, with tea. Love... I scratched my chin. *Love, Nina!* of course. I wrote it on the card as best I could. My hand was a bit unstable since I hit it on the side of the bath.

"To Nina, with tea. Love Nina." I read quietly before folding the tag back into a closed position.

"What?" asked Claire, motioning towards the bag. She dropped into the chair across from me, plate with toast in one hand, cup of black tea in the other. "What was that?"

"A gift."

"I gathered that, what with the gift bag and all. For who? What is it?" she asked.

"It is yellow tea. For Harvey," I said.

"Ooh," said Claire, a mocking glint in her eye. "For your *boyfriend!*"

"Oh, shut up, Claire," I answered. She stuck out her tongue. "Seriously?" I pretended to be angry.

"A special gift for your secret boyfriend... So romantic!" said Claire.

"How is he a secret boyfriend? You know all about—"

"Does Rachel know?" asked Claire. "And Tom?"

"Tom knows," I said while standing up. "Anyways, I have better—"

"You still haven't told Rachel?" she asked.

I turned to face her. "Told Rachel what? She knows about Harvey, she knows that we are friends, do I really need to give her any more details?" I asked.

"So that does make him a *partial* secret, does it not?"

"What does that even mean, Claire?" I asked. I could feel my temper flair like a plastic bag caught in the wind.

"Here, let me text Rachel right this minute!" she took out her phone from the pocket of her hoodie.

I turned and walked out of the room.

"Mom?" said Claire. "Where are you going?"

I stopped in the doorway. "Claire... You're not funny."

"If this isn't funny then imagine how Rachel will feel when she finds out about Mr. Partial Secret? Feeling all left out and alone in—"

"Claire—"

"Just imagine the look on her face when—"

"Claire!" It is difficult to explain how her words had such a strong physical affect on me... My hands began to shake.

"Mom?" She stood up and walked over to me. "Sorry, Mom," she said. "I don't know why I'm going on about this. We both know how Rachel would react. I know all too well how sentistive she is about the feeling of a 'replacement father' so soon after Dad's death..."

"Is she right?" I asked. "Is it too soon?" I felt my light heart get heavy. The sun drained away.

"Oh, Mom, I shouldn't have bugged you," she said. "I don't think it's too soon at all. I'm sorry." She gave me an awkward hug. I pushed her away.

July 15

It was such a weird afternoon. I tried to read in the solarium, because the sun was big and bright in the sun sky, without being overbearing. But I just couldn't. my eyes were too tired, I think. The pores on the pages were so large... It was like I could only see the paper, but not the words inscribed on the paper. Maybe the sun was too strong?

I fell into an eerie sleep.

i was walking along the beach. For a while, I thought that I was alone. It was a warm night, the stars were bright. The moon hung low, very near to the horizon. There was something in the water – algae? fish? – that was lighting up the sky.

Then, suddenly, I heard someone shuffling beside me. I glanced over my shoulder, to the side with the water. There was a man. He was tall and thin, his face covered by a hood. Only his long nose stuck out from behind the hood. The skin from his hands seemed transluscent in the moonlight. So pale. His gait was strange, as though he had one leg that was longer than the other, or maybe one leg was shorter than the other. The wind picked up, pushing back the hood. His face was horrific, disfigured, as though it were made of melted wax. The inside corners of his asymmetrical eyes were full of puss.

I gasped.

He pulled the hood back down.

"Hello, Nina."

He continued walking. I caught up with him.

"How do you know my name?"

"I have been here all along."

"What? Since I started walking on the beach?"

"No. I am you, Nina. I live inside you."

"I dont understand."

"I am here to save you."

"I dont need saving.

"There is someone following you, Nina. Someone very bad. Someone who wants to take everything away from you. But I wont let that happen."

"Who is following me?"

"Nina. There is a man. And he knows what you have done in your life."

"Who is he?"

"An angel. Azrail. And he knows what you have done."

"What have I done?"

"Think, Nina. Have you brought more good, or more bad, to the people around you?"

I thought.

"You will find the answer upon his face."

I thought.

"If he appears as a handsome man, it means you have lived a good life."

I thought.

"But if he is a monster, well…"

"Well?"

"Well. He will take you to hell, Nina."

Nina. Nina. Nina?

I awoke with a start.

"Nina?" said a familiar voice.

"Who is there?" I asked.

"Claire let me in. Did you still want to meet for tea?" asked Harvey. "If this is not a good time…"

He was standing in the doorway of the kitchen, leaning forward into the solarium, his perfect brown and salty-white hair full of body and movement.

"No. I'm coming, Harvey."

I could smell his cologne over the earthy, pungent odor of the plants.

"I thought we could go to my house and try the yellow tea," he said.

"I'd love that."

"There was one thing I wanted to as you though," he said as we walked through the house. "I am not sure what you meant by what you wrote on the tag."

"Oh," I said. "I wasn't sure either. I mean, I didn't know if I should write on the tag or not... But Claire told me I should."

Harvey frowned.

july 19, 2016

never had intended to make a life for myself with anyone else. I was selfish, it is true, but there is more to it.

Probably, people would be happy to judge me as a self-centered, narcissistic, cold woman. And they would not be wrong.

But I never intended to hurt anyone. I held no hostages. It was just my imagination...

Every encounter bloomed in my mind into an infinite number of possibilities. Each man a different life in a different country, a different home, a different job.

I loved meeting people. I loved measuring my capacity of attraction.

Probably it all comes from a high degree of self-loathing. New prey meant new valorization is someone else's eyes.

Im no psychologist. But pop self-analytics would say that I just wanted to be good enough. No attachment. That would involve commitment. Work on myself. Sleeping around, that was much easier.

A one-night stand is a fantastic tool for calculating one's personal value on a strictly porous level.

Besides that, the benefits are slim to nil, especially if you're a woman.

When I was younger, and busy sleeping with various men, I always thought that I was truly living it up.

When Elvis entered my life, I became enchanted with the idea of being a mistress. Was there a part of me that felt guilty for duping his old lady? Not really. I thought that in the end, people who get angry about that sort of thing were just taking life too seriously. There was something alluring about being the woman that he *wanted*. Sure, he had someone to go home to, but instead, and despite all of the complications, he came to me.

When things with Elvis became more serious, I began to resent the other woman, the first, the genuine, the official. She was not obliged to go halfway across the island just to have drinks or grab a cone of soft-served. She did not have to call and hang up, depending on who answered the telephone. She could share a bed with him all night, not just for an hour or two.

It was very difficult for me to come to terms with the idea that I wanted to wake up next to Elvis. Falling pregnant changed everything, but still... I could not let go. I was a very hard person to be with, no doubt. Elvis was up for the challenge. Bless him. what a sweet life we made.

One gets used to waking up next to someone in bed. At least, I did. And then it became harder and harder to fall asleep without Elvis by my side. But then... It is strange how comfort can lead to boredom, anxiety, depression even.

When Elvis died, I struggled through countless sleepless nights. I would have nightmares, terrible nightmares, some realistic and others far-fetched, but each as disturbing as the next. Even now, my sleep remains clouded in nightmares and the feeling of falling off a cliff.

The first night that I spent with Harvey was the worst night since Elvis' death.

Everything leading up to it was perfect. Harvey and I had spent the evening talking by his massive fireplace, drinking mugs of bourbon mixed into warm apple juice, stirred with a stick of cinnamon.

"This lighting suits you so well, Nina..." he said, moving closer to me on the large leather couch. I had a heavy knit blanket over me, my feet resting on the old trunk that he used as a coffee table. The sky was inky and thick, the snow was falling gently, clinging to the bottom of each square of the window panes.

"You're drunk," I said, making as if to push him away, but instead leaving my hand against his chest.

"That is true, and you must pardon me for it," he whispered into my ear. His breath was sweet with only a short alcohol finish, his beard bristly against my skin. "I am going to take a shower, then I am going to bed. I'd be pleased if you followed me, but I would understand if you did not."

Harvey kissed my neck gently, then got to his feet. I was in a daze, on a cloud, drunk and warm. He went into the kitchen and I could hear him rinsing dishing in the sink. Then silence.

"Am I ready for another man's sheets?" I asked myself. I heard a shower go off in the distance, somewhere above my head.

I stood up, folded my blanket, and looked for a piece of paper upon which I could write Harvey a short note. I found a notepad near the telephone, but no pen. I found no pen in my handbag. No pen in the kitchen. I went upstairs to Harvey's bedroom, pad of paper in hand. Upon his desk, which was in the corner of the room and set right under the window, was a mug full of pens and pencils. I sat down in the solid wood chair, and only then did it strike me that he had lit a half dozen candles. Smug bastard.

"Nina," said Harvey from the doorway. He was wearing a towel around his waist and his hair was wet, yet it still fell perfectly around his face. "I am so happy to see you here..." as he walked by to close the dark drapes, the smell of his soap took me by surprise. I shivered. My mouth watered.

"I am not sure that I should be here, Harvey..." I said. What made me feel most guilty was the fear that I would compare everything about that night to being with Elvis. He deserves better.

"No pressure, Nina. Just pleasure." He came behind me, rubbed my shoulders. He ran his finger along my neck, across my collar bone, down my shirt.

No man had ever made me feel as weak as I felt at that very moment.

As best he could, Elvis kept me sane. But he couldn't keep my imagination from straying, from multiplying my life into an infinite number of possible lives.

July 27, 2016

<u>The Human Experience</u>

In a universe so vast
That it takes philosophy to grasp,
With light moving so fast.
And the wind
In the stars
        just blows...
The universe is not concerned with you, little girl,
Because the universe has no care in the world.

But within you is a power that is stronger than the starwind,
Stronger than the waves of the sun,
Stronger than the steely rings of the metallic planets.

Oh, yes, girl.
So do not be afraid.

Within this very plain,
Very commonplace,
very extra *totally* ordinary
        Human experience...
You are the brightest of all the stars.

It is true.
Bright star girl,
Disappointment will eat at your soul,

Alyson Hope

It will taste bitter,
> Bitter,
>> More bitter than burnt bitterness.

You will wish and hope and pray,
Sweet girl.
You will do everything right.
You will follow the rules!
Show up, act tough!
But...
You will still not have what you want.

The universe,
(the stars that are suns and the planets and the lady moons)
Will whisper quietly in your ear.
Breathe, girl. Hear girl.
Heal, girl.

No.
You will not always have what you want.

The time has come,
A classic start,
Will say the universe to your heart.
To be happy.

Oh yes, precious girl.
For if you wait to be happy...
You will miss out on
> the human experience.

August 2, 2016

"Table for two. And it had better be a good one. Did you see my wife's legs?"

The Maître D bowed his head respectfully and walked away.

"Gianni!" I said, hitting him playfully on the chest.

"Today, you call me Robert. And I call you Stella."

I laughed. "Can I call you Bob?"

"Do so and you will regret it tonight."

I gave him the eye.

"Sir, Madam, right this way please," said the Maître D. He took us to a table by the window. The view of the city was breathtakng; the restaurant was just below the line of fog, which meant that we could see the buildings below, but nothing above... Like being inside a giant snow globe.

"I hope that this table suits you?" said the Maître D.

Gianni puffed up his chest, nodded, then put a bill in the old man's suit jacket pocket. The man flinched slightly. The gesture was arrogant, rude even. For the first time, the spell that Gianni held over me cracked, if only slightly.

"That won't be necessary," said the Maître D, reaching into his pocket.

"Keep it," said Gianni, putting his hand up. "You need it. For a new pair of shoes, maybe."

"Gianni," I said under my breath. Elvis would never have done such a thing.

Gianni reached across the table and took my chin in his hand. "Stella, did you just call me by the name of you ex-boyfriend?" He spoke in a voice just above a whisper. He squeezed my chin with his hand.

The Maître D bowed and went back to his post, no doubt feeling the uncomfortable tension.

"Sorry. I just don't like—"

"Get used to it, Stella. Money is the bottom line here. You've never even written on a paper as expensive as the ones they use to wipe their asses with in this place." He looked at me from head to toe. I felt naked. "You look the part. Now learn to act it."

"Would you like an aperitif?" asked the waitress. She was a short red-head with a pretty, young face.

"Give us your name," said Gianni. He did not smile.

"Sorry. I am Sam." She picked at the skin around her finger. "Sorry. Anything to drink then?"

"Sam, dear. My husband here needs something stiff. Let's do a whisky. Whichever Macallan you can find back there... He's had a long day. And I'll have a glass of white. Something light, floral. You decide. Thanks," I said.

Sam looked at me and nodded, then turned away before anything more could be said.

A small smile broke in the corner of Gianni's mouth. "That's my girl. That's why I hired you."

"You're not my boss today, Robert." He chuckled. So he was the kind of man who liked to be led by the balls. Got it. "Now take it easy," I said.

"What do you think of this view?" he asked. "Chicago. Windy City. Moody City. I do love her..."

"So far, it is very pretty," I said. He was looking out the window. I looked too. We could see directly into the windows of the tall apart-ment buildings across the street. Each place was so different... For a moment I entertained the idea of leaving everything behind – Elvis, the kids, Montreal – and moving here, to Chicago, to live in one of those posh high-rise apartments. Everything would be made of either glass or stainless steel... The cleaning lady would come in once a week... We would have cocktail parties and go to art galleries and movie openings...

"... speakeasy?" asked Gianni.

"Sorry?" I asked. With a blink, the alternate life was lost forever.

"Have you ever been to a speakeasy?"

"No. I have seen them in those Al Capone movies... But I didn't even know that they still exist."

Sam arrived with a tray and gave us our drinks.

"Will you be ready to order a starter?" she asked, looking mostly in my direction.

"I'll have the French onion soup," said Gianni. "And bring Stella a garden salad."

"A salad sounds nice, thank you," I said.

Sam took out her little pencil and scribbled a few lines into her notebook.

"Are you ready to order your main dish now too?"

"We'll wait," said Gianni.

Sam smiled apologetically and was off.

"Nice ass. No self-confidence though." He watched her walk to the kitchen. "But... Those kinds of girls are usually better in bed."

What?" I was taken aback.

"Sleep with a hot woman like you, she is probably lazy, selfish even. You know that you have the face, the body, to get whatever action you want. Men flock to women like you, Nina. But sleep with a girl like Sam... Now a girl like Sam has something to prove. She is cute, but not... Not stunning. So she wants to please men like me. She'll go way out of her comfort zone for me. And I don't have to worry about my performance... Because she'll be satisfied either way, just being able to tell her friends that she took me to bed."

"That's kind of—"

"It's a win-win situation, if you think of it. It's the same when you sleep with a guy who is a few lightyears below your league... No?"

Gianni. Such a bastard. Only... Only he was truly the best-looking man in the restaurant. By far. Most of the women around us had taken notice of Gianni... And I liked being in his limelight. I wanted everyone to look at me. I felt proud. Not a hint of shame.

"I guess," I said.

"Obviously. Take that husband of yours, for example."

"Off limits." My voice was cold. It was not a challenge, but a demand.

Gianni laughed. "And you told me to take it easy? Who is being all uptight now, Nina?"

I leaned towards him. "I am Stella. Now drop the subject or you will regret it tonight."

Gianni nodded.

August 10, 2016

Elvis used to say to me that he could never bring me home to his family. "They'll never let you leave again!" he would say. "They'd want to keep you on a shelf, just to stare at you all day."

"Come on," I would say, "you're being silly."

"You have never actually been to Italy!" he shouted. The other pregnant women in the waiting room glanced over disapprovingly. "If you would go—"

"Elvis, I spent multiple weekends in Italy before we ever met. Sometimes you forget that, that I had a life before you entered it."

And a life after you left. It is a struggle, but I am getting there.

"Nina," he said. "You are so very beautiful, everyone would stop you to ask if you were a famous actress!"

"Oh, because they could see from my face that I am good at memorizing lines and the could tell that I can express 14 different emotions with a single eyebrow?" I said, rolling my eyes.

"What?"

"As far as I know, there is a whole lot more to being an actress than having perky tits..." I said, receiving a few critical stares myself.

"There is?" asked Elvis.

I cut him with my eyes.

"Joking!" he shouted. he looked around, finally noticing that were creating a small scene. "Italians love beauty. That is true though," he said.

"The whole country. More shallow than a boot?" I asked.

"There is something that you aren't understanding," he said. "You judge, but you do not know what it means."

"Pray. Teach."

"Italy has been through a lot of instability throughout its history," he began. "It was conquered and re-conquered so often, there was coup after coup, political crises, barbarian invasions... the list goes on."

"Crises," I said.

"Exactly. So with all of this trouble, it was hard for people to be able to rely on anything. From one second to the next – bang! – everything could change. New language, new culture, new money, new emperor. But along the hundreds and hundreds of years... One thing remained stable."

He took a pause, waiting for me to ask him to go on. When I did not, he continued.

"Beauty. The only thing that has remained in Italy is beauty," he said.

I raised an eyebrow, trying to be less than moderately interested.

"The only constant for Italians is beauty. That is why we worship it so much. That is why we are so... preoccupied with beauty. It is the only thing of value that has stayed."

"That is very strange."

"No," he said. "Not strange, Nina. So logical!"

My name was called and we went into the doctor's office.

After a quick exam – I'll let you imagine what that entails – the doc said to go home.

"Your son is far too comfortable to join us yet," he said. "Wash a few floors, that may shak him up enough..."

"Nina, clean a floor? Keep dreaming," said Elvis.

August 13, 2016

I ran into May yesterday, as I spreading so early fallen leaves across the yard. it is actually quite affective for nurturing the gras.

"Hi, long time no see," said May from behind me.

"Oh!" I exclaimed. "I didn't see you there. How are you, May?"

"Good. Feels good to be out now that it's a bit cooler, doesn't hit?" she said.

She was wearing shorts, boots and a long cardigan. Her hair was long now, tied in small green and brown braids.

We chatted back and forth about her job and her parents.

"So," she said. "Can I invite you over for tea sometime?" she asked. "I miss... when we used to have talks and stuff."

"Me too."

"Okay," she said, waving shyly and heading back across the street.

"May," I said. "I haven't seen Claire for days. What do you say? Would you like to come over? We can order pizza, watch an old episode of Dr. Phil or something," I said.

"Are you sure?" she asked. "About Claire?"

"Even if she comes home tonight, she won't be back until much, much later."

"Reruns and pizza. You've got yourself a deal," said May.

We walked into the house together.

"So, I guess Claire is living with her new girlfriend?" she asked, too casually not casually.

"No, she still lives here!" I said. I felt badly. Did she not know how serious the relationship was? Did she still keep a piece of her heart for Claire?

"Oh, cool," she said. "So I've seen you and Mr. Gibson chatting a lot lately..."

"Did you order the pizza?" I asked, letting myself fall onto the couch. I reached across for the remote.

"Right. Food first," said May. "Then gossip."

She took out her phone and called for a two-for-one order of medium pineapple and mushroom pizzas.

"I guess you still remember," I said. It was a sweet moment, reminiscing with her.

"No one else in the world eats the same pizza we do," she said.

"We had so many interesting conversations over pizza, didn't we?" I asked.

"You were like a mom to me, you know," said May.

"That's really sweet."

We sat there, just the two of us in my warm living room, thinking back on the days when May spent more time here than in her own home.

"Especially when my parents found out that I was in a relationship with Claire..." she said, taking me away from my black and white film of the past. "If I didn't have you to guide me through it... I'm not sure what I would have done."

"You're sweet, May. But I just did what I was supposed to do."

"No," she said. She crossed her legs and adjusted her shorts. "No. Were really there for me, Nina. Even after Claire and I broke up..."

"It was a rough time for all of us," I said. "I mean, what Claire did..."

"Water under the bridge," said May.

"It has been a few years, after all."

"Four," said May, a little too quickly. "Or so."

"You were her first love, you know that, right?" I said. "No matter what, you will always be her first love."

She smiled, but it was a sad smile. "We were so little. And she was so full of life. She was indipendant, that is what I admired most about her. Even as an 11 year old, I knew that she had a special spirit. She was so creative, so down-to-earth and yet, at the same time, she created a world of fantasy all around her. Do you remember on the rainy days, when we would sit and watch the droplets fall down the windows, trying to guess where they would end up?"

"I remember the time that you went running outside during a thunderstorm, and you slid on the grass and landed on your knees in the driveway..." I said, the film slowly taking up again.

"My mom freaked out when you called her from the hospital!" said May. "Do you remember how many stiches I needed?"

"I remember how many rocks they had to take out of each knee!"

"It was so gross," said May, looking down at the light scars on both of her knees. "Claire loved it."

"No," I said, shaking my head. "She loved the stiches. But the procedure? The needles?"

"I had totally forgotten!" May laughed. "Didn't she faint?"

"Yep, she ended up in a stretcher in the ER."

"It took hours to clean the mess out of the car," I said.

"I felt so bad," said May. "But I wasn't allowed to come help..."

"You mom wasn't fond of us at the time, was she?" I asked.

"There were a few reasons for that. She blamed you for not telling me not to run on the grass in the rain. There as than..." said May. "She thought that you were all a bit crazy."

"She wasn't wrong about that one," I said.

We saw a few lights though the glass door and after a few more moments, we heard movement coming from the front stoop.

"Pizza," said May. "I'll get it!"

I went into the kitchen to take out a couple of plates, forks, knives.

May walked in, her face grim once again.

Claire followed in after her, along with Robin.

"Hi, Nina," said Robin, coming over to me. She had to bend down slightly to kiss me on both cheeks, which is rare, as I am rather tall for a woman. Robin looks like she just got off the boat from Ireland: fair skin, fiery red hair, freckles, dark eyes.

"I wasn't expecting you, or I would have changed and tidied up a bit," I said, realizing how dirty I had let my kitchen become.

The doorbell rang.

"I'll get that," said May, slipping away without waiting for a response.

"It is weird. Isn't it weird to walk in on your mom and your ex?" said Claire, her dark eyes blazing.

"It's fine," said Robin as she helped herself to a large glass of water from the tap. "Nice day today, wasn't it?" she asked.

"I'm not sure," I said, distracted. "I guess we'll see."

"Yeah," said Robin politely. "Can I help you set the table?"

"We were going to watch TV, actually," I said.

"Seriously?" said Claire.

"What? It is my house, isn't it?" I said. "I can eat wherever I please! You're the one who walked in..."

"Nina, if we're walking in on something, we can go grab—"

"No," said Claire, cutting off Robin mid-sentence.

"I'm going to go see what is taking her so long at the door," I said.

Walking to the front of the house, I realized that it was strangely quiet. The two boxes of pizza were sitting on the bench next to the door, but May was nowhere to be found. I turned on the light and saw the receipt from the debit transaction sitting on top of the pizza boxes.

I brought the pizza back into the kitchen.

"Where is she?" asked Claire.

"May?" I asked.

"Who else?" said Claire, waving around to show how obviously there was no one else missing from the group.

"She left."

August 29, 2006

I just got back from visiting Tom.

Laci is well, seven months old now, smiling and kicking and things.

I had a strange conversation with Tom, it has left me feeling feel kind of bad.

We were sitting around his kitchen table, just finishing lunch. i had brought some Montreal bagels, Fairmont of course, as if there were any other choice.

"So what will you do when Claire leaves?" asked Thomas. "Have you made plans to move into any home yet? Have you visited at all?"

Now this is a difficult subject for me, like for most elderly folk who at some point are told that they can no longer live alone anymore, because they will burn the house down by accidentally making soup in the dryer or something. Fine. But my house... My house is even more important to me. My house is the house I built with Elvis. My house is the place where all of my children were raised. My house is Elvis' final resting place.

"When did we ever discuss moving out?" I asked. "When Claire leaves, I will go on doing as I did before she arrived, Thomas."

"Things are different now, Mom," he said.

Zandra cleared her throat, excused herself from the table and went into another room. "She does that a lot now, doesn't she?" I said.

"This is a personal matter," he said. "She doesn't want to offend you."

"Hey, Zandra!" I shouted. Tom gave me a nervous glace.

"Yes?" she called from another room. I heard her walking and a few seconds later she came back from around the corner. When she walked into the kitchen again, she had a sleeping Laci in her arms.

"You didn't have to leave," I said.

"I know," she shrugged. "But this is none of my business."

"Can I ask you something?" I said. "Since you've got a more objective view of the whole situation?"

Tom and Zandra exchanged looks.

"Sure," she finally said.

"Do you think that I need to move into a home when Claire leaves?" I asked.

"A home?"

"Like, a residence for elderly people," I explained, realizing her language barrier.

"Oh. Well..." she said. "I imagine it would be best to follow Dr. Lee's recommendations."

Thomas turned to Zandra, his eyes wide.

"What do you know about her recommendations?" I asked, trying not to raise my voice.

"She thinks it would be safer for you not to be alone," said Tom.

"How do any of you know about the private things that are said between me and my doctor? What ever happened to my privilege, to her oath of silence! I haven't been served a certificate of innaptitude just yet, have I?"

Tom cleared his throat. "Mom," he said, his voice very quiet. "You told us. You told us in the car as you drove home from your appointment."

"I... I did what?" I was so confused!

"You called us from the car speaker... You told us all about your appointment..." he said.

I felt myself become weak. My stomach fell. my mouth tasted of metal.

"It's okay," said Zandra. "A lot has happened since then. Would you like to hold Laci? I have to take a shower," she said as she dropped her daughter into my arms.

Tom shook his head, but said nothing. That was even worse than his speech about sending me to a hospice.

"I know you're just worried about me," I said after some time. I smelled the top of Laci's little head. Divine. "But I'm okay, Tom. Really. I have lived alone for some time now. And even when your father was around, he wasn't actually *around* all that often, was he? And I still figured things out."

"Mom, if you would just let me be honest with you..." he said.

"Of course."

"I think that it is quite clear that your... situation... has been changing since before his death. Don't you remember the time—"

"Stop that, Thomas," I said. "You won't get anywhere by walking down that path."

"There are a lot of examples, Mom."

"Examples!" I shouted, making Laci's closed eyes flinch. "Examples!" I whispered. "I am not some math problem that you've come across at school, Tom. I—"

"You are a proud woman. You fought very hard to become what you did. All of the odd were against you. You should be a vagrant, or a compulsive gambler, or maybe you should already be dead. But you're very much alive. Fiery. Mom, you prevailed. And you did it because of your strength, your determination, intelligence. But Alzheimer's..." he sighed. "Mom, Alzheimer's is not the same game. You can't outsmart it. You can't will it away, not matter how resolute you may be. You need to make some plans. You need to be responsible in this new chapter of your life."

I tried to take a deep breath, but my lungs seemed like they were already full of air. "I'll be fine, Tom," I said. "For a few more years at least. I have only just been diagnosed with the disease. I'm young! You don't just up and die from Alzheimer's at 64."

Tom frowned. "You're not 64..."

"That is not the point!"

Anyways, yes, technically, you can 'just up and die at 64'. Or at 66. There isn't an age for Alzheimer's, you know. Even people in their 20s have been diagnosed with it."

I shook my head. Or what it just trembling on its own? "I'm okay, Tom. Really," I said.

"That is what bothers me..." he said.

"It bothers you that I'm okay?"

"It bothers me that you *think* you're okay. Which leads to the other not-so-cool part... It is hard for me to know when this all started, to get an idea of the progress of the..."

"Descent?" I said, finishing the sentence that he dare not finish.

"It's all part of it. The more information, the better."

"What does it matter?" I said. "I'll live each day, one at a time. Come on, Tom. Can we talk about something else?"

"I am worried about you. That's it. I can't help it."

"I don't need you to worry," I said. "You have so much going on in your life right now. focus on the positive. Leave me out of this."

"Mom..." said Tom. "you don't get to decide what I worry about."

September 3, 2016

"Harvey, you look absolutely dashing," I said.

"Stop, you're making me blush!" he said, winking at me.

"Where to?" I asked.

"Nina, I can't tell. It's a surprise! You know that!"

"Okay," I said. "But for the record, I am being pretty subdued for a lady who hates surprises."

"That is because you have never been surprised by me before!" said Harvey.

He opned the door for me and I turned to lock it.

"Do you think the weather will pick up soon?" he asked as he opened his umbrella. Heacy rainfall over the last few days had leaving the ground wet and soggy, as though it just had no more place for any more water, so it just sat on the surface.

We took the metro downtown and ended up somewhere on the Plateau Mont Royal. The rain let up slightly, but the sky remained a dark grey. We crisscrossed through a few streets, arm in arm, Harvey holding the umbrella high above both of our heads.

The Plateau. The Plateau is a charming borough, it is undeniable, with those iconic outdoor staircases, built for the mostpart in the 19th century, that snake up and down the streets. A few years ago, the Plateau had a genuine eclectic hippy vibe. Now, there is something saccharine about it. To me, it feels like a place that tries too hard to live up to the image it has of itself and falls short.

Finally, I could hear music in the distance, the rain stopping as if by magic.

"What is it?" I asked.

"Outdoor concert, said Harvey as he closed his umbrella.

There was a small gathering of people, dressed in varying degrees of layers: raincoats, wintercoats, barelegs, rubber boots... Everything entirely rainy Montreal days.

I looked more closely at the three women with bare legs.

"Ballerinas," said Harvey as he took my hand into his. "Pop-up performance."

An elderly man sat playing the piano gravely, and a young girl played the violin. The clouds rolled away and they were washed in timid golden sunlight.

We watched the dancers from across the street as more and more people gathered around us. They were elevated slightly, on an unfinished wood platform.

Oh, Harvey, man of many aces up his sleeve.

"What do you think?" he asked.

"Begging for a compliment, are we?" I asked.

Harvey ruffled my hair.

"Don't!"

"Well then? Neat find, or not?" he asked, his eyes glowing.

I kissed him on the neck. "Where did you hear about this?" I asked.

"There was a poster in the washroom at the café on 45th Avenue."

We watched the performance, which lasted for three more songs. The ballerinas moved about with such fluidity, I was reminded of branches caught in a breeze. It was tender, sweet, simple.

The music drew to an end and the little girl who had been playing the violin took a deep bow. The crowd laughed and applauded, which surprised the little violinist into standing up rigidly, awkwardly, arms crossed over the instrument. The dancers came beside her and bowed. She followed suit.

The crowd dispersed little by little, as did the musicians and the dancers.

"There is always something going on in Montreal, isn't there?" I asked.

Harvey took me by the hand. "Hungry? Thirsty?" he asked.

"Sure," I said. I looked at my watch. It was nearly 1 PM.

"Any specific craving?" asked Harvey.

"Surprise me," I said, winking.

Harvey laughed.

"I don't really know this neighbourhood as well as I used to," he said.

"You lived here?" I asked taking Harvey's hand.

We started walking down the street again.

"I had a few musician friends who worked at the Café Minuit," he said. "That is where I met Colette."

I felt a pinch in my heart. Colette. Elvis.

"Every Saturday and Sunday night, my friends and I would sit in a booth near the front and watch the guys play. Those nights..."

"sounds like you spent a lot of money on beer," I said. "Money and time!"

"No, not beer," said Harvey. "We went straight for the hard liquor. Less headaches."

"Really, no headaches?"

"No," said Harvey. "I said less, not *none at all*. I remember everything in sepia, isn't that strange?"

"You're such a romantic," I said. "Sepia glasses. I bet that all of the bleary-eyed mornings after are sweet, fluffy memories too?"

"Oh, some," said Harvey. "But not fluffy. Mostly fuzzy."

"I never pegged you for that type," I said.

"Hey, everyone has been seventeen years old, Nina," he said.

We stopped in front of a door that opened on the coner of the street. The name Wilensky was written across the glass in big yellow capital letters.

"A usual haunt?" I asked.

We sat down on the round bar stools. The walls were plastered in vintage newspaper clippings and retro menus from when you could buy a meal for your whole family for less than a dollar and still get back some change. The whole shack probably hadn't changed at all since Harvey came here when he was a teenager. A grumpy hundred-year-old woman grunted our way.

"I'll have a Wilensky Special," said Harvey. "With a 7up."

The woman behind the counter grunted at me.

"I'll have what he's having. But can you hold the mustard?"

She shook her head and walked away.

"Oh boy," I said. "What did that mean?"

"They don't modify their recipes," said Harvey.

"Modify? I hardly qualify 'no mustard' as an alternative recipe."

"I guess it is a matter of perspective," said Harvey.

I tried to act normal, but that whole thing about the mustard had really bothered me. Since when don't clients decide what fucking condiments they want on their sandwich?

The waitress shuffled over with our drinks. A few minutes later, she came back with thick round sandwiches on rectangles of wax paper.

"Two Wilensky Specials," she said.

"Right here," said Harvey.

She placed both sandwiches in front of Harvey and turned away.

"For you," he said, dragging mine in front of me from a corner of the wax paper.

"She new it was my order... She just took it five minutes ago," I said.

"Don't take it personally," said Harvey as he took a bite of his thick sandwich. "It's just an act. It's all part of the experience."

I shrugged and took a bite.

"So?" he asked.

"Too greasy," I said once I was finished with my bite.

"You've got a little something here," said Harvey, pointing to the corner of his lip.

I tried to wipe it away.

"No, the other side," he said.

After a few more unsuccessful tries, he took his napkin and wiped it for me.

"Mustard," he both said at once.

September 8

I went back to the shrink with my daughter today. She tried, as usual, to create an problem between myself and Claire.

"How has the progress gone?" he asked. "Did you do the homework that I asked of you?"

Rachel tensed up. She clearly was uncomfortable with the idea of not having done her homework, even in this context... "We haven't had the time," she said.

"It has been almost four—"

"I meant we didn't have the time to heal. To get over past events. To revaluate what it all means."

"Speak for yourself," I said.

Rachel tightened the nerves in her neck. "im not ready to see her outside of this office, I have nothing constructive to say."

"What I am hearing is that you are very angry," said the psychologis. "But you have to understand that anger is not a constructive emotion. And on top of it... It tends to hide some other emotions. Less aggressive ones. Like sadness, or disappointment."

"Yes, I agree," I said. Rachel looked over at me. "Why are you so aggressive?"

"Do I really have to take this?" she asked as she crossed her arms. "How can I have any discussion at all with her? She is incapable of hearing anything that comes out of anyone else's mouth. All she hears is a... a transformed series of lies she tells to herself."

The psychologist straightened up in his chair. "Rachel. She is your mother. And to become a real, normal, functional adult, you have to be faced with the fact that your parents are not perfect. None of us are, and chances are, you won't be a perfect parent either, if you decide to have children yourself."

"Not a chance," she said.

"That is not my point though," he continued. "What I am trying to say is that no person is perfect, not your mother, not anyone—"

"So you're suggesting that I lower my standards?" asked Rachel, interrupting once again. I scowled at her and she rolled her eyes at me.

"No. I am suggesting that you need to let go. There are things in this world that you cannot control. Like, for example, the choices that your mother made in the past, or the ones that she will make in the future. Nor can you control your mother's disease. And so, if you want to take advantage of this time that you have left with her... Well, then you have to learn to let go. Because even worse than this feeling, I promise you, is the feeling of regret when face when a loved one has passed away."

"I'm sitting right here!" I shouted. I could feel my scalp tingle with sheer rage. That feeling always scard me because I never knew what would come next.

"I wouldn't regret anything," said Rachel. "I'm not big on regrets. Especially when there was nothing that I could have done to change things. Doctor... You have to see how I have tried. You have known my mom for a year now... You know how difficult she is."

"Interestingly," he said, tapping his chin with the butt of his pen, "I see many of the same qualities in you."

"Pardon me?" we both asked at the same time. A hint of a smile tugged at my lip, but certainly not at Rachel's.

"Mrs. O'Connor is an independent, strong-willed, resourceful woman. She is rounding the corner into middle stage Alzheimer's disease—"

"She doesn't live alone anymore," said Rachel. And then she went too far. "Claire moved back in because she was worried that Mom was going to harm herself."

"What?" My saliva became watery. "No. You're lying, Rachel. She *needed* to move back in. she needed a place to stay because she was having trouble with her boss and—"

"Two things," said Rachel, the most evil sneer across her face. "First, Claire moved back in because she was afraid for you. Did it never occur to you that she would have just moved in with her fiancée, Robin, if she really needed a place that badly?"

It had never occurred to me.

"Second," said Rachel. I was disgusted by the degree of pleasure which shone forth in her eyes. "Can you blame her boss for being pissed? Claire had been selling drugs from behind his desk. When she couldn't pay her supplier back, she gave them a key to the gallery, so they could let themselves in and make off with their due in material items." Rachel stretched both of her legs forward. "Do you mean to tell me that your precious Claire didn't tell you the truth?"

When I got home, Claire was in the kitchen cooking supper. She had opened a bottle of wine, and it was about half empty.

"How did therapy go?" she asked.

I shrugged. "I thought that you don't want me to talk about Rachel in her back anymore?"

"Don't be cruel, Mom," said Claire. She dumped a whole pack of spaghetti into a pot of cold water, then covered it in salt and pepper. "I don't want to be mean about the whole thing. I just hope that you're... That the two of you are getting along better." She stood by the stove moving the chuck of pasta in a small pot with a fork. She scratched the bottom of the pot and the sound gave me goosebumps.

I took of my wet coat and threw it over a kitchen chair. "I know that you don't want to get into it, but Rachel said something nasty about you today."

Claire turned to look at me in the eye. "You're right. I don't want to get into it."

"Okay," I said. "I just didn't think it was fair, because you weren't even there to defend yourself..." I left myself drop itno the chair. My body felt heavy, tired, water-logged.

Claire went back to stirring the pasta. She was quiet for a moment. "Isn't there a thing about patient confidentiality?" she finally asked.

"Like isn't it illegal to talk about something someone said to a doctor privately?"

"No. I think that it is a code for doctors and things. But not for patients. I don't think."

"Anyways..." said Claire.

"Anyways," I continued, "I was wondering. I had a thought." I watched as the water began to boil over the sides of the pot. The parts of the spaghetti that were sticking out stuck together tightly. "Why didn't you decide to move in with Robin?"

Claire turned to me again. "Mom," she began. The boiling water spit and sizzled behind her. "I told you. We're waiting for the renovations to finish at Robin's place. She's staying in a tiny studio right now. Remember?"

I nodded.

"So there was no point in moving out now. It was easier for both of us this way," she said. "Know what I mean?"

I nodded again but I wasn't sure that I understood.

"Also, I was wondering abot your conflict at work..."

Claire's eyes shot towards mine. Even in the best of times, I am not sure how well I could have red them.

"Yes?"

"Did you... are you..." I started.

Then, from somewhere deep inside came a voice that sid drop it.

September 18, 2016

Two people lay side by side in a bed. Both are in the same position: straight arms, straight legs, facing the ceiling.

They are so close that they can feel each other's warmth. And yet they are so far that there may as well be a continent between them. But something far more sinister has set them apart.

He is aching to reach over and touch her. His fingers burn. He is wide awake.

She is aching to reach over and touch him. Her heart is heavy. She is wide awake.

The tambourine rain plays softly against the window. The wind interrupts its song.

She lets out a sigh.

"Nina," he whispers. Are you awake?"

"Yes." The darkness swallows up those three little letters, like a drop of water poured from a rusted watering can into a dry flowerpot. He does not hear her.

He sits up, throws his feet over the side of the bed, and shuffles out of the room, quietly closing the door behind him.

"What have I done?" she asks. She feels cold. The night will be long. "What have I done."

September 29, 2016

I wonder sometimes if getting older is inevitably synonymous with loneliness. Hacing Claire here has not been easy. I hate feeling like charity. And there is that nagging feeling about the drugs. Drugs. What kind? Is she selling here now? She is closer physically, but I have never felt so far from her.

I am starting to see myself as a tired, lonely, isolated old woman. I have entered my period of decline.

The advantage that I had as a young woman – which does not feel so much like an advantage to me anymore – is that I had no older relatives with whom I was close. It felt like an advantage when I was in the throes of getting my career off the ground because I had the freedom to do my own thing without any meddlesome family members trying constantly to give me unsolicited advice. I watched as my friends went through the loss of their older aunts and uncles, and their grandmothers and grandfathers, but I felt only sympathy, not empathy. Had I been around older people as a teenager, I may have learnt better coping methods for aging and communicating with dignity.

My mother had raised me alone and had never been on talking terms with her own parents or siblings. Truth be told, I've never been sure how many brothers and sisters she has. There was only one cousin, Alfred, with whom she was close, but I had never been particularly fond of him. And so, in being such an outcast – even rejecting her own daughter in many ways – my mother effectively liberated me of all filial duties.

My very good friend, Louise, with whom I took my real estate agent courses, lost her mother at the age of 23. Apparently, her mother was murdered by hoodlums who broke into her place. They made off with a bag-full of silverware and $20 dollars from her wallet. They found the killers, who turned out to be two teens from her neighbourhood, within a few weeks. In their defence, they explained how they had always assumed that she was some sort of rich widow because her lawn was so perfectly manicured. They went on to explain that they had not intended to kill her, only keep her immobile and confused. It was a shock to the teens when they realized that tying a plastic bag over a frail little woman's head for the better part of an hour could actually suffocate her. Their parents paid for top lawyers and the judge was sympathetic to the boys' story.

Louise and her twin sister Lucy were – understandably – revolted by the whole thing.

I tried to comfort her as best I could, but how could I take the pain away from a friend who lost her mother is such a hideous way? It made me re-evaluate my relationship with my own mother, made me wonder if I should not try to mend broken ties. I tried briefly, as people do, full of good intentions and emitonal motivation. In the end, I decided to leave things as they had settled on their own.

Before Elvis, my friends were my family of choice. When I married Elvis and we had our three children, I lost touch with most of my friends of young adulthood.

I did try to reach out to my mother when Thomas was born, but she was not particularly interested in cultivating a relationship with him.

To this day, my mother remains just as distant, not only with me but with her grandchildren as well. I am not even sure that she has called Tom to congratulate him on the arrival of Laci.

I wonder if she feels as lonely as I do sometimes.

October 1, 2016

"Mom," I said. "Give it up. I don't have time for this. Are you coming to the hospital with us or not?" Another contraction shook me.

"Well, dearest Nina," she said. I realized that her voice was slurred. "I don't know." She rambled on, but I could not understand the words.

"What?"

"Nina! I have something things to go over first, some stuff to do, and so forth, so on and such and such."

"Nina!" this time it was Elvis. "Do you want to give birth right here on the living room floor? We have to go."

I nodded. "Mom. come if you want. Or just forget it. I have to—" Contraction. Breathe in, breathe out. "—go now. Good—"

She hung up the phone.

"Well?" asked Elvis.

It was four o'clock in the afternoon.

"She can't make it. But it's fine. I've got you. Let's go."

"Are you ready for this?" Elvis asked. He smiled in such earnest that my heart grew. He looked so foolish, standing there in flip flops, a thick plaid shirt, sports shorts and a fishing hat, all while holding my little pink suitcase with wheels. The thought that just over a year ago, that very suitcase held all of my skimpiest bathing suits and tightest dresses, ready for some excursion or other in a distant land... Fast forward and it is full of slippers, a housecoat, some baby clothes and extra-absorbent pads.

"What?" asked Elvis.

"You're adorable," I said. "Now go get the chariot."

We went to the hospital together.

"We will send for you later, Sir," said a small, dark-skinned nurse. "When the baby arrives."

"No," said Elvis. It was a flat no, a clear no, not a threat but an irrevocable statement.

The nurse shrugged. She pushed my wheel chair into a room where another woman was sitting up in bed, reading a magazine. She did not seem to notice us enter, and the nurse quickly pulled the curtain between us.

"My name is Meena," said the nurse as she helped me into the bed. She went about clipping things to my finger and gluing things to my stomach. All tubes and wires. "Please call me if there is anything. A doctor will be in, sometime in the next hour or so. Mr...." she looked at her clipboard. "Mr. O'Connor. You cannot—"

"Rossi," we both corrected at the same time.

"Mr. Rossi," she said, sighing. "You must stay with your wife. Do not leave this room, do not wander about, and for heaven's sake..." she rolled her eyes, as if Elvis had made some sort of obscene gesture in her direction, "do not get in the way."

"No ma'am," said Elvis as Meena walked out of the room. He came to the side of the bed and reached for my hand. "How are you doing, champ?" he asked.

"I'm okay. The contractions aren't very strong right now..."

"You can do anything you put your mind to, Nina."

I nodded. He kissed my forehead.

Thomas was eventually born – 44 hours later – and Elvis stayed by my side the entire time. It was not a pleasant experience, not by any standards in the world...

When Thomas finally made his entrance into the world – his bald pink head first, then slim shoulders and long body – he gave one great big wail, then quieted down immediately. Elvis was crying, wiping his runny nose and eyes onto the sleeve of his stupid plaid shirt. Everything accelerated after that moment, as though the hours and hours of labour were actually just a few minutes, slowed down to an extreme as I suffered through it, for some cruel and unexplained purpose.

They scrubbed Tom down, then placed him on my stomach. It killed me, the fact that I still looked and felt like a whale, even though he was no longer sitting inside me, just below my ribcage.

"Oh, Nina," said Elvis. I smiled through my tears, through my fear at the recognition that I felt nothing at all for this tumor of a human being mewling on my belly. "He looks so much like you!"

I nodded. I just wanted him to be taken away for a while... I needed a rest...

Lying there in the hospital bed, the world moving faster to make up for all of the slowed hours, I thought about all of the mothers who give birth to stillborns.

I know. All of this sounds terrible.

I thought about what it would have felt like for Thomas to be born purple, to be rushed out of the room, to have a snotty nurse come back, apologetic, to tell us the terrible news.

I imaged being wheeled out of the hospital the very same day, empty handed. I imagined all of the people around me asking about the baby that was supposed to have arrived. I imagined strangers in the street looking at my saggy, post-pregnancy belly and asking when I was due. I imagined a tiny coffin, a simple ceremony, a grieving couple all dressed in black.

"What is that?" I asked, feeling a warm liquid drip down my side.

"Don't worry," said Meena, who had apparently returned. "I'll get you cleaned up now."

October 9, 2016

After hours. The halls were dark and I had stayed behind to file the files that had gathered atop my desk. I thought I was alone until he showed up in my doorway. He let himself in, closing the door. Locked it.

"Nina?"

I had been putting on my coat, about to leave.

No answer.

"You knew that this was just about the sex. Didn't you, Nina?"

I turned away.

"Oh come on," he continued. "You didn't really think that it was more than that... Did you?"

He stood so close behind me that I could feel his quickened pulse. I froze.

"Nina," he said sofly. "I'm your boss. It would be so... *unprofessional*. Let's keep things cordial." He reached out and grabbed my hips, pulling me towards him. He moved my hair aside and licked the side of my neck.

I stood there, still frozen.

"We had our fun. Let's quit while we're ahead." He ran his fingers down my spine. "Didn't you have a nice weekend? Didn't I give you everything you wanted? I payed for it all! Your little weekend would have cost a year's worth of your salary. What more do you want from me?"

I closed my eyes.

"Nina, if I chose to invite you... If I picked you... It is because you are the perfect ice queen. Didn't I say that? You're not soft. You're not vulnerable... You were just looking for fun too, weren't you? You needed this escape as much as I did." He turned me around to face him. "You didn't really fall for it, did you?"

I could not look him in the eye. How to tell this man that I had indeed fallen? Not for him, per say, but for the life that I had fabricated and projected onto him?

I was an unfulfilled woman. I was a miserable mother. I was exasperated, upset, worn-out. I felt like a flower looking out a diry window, starving for daylight. I could see the sun through the streaks, just barely, but I could not get enough. No. I needed more.

Gianni was the new sun that I desired desperatly. Only, clearly, he too left me in the dark.

"Nina, don't pout now," he said. He had the ugliest sneer across his face. "Won't you say something?"

Ice queen. Ice Queen. How did I ever get that reputation?

I knew the answer, of course.

Fool me once, shame on you, you bastard. Fool me twice, shame on me. Get hurt often enough, and it becomes a battle of who can lure who into the ship, then jump out first.

"Nina?"

"Get out of my office, Gianni. Or I will tell everyone and their mother about your sardine-sized dick."

He gave a surprised laugh.

"That's my girl," he said as he pretended to swing me a punch in the jaw. He let himself out of my office, still chuckling to himself.

What a prick. The alternate Nina-and-Gianni universe evaporated.

So be it.

"I don't need him," I said as I wiped a tear from my face. "Stupid, stupid Nina."

October 16, 2016

Everything is broken.

Last night was Claire's birthday party. She decided to have a small gathering, including Thomas and his family, Rachel and her new boyfriend, Robin and her sister Samantha, and Harvey.

"Hey Mom," said Claire, "it might be a fun time for Harvey to finally meet the rest of the gang. What do you think?"

"I'll ask Harvey," I said. I called him, unsure how to phrase the invitation.

"Hello, Nina," he said.

"Harvey. Are you busy Friday night?" I asked.

"No, I'm never to busy to make time for you, Nina."

"Okay. Well. Claire is having a little get together for her birthday. Here, at my place. she wanted to know if you'd like to come?"

He accepted right away.

Tom, Zandra and Laci arrived in the late afternoon, just at the point when the sun tastes like iced tea. It was a warm day for October. The leaves around us blazed. We talked about Laci, and about Tom's anxious return to teaching. It was a nice afternoon, all of us sitting on the back porch, little Laci bundled close to my chest. I was overcome with such feeling of calm... Like everything was exactly how it should be.

Claire was sitting at the end of the table, her chair leaning on both back legs and a cigarette in her hand, when Harvey came in.

"Claire," he said, nodding in her direction. "Happiest of birthdays, sweetheart."

Claire stood up, crushing her cigarette into the bottom of a sliced beer car. "Harvey! You made it!"

"Across the street?" he asked with one eyebrow up. "I am not yet that old, Claire..."

They hugged each other in a sweet, familiar way.

Tom stood up next.

"My how you've grown!" said Harvey. "You are not that lanky, awkward, brooding, teenager that you once were! Only yesterday, it would seem..."

Tom blushed. "Not too loud, Harvey. Zandra doesn't need to hear—"

"Oh yes I do," said Zandra, standing up too. "I am all ears."

"Portuguese?" asked Harvey.

"Sim!"

"Harvey, you devil," said Tom, laughing. "Do you really like literature, clean gutters, *and* speak Portuguese? That is indecent, man... Think of how you make men like me look!"

Harvey winked, then went over to take a chair next to Zandra. And just like that, the two of them were off having their own conversation.

Claire's phone began to ring. "Hello?" she said. "Oh yes, come on in, right through the to the back. You'll have to walk through a solarium greenhouse thing... No... No, if you've hit a bathroom, then you've gone—"

"Claire!" admonished Tom. "Just get off your ass and go. Is it Robin?" he asked.

Claire stood up, giving her brother the finger, and went into the house. A few minutes later, she was accompanied by Robin and Samantha.

"Robin," I said, standing up with Laci. "So happy you could make it."

We exchanged kisses.

"This is my sister, Samantha. You can call her Sam," said Robin. She was wearing the perfect olive summer dress to offset her red hair. Sam, on the other hand, looked more like Claire than she did her own sister: short, on the round side, dark hair and eyes.

"Nice to meet you all," said Sam. She smiled shyly. "Thanks for the invite guys. That baby is very cute."

I smiled back. My heart was so light.

"You didn't bring Winston?" asked Claire.

"I didn't know if he would be welcome," said Sam.

"Your boyfriend?" I asked.

Claire, Robin, and Sam laughed. I felt silly, but had no idea why.

"What?"

"Winston is my Great Dane," said Sam. "But there is not always quite enough room for a dog like him. And some people just don't like dogs."

"Me!" said Harvey.

"We have a bit of history with dogs," said Claire. "Not an easy one though."

"Are you talking about Poppy?" asked Thomas.

"You never told me about Poppy," said Robin.

Claire shrugged. "She died when I was pretty little."

"Committed suicide," I said at the same time as Tom.

Robin coughed. "What?"

"True story," said Tom. "When we first got her, she tried to eat a handful of nails that my dad and left in a coffee can on the floor next to the door."

"No kidding," said Sam.

"That wasn't the first attempt though," I said. "Tom doesn't remember this, but there was once a time when she jumped onto the counter and tried to drink a glass full of Windex."

"Why did we have a *glass* full of Windex?" asked Claire.

"I had dropped the bottle, the plastic spray bottle thing, and it was leaking out. So I poured it into the glass," I said. "It had been on the counter – right next to the sink, at the very back! – for less than a minute when the dog got to it. I was trying to find a container with a twist-off lid or something when Rachel started crying. So I went to grab her, and when I came back, the dog had jumped from the floor to the top of the garbage can to the top of the counter and was drinking the damn Windex..."

"That is so strange," said Sam. Everyone had stopped talking and was listening to our conversation about Poppy.

"Is that the red dog that would bolt from your front door and into the street and run after moving cars?" asked Harvey.

There was a general gasp from the crowd.

"Not after moving cars," I said. *"In front of."*

"Yes," said Thomas. "I remember that. Didn't she once get hit by a kid on a bike?" he asked.

"Oh my goodness!" I exclaimed. "I had forgotten that! Poppy broke out from the door once, when Elvis was coming in with his arms full of groceries or something, and he didn't notice her. She threw herself in front of a teenager on a bike. It was a rainy day. He slipped, fell on his head..."

"People didn't wear helmets back then..." said Tom.

"What happened?" asked Claire. "I don't remember this part."

"He cracked his skull, actually. He was taken away by an ambulance. We actually have no idea what happened to him in the end... The police asked us a few questions, then they were gone too. We tried to find out what happened, checked the paper and stuff, but we never saw anything about the incident," I said.

"Did you tell the police what actually happened? About the dog?" asked Zandra, her elbows on the table and leaning in.

"We tried," I said. "But they didn't quite understand us. Or believe us."

There was a moment of silent reflection.

"How did Poppy die?" asked Robin.

"We had taken her to a cottage up north for a family vacation. My mother had even come..." I said.

"There were three floors to the place," continued Tom.

"It was a good place," I said. "Right on the water. Very nice looking."

"And that is where she commit suicide?" asked Sam. "She drown?"

"No... Poppy finally threw herself out the third story window." There was an audible gasp. "She broke her neck. Rachel found her."

"Who did I find?" asked Rachel, coming through the patio door with a tall, dark, handsome young man. "You all look so serious," she added.

I stood up and went over to greet her. "We were just talking about Poppy," I said. "But we can talk about something lighter. How are you, Rachel?" I asked.

She did not answer me, but nodded at everyone who was gathered around the patio table. "I'm starved. Can I bring out the food?"

"Sure," I said.

"Let me help," said the man. They went inside.

"Who is that?" I asked Claire in a whisper.

She frowned at me. "Rachel's boyfriend... You met him at her birthday. Don't you remember?"

"Oh yes! Rachel's boyfriend. What is his name again?" I asked.

"Adil."

As though being summoned, Adil came out with a plate full of fruit and cheese. I helped him set it out on the table. Rachel soon followed with the plate of cold cuts and nuts.

"I couldn't find the baguette, Claire," said Rachel, addressing me directly for the first time.

"Oh, true! I had meant to stop by the... The..." I just could not remember. The breadery? The bread store? "The bake place? The place where they make bread?"

"The bakery, Mom?" said Rachel.

"Oh, for goodness sake! Yes, the bakery. Where is my mind these days? So I had meant to stop by—"

"What do you mean?" said Rachel.

I looked over at her, my mouth still open like a goldfish. "What?" It came out with a set of bubbles. I glanced over at Harvey. *Shit.* He was listening.

"It is a pretty obvious symptom of—"

"That is not necessary," said Claire.

"Rachel, don't..." I said, my eyes set on Harvey.

"Symptom?" he asked.

Rachel squinted her bright blue eyes at Harvey, then at me. "Mother. He does not know." It was not a question, so I did not feel the need to answer.

"What don't I know?" asked Harvey.

The hair stood on the back of my neck.

October 28

What happened since that last entry, I have been trying to make sense of all week,

It hurts so much.

Harvey, beiung the adult that he is, spent the rest of the party being charming and courteous...

Then, we saw each other on Thursday. I sat down on the couch and pulled a pillow onto my lap. Harvey sat next to me, but further than usual. Was he really sitting further? I wondered if I was not reading too much into things, if I was not projecting my own insecurities. Like when you think something is happening so you igmaine that everything is a sign of that thing happening.

"Harvey, what is it?" I asked.

"Nina..." he looked down, fingered the top button of his button-up shirt.

"What is it?"

"I spent so much time trying to run after you, Nina," he said. It was Harvey speaking, but I could hear Elvis in the periphery of his voice. "It took such a long time for you to trust me. And that was okay. I knew you had just lost your husband. And you were worth the wait."

I nodded. Despite the things that he was saying that seemed positive, I knew there was something more coming. Something bad. My heart felt yellow.

"I trusted you straight away, Nina. Right from the start. I opened myself to you, knowing full well that I may not get the same in response.

At least, not right at first..." Harvey looked out the window. I followed his gaze to the little playhouse in the corner, darkened, moldy and falling to pieces. "What is a couple without trust? I'm not sure if we were a couple, Nina..."

Were?

"But whatever we were... We were *something*," he said. "we had something, Nina. It has been a whole year. But now we don't have that. We have nothing. We are two people who have nothing anymore, except maybe that we are neighbours. I was so blind. I had such a bad feeling..." He sighed deeply, a sigh that reached straight through to the bottom of the ocean. "When you gave me that gift. The—"

"The tea. It was just a spelling mistake, Harvey... Grammar or syntax or something. But it doesn't have to be this way."

"That isn't it..." he said.

"What does any little mistake mean?" I asked. "It's just writing. it means nothing!"

Shrug. "I think it does."

"Harvey, why?" I asked. I was holding back a sob. I felt my heart grow yet more brittle.

"Nina, I have loved and I have lost. I watched Collette get sick... I watched her lose her autonomy... I held her hand as she died in that sterile hospital bed, tied to a million tubes and wires... I just cannot go through it again."

"We all die," I said. My voice sounded metallic to me, robotic. "You didn't mistake me for immortal, did you?"

"You can't just expect me to get—"

"Trust me, Harvey—"

"That is exactly the point!" he shouted above me. "There is no more trust. How could I ever trust you, Nina?"

"Well fuck you, Harvey!" He looked over at me, his startled expression mirroring my own sense of surprise.

"You've become so aggressive," he said, standing up bolt right. "Does it comes from the dementia?" He took a few long strides to the end of the living room.

"What does any of this have to do with trust?" I shouted at the back of his head.

Harvey turned to look at me, his face sad, his body still facing the doorway.

"Why cant you trust me?" I asked, insisting.

He sighed. "Nina, how long have you known that you have this disease?"

"October."

"Why didn't you tell me?" he asked. His face looked strange, contorted to look back at me with his body still facing away.

"I don't know what you mean."

"Nina..." he finally turned to face me. "Why? Why didn't you tell me?"

My breath caught in my throat. I felt overwhelmed, ambushed, angry. I did not want to say it out loud. I could not. Delivering words from my lips to his eardrums would make them real. Forever words. They held too much power.

"I..." I started, but failed to go on. I was having trouble speaking. "Harvey..." I shook my head. For a long moment, I averted my gaze, staring instead and the details in the woodgrain of the floor. So much time had I spent making out different shapes in the wood patterns: a monocle, a cup of tea, a sea lion, a bowling pin...

"You didn't give me a chance, Nina," said Harvey.

"What?"

"You let me fall in love with you. That was unfair of you. Knowing what I have been through... You presented me with a false reality, Nina. Had I known before... Had I known the truth... Well, who knows what I would have chosen? But this is not a way to go about things, Nina."

"Harvey. You know now, Harvey..." I looked up, locked eyes with him. "I am still the same Nina as I was yesterday."

"I resent you." For the first time since we had gotten to know each other, I felt a cold, an absence, in his eyes. "You are one of the most selfish—"

"Love is always selfish!" I shouted. "Harvey! Why do we ever fall in love with anyone?" I was on my feet, walking quickly towards him.

He took a step back. "To be loved back, of course! We only love to be loved in return. To feel appreciated. To be taken care of. To be less lonesome..."

"Your vision of love is distorted. I loved you for you, because I cared deeply for you... I wasn't trying to gain anything from you, Nina. And all along, you stood back and watched me get attached."

"Be fair, Harvey," I said. My voice was pleading, which made me embarrassed. "I did not draw you in, I did not insist on anything. You kept coming. *You* insisted." I looked away. I felt dizzy. "Harvey, I watched you get attached the same way I watch myself get attached. And then it was too late..."

"Nina, may the Lord have mercy, you are a wicked old woman."

"What have I done, Harvey?" I asked. "What have I done! I love you just as much as you love me..."

"What did you do? he asked. "You let me fall in love with you without telling me that you're sick." He grimaced, as though he had smelled something foul. "That is immensely dishonest. I have been tricked into battle... Unarmed."

"Are you really angry with me because you think that I am going to ring you in as a nurse? Is your concern that... That... Do you believe that I am trying to get at your money to be able to set myself up in a better hospice? Is it that you're afraid that I'll need you to wipe my ass? I don't need you to watch me die, Harvey. I don't need you to wipe the spit from my chin. I wouldn't allow you that honour. I just want some more... Some more good times. With you. is it because you think I'm—"

"It is that you lied. That you did not let me make an informed decision about you. You lied to me, Nina! Once a liar, al—"

"Oh, bullshit!" I shouted. "Listen. Can't we just act like two adults? I want to take advantage of the time that I have left. Can't we do that? Can't we act like nothing else happened? And when... And when you feel that... That you need to walk away..." I could hardly see Harvey from behind the tears in my eyes. "When my condition becomes too much for you to handle, you can just say goodbye." I wiped my tears with the back of my hand. "Harvey?"

Harvey shrugged. I had never seen him with such a lack of personal composure: it made him so much less attractive. "I guess that makes sense."

"What?"

Harvey shook his head. "It makes sense. To tell you goodbye when it is all too heavy." He leaned forward and kissed my forehead. "You've given me permission to walk away when things get too difficult. Honour your word, Nina. I choose to leave now."

The world shifted, spinning on a new access.

I am sorry, Nina..."

"Don't be sorry, Harvey." I felt the back of my scalp tingle. "There is nothing to be sorry about. And sweetheart? Let me tell you. Let me just say..."

"What?" he asked.

"I will be fine without you."

November 1, 2016

Sometimes, adults treat children like shit. Like when a kid is sad. I can promise you that when a kid is sad, no matter the reason, they should be taken seriously.

"Aww, you had a widdle fight wit your widdle friend? Oh well! Just wait until you can't find the money for your car payment *and* your mortgage! Do you pay for the roof above your head, or the wheels that get you to work to keep the room above your head?"

My mother did get sober for a while. I don't know for how long, really. I was a kid. When you're a kid, time is not measured in minutes or seconds. No. Time is a feeling measured in fun days, those slip away in the blink of an eye, and not fun days. Those stretch on for miles and miles.

We were living in a cardboardbox on Saint Denis Street, right above a fussy jewelry store. The way that the apartment was made, we had only one small window in the bathroom, which overlooked the alley-way behind, and one in the kitchen, right above the sink.

I have no one to meet,

And the ancient empty street's too dead for dreaming.

Bob Dylan was blaring from a neighbour's window. I had just gotten home from school. I must have been eight, maybe 10 years old?

"Nina?" called my mother in her shrill, impatient voice. "Is that you?"

She came into the kitchen – that is where the door lived – wiping her hands on her purple velvet pants.

"Yes, obviously who else are you waiting for?" I asked.

"You deserve a smack on that smart mouth of yours, little daughter," she said. She walked towards me. I felt my stomach tense. Why did I eat so many of Jenny's sour raspberry candy?

"But I won't lay a finger on you," said Mom, taking a strand of my hair into her fingers. "Because I know better, child. I know better and I have someone to introduce you to." She let go of my hair.

I let my backpack fall onto the floor.

"Come, sit," she said, inviting me to take a seat on the broken chair. I pulled myself up, my finger getting stuck in the sticky table surface.

She paced from the stove to the fridge.

"Nina, do you know who helped me beat my disease? Do you know who got rid of the devil that lived inside me, Nina?"

Her heavily made-up eyes were full, clear, unclouded. She reeked of sincerity.

"No."

She tucked her hair behind her ear, leaning down on one knee. I smelled her breath. It was... it was... normal.

I was terrified. How long had she been this way before I had noticd?

"First, Nina, it too a lot of work to admit to myself that I had no power in the thing. The alcoholism. And then I met Him."

"Who?" I asked.

"The love on my life, Nina. The love—" she put her hand to her heart, "--of my life."

I looked around, half-expecting a man to walk into the kitchen from our shared bedroom.

"You idiot," she said. "He is not here, Nina. Well. In a way, I guess that he is. He is everywhere. So I guess he is here too. Anyways. Do you know who I mean?"

"Santa Claus."

"You idiot. Anyways, haven't you noticed that I'm doing much better these days, Nina?" she asked.

I could not follow her. The thought creeped up that she was somewhat less confusing when she was drinking.

"Nina, step two. Step two and step three. I have found God, Nina."

"What?"

"Haven't you learnt anything in your religion classes in school?" she asked. "Our Lord is the love of my life."

I half wondered if she was talking about our LANDlord, a certain very tall, somewhat obese man with a pointy face and face hair.

"People, Nina, need God. Without Him in our life, well, that is when we get lost. I was lost, Nina. And I am sorry for taking you down that path with me. But those times are over!" She reached for me, tried to hug me, but it just felt off. She squeezed my face into her chest as she spoke. I could hardly hear her speaking anymore, my face crushed against her, my ear covered by her hand. "People need God... good... God... people... God... needs... God needs People."

God needs people. It is not the other way around.

Her sobriety was maddening. Suddenly, I had a basket full of new concerns. "Nina, did you make your bed? Nina, where are you with your homework? Nina, you get home before the sun sets!"

For a while (who knows how long?) I wanted my old mother back. I wanted to be allowed to dress how I wished, to walk around barefoot in the winter, to skip school on Friday afternoon to watch television curled up on the couch...

She began to dress sharp. She had the perfect cat-eye eyeliner. Her hair was in a magnificent round cut. Her nails were hot orange. Even the apartment began to reflect her lightly-shambled dignity.

I started to get used to my new and improved mom. Going to bed at a regular time wasn't so painful after all. Having a belly full of warm food didn't hurt either. I was even doing well in school.

"Nina, you are so graceful," said my mother one cloudy afternoon. "You should be a ballerina. Would you like to dance?"

She bought me my first ballet slippers. She put my hair in a bun and I walked down the street to my first lesson one Sunday morning.

"Show me what you've learnt!" she exclaimed.

Petit plié, grand plié, piqué, piqué, piqué...

"Oh, Nina!" she exclaimed. "You're really learning!"

I felt something growing inside my chest, making my cheeks puff. Pride? It was pride. I liked the feeling.

Then, one day, things that were sure to happen did just that.

I came home from school and the back door was locked. Strange. "Mom didnt mention being busy tonight..." I thought.

It was springtime, mornings were warm. I had gone to school in a light sweater, but with the sun falling rapidly, the temperature followed.

I sat on the steps, my back against the door, reading the book that I had just taken out from the library. It was about a ballerina, of course, who got lost in an enchanted forest. The pictures were bright and there were even sparkles on some of the pages.

I shivered. "How long have I been waiting?" It had gotten too dark to see the pages of my book.

"*Petite fille?*" came a voice from my left. "Bonjour. What are you doing out here?"

Never tell a stranger that you're alone, my teacher had taught us.

"My mom went to get my little brother at the neighbour's house. She'll be right home. I'm waiting for her."

He laughed. The quickly fading light hit strangely on his teeth. "*T'as pas de frère, menteuse...*" he said. "Why do you lie?"

I said nothing. It was enough to come up with the first fib, my imagination could not stretch far enough to come up with another.

He stepped closer. He smelled terrible, like a dumpster. All of my instincts were sceeaming at me to run. Hide. Get away, Nina. get away!

That is the first time in my life that I remember feeling my heart *actually* break. I can't explain the science behind it, I can't draw you a drawing. It is a thing that one simply knows.

Nothing is more painful than a broken heart, and that is true not matter how old you are.

November 10, 2016

Well, I guess everyone is aware of what happened last night. that was QUITE the shocker... when I woke up this morning to see that results i was sure it was a prank...

if I were still in the real-estate business, well, I can tell you that this election would have been a godsend!

With this president, it appears that many higher-class liberal-type americans will want to come live here in Canada, and Montreal is a close city to the border.

I bet that the real-estate agents are pretty excited about this news.

i didn't expect it tho! oh boy...

June 01

Claire informed me today of Rachel's engagement to Adil. She showed me a bunch of pictures on her phone.

"Who are all those people?" I asked as she quickly scrolled by a large group photo. There had to be at least 30 people in the picture, cramped into a small living room.

"Oh," said Claire, continuing to flip through the picture. "Adil invited a few close friends to surprise her afterwards."

I felt a lump in my throat. "Family too?"

"Well, some family... he is really close to his parents," said Claire. She clicked off her phone and threw it onto the footrest.

"You were there..." I said.

She nodded.

"Tom?" I asked.

Again, she nodded.

"Really? All the way from Ottawa? Why didn't he mention it to me? Where did he sleep?" I asked.

"They rented a hotel room," said Claire.

"*They?*"

"Well, for Zandra and Laci too..."

"I see..." I said. "Why didn't anyone tell me?"

Claire shrugged, looked away.

"Claire?"

It was a strange feeling, that of being left out from a place that I wanted to be. It reminded me of why I had kept my guard up for so long. When did I become so vulnerable? Was it when Elvis died? My security blanket, my sure thing, my stand-by...

"Rachel didn't want you there, Mom," Claire finally answered, in a voice just above a whisper.

"That makes no sense," I said. "Think about it, Claire! Rachel didn't plan that day... Adil did. What the hell does he have against—"

"Mom, he's got nothing against you! Don't be ridiculous. Don't you see... They talk about stuff together. And obviously, Adil knows how Rachel feels about you," said Claire.

"How she feels *at the moment*," I said. "But that can change. And no matter what, I will never have been there. I won't be in any pictures. I didn't get to meet his family. I didn't get to congratulate them... Nothing." I felt so insignificant in that moment, so unimportant, cast away like rubbish.

"I'm sorry, Mom," said Claire, moving closer to me on the couch. "This sucks. It's really just a timing thing though, I'm sure. If things were easier between you..."

"Doubt it. It's Adil, I'm nearly sure of it."

"What do you mean?" aksed Claire, pulling her arm away.

"I've always known that he had something against me," I said. "He never went out of his way—"

"Really, Mom... just don't go there. Trust me, it had nothing to do with Adil."

"Well," I said, "maybe not. But he isn't the most friendly with me regardless. Remember when we were at his birthday party—"

"It was Rachel's birthday," she said.

"That is what I meant. You knew what I meant. Anyways, at the party, he was rude. Didn't you find him rude?"

Claire looked into my eyes. Dark into light, brown into blue, indifferent daughter into dejected mother...

Mom, take it easy. Really. Adil had nothing to do with it.

"Fine. Anyways, where were they engenged?" I asked. Not as if I care...

"He proposed on the top of Mount Royal," said Claire. It was a perfect spring day, the leaves were in their first blush of green, the birds..." she smiled.

"So everyone hid in the parking lot?" I asked. Lame.

"No," said Claire. "The surprise supper was at Robin's place."

So Robin knew too?

"Everyone..." I said. "But me. You're all preparing for when I'm actually gone. I guess it makes sense..."

"No, Mom... Please," said Claire.

"Listen. It makes sense. If you get detached now, it won't be so hard to see me alone in my hospice bed, shitting my pants and eating through a tube."

"Mom, I—"

"It doesn't matter, Claire. I won't know who you are even if you do decide to visit."

"Mom, please just—"

"So let me get this straight." I felt my face turn to an ugly sneer. "Robin's place is too small for you to move in, but big enough to have a party with 30 people? Come on, Claire...

I stood up and left the room.

December 17, 2016

It has been hard to pick up the pen again. how long has it been?
30 days. I just checked.

But if i wrote on the 17th, the and then the 17 December, does that make it 31 days? Or 30? anyways.

The psychologist insists that it is best for me.

Remind me again why I see him?

I guess that without him, I don't really having very many people to talk to.

It is nice having Claire live here with me, but she only ever comes and goes...

She has never been the most reliable.

Harvey and I only had one argument before he... left me... We were having a conversation about and argument that I had had with Claire. The issue at hand was May. May is my neighbour. She has lived on this street for as long as I can remember.

"Nina, really..." said Harvey. It was the first time since I had met him that he showed a sign of impatience towards me. "You're just creating a storm within a glass of water."

"What?" I asked, in a tone reflecting his own aggressiveness.

"You're busy making grand gestures to remedy an issue on this end of the glass, but in reality, you're just making a mess of the other, it's all confined, it is stuck together, this problem..." he said.

"And then what do you suggest that I do?" I asked.

"First, be calm, for heaven's sake, Nina..." he said. "The more you upset things, the murkier they become. Let the sediment—"

"Jesus!" I shouted. "What are you, the fucking sphinx?"

His shoulders tensed.

"For the record, Nina, I will not be spoken to like that. I'm leaving now." I did not walk him to the door. I heard it shut quietly behind him as he left. That was bad. I wished he would have slammed it, punched a hole in the wall, shouted curse words at me... But this reaction? This flight? It made it seem like I was not worth the fight.

"Mom..."

"Claire!"

She moved towards the light. She was standing in the living room.

"How long have you been standing there?"

"I live here."

"So do I and sometimes it would be pretty nice not to have to creep around for privacy..." I said.

"You were talking about me," said Claire. "I have the right to hear what you say about me, don't I?"

"You made your thoughts very clear, Claire, and—"

"You know, you really should just shut up and listen to Harvey, Mother."

"Don't talk to me like that," I said. "You're the one who can't just get over things."

"You're bringing her up again? Seriously?"

"Claire! I can invite whoever I want into my own damn house!"

"I swear," said Claire, "that I understand what Rachel feels right now. You are impossible. *Impossible.* And instead of just thinking about things, you go about like a fucking harpy trying to find someone who will agree with you."

"I need to talk about my feelings, Claire, I won't apologize for that either!"

"It is not just talking. You're unbearable! You just don't stop. You make everything so much worse than it needs to be. You're so aggressive!" Claire was getting worked up. It wasn't like her to be so agitated.

"So, clearly, Claire, you do still have feelings for may..." I said. I knew how to prick her just the right way.

Her face became red, her eyes full of water.

"Well, Claire, that is the problem, isn't it? Not just the fact that I have her over every once in a while..."

"No!" shouted Claire. "Oh my god, you are so fucking stupid... I am getting married to the woman of my dreams. I love Robin. I don't want to jeopardize it for anything in the world. And one day, I show up, and well if it isn't my ex-girlfriend – to whom I was also engaged, in case you've forgotten! – sitting in my living room. And then you—"

"Stop saying things like that!" I shouted. I was losing control, losing my edge.

"What?" asked Claire, her face becoming smaller.

"In case I forgot. It is so rude! Stop rubbing it in my face!"

"Jesus Christ, Mother. Get over yourself! Even normal people forget things!"

"Normal people!"

"You're a magnet, you know that?" she said.

I looked at her, folded my arms, refused to ask her what she meant.

"No matter the situation, no matter who is concerned, you always drag it back to yourself. And you are always the victim, too."

"Oh, shit, just shut up, Claire." I went towards the stairs. "I'm done. Pack your things, if you want. i don't need you here."

Claire's eyes glazed over. "Do not invite her over anymore. It is fucking weird. You saw how the night ended last time... It's all so fucking weird! That you hang with a girl in her thirties. That you hang out with your daughter's ex. That you don't have friends your own age. It wasn't that big a story... But you always know how to—"

"She invited herself over, Jesus, Claire. She came to knock and—"

"It doesn't matter who invited who!" Claire looked like she was about to burst a blood vessel in her brain. "It is still fucking weird!"

"Since when are you my mother!"

"Seriously, Mom?"

"I can be friends with who I want," I said.

"You can be freinds with whoever you want. I do not give a serious fuck. Just not *HER*."

"Anyone but May?" I said. Claire's eyes shot me a deadly look. I laughed. "And I guess that would explain why you're so pissed for nothing."

Claire shook her head. "What?"

"Claire," I said, taking her hand into mine. "Are you having second thoughts about your marriage? Is that was this is—"

"No!" she shouted, letting my hand fall. "And anyways. Why are you lying about it?"

"About what?" I asked.

"About inviting her here! She never knocked—"

"Okay, Claire. Okay. I'm done. Goodnight!" I went up to my bedroom. I heard the front door slam.

It didn't much bother me what had happened with claire, I knew that she would be fine, but I was really concerned about Harvey's reaction. It was just too easy for him to walk out on me.

I walked around a bit, took a shower, got into bed.

That night I dreamt Harvey left me. For May, of all people. And he did leave me. i guess that makes my dream a kind of profesy...

I studied King Lear in high school. I always kind of liked literature. And I liked the idea of liking literature, if that means anything.

Anyways. This came up with the shrink last appointment.

He asked about what models I had of old age. I answered King Lear.

I don't remeber a whole lot about the play, beyond that it was about an old feeble king being betrayed by his three unfaithful daughters... But anyways, there was this one phrase that has stuck in my mind all of this time. I don't remember it word for word or anything, but it goes something like this: King Lear banished his loyal servant, like a patient who kills his physician, preferring instead his mortal disease.

December 21

I do not talk about my childhood very often. They were not happy days. Mostly I remember being very, very lonely. Thinking back, that probably explains why I decided that I did not want to have children: what model did I have to base myself upon?

My mom spent a lot of time telling me the 'truths about life.' I remember these conversations from when I was very little, much too little to understand any of what was being said.

One day, I must have been no older than six, I was standing in the bathroom brushing my teeth when my mom wandered into the room. I remember it being a filthy little space, especially the toilet: I was afraid to use it because of the brown rings which marked up the inside. In my little child's mind, I was sure that they were cracks, and that sooner or later when I took a seat I would fall right into the sewer.

So I stood there brushing my teeth, essentially about to put myself to bed, when my mom barged in.

"Nina, sweet Nina, she smelled of rotten fruit. "You know about your father?"

I spit into the grimy sink and wiped my mouth with the back of my hand. "Yes Mom. I know. He's gone..."

"Nina, you know what made hm go?" She stood unsteadily in the doorway. I braced for what I knew to be coming next.

"Yes Mom," I said. "I know."

"I could have been a professional actress," she continued. "I had natural talent. And I practiced all of the time, and your father was such a big supporter of my career..."

On the good days – of which there were few – my mother would break into spontaneous recitations of monologues, soliloquies, and fragments of dialogue, with perfectly smile on her face... Those are some of the only memories in which I remember my mom being happy.

I put my toothbrush into the pink ceramic cup. "I'm sorry about all that, Mom."

"You're right about that," she went on. "You're right to be sorry. Look at this shack that we live in, all alone, and I don't even know where I'll get my next paycheck from..."

I left the bathroom as quickly as I could and went to bed. My mother never really bothered following me, and I was thankful for that small grace. I turned on my clown-shaped night lamp and looked through a crumbly old clothing catalogue. My mind always wandered when I got to the children's section; pretty little blonds with pretty little smiles and pretty little clothes. I switched off my lamp then pulled my blanket over mysel, turning it just right so that the holes would let in the least amount of cold air.

Sometimes I would heard the door open, which could mean one of two things: my mom had left, or a man had arrived.

I would push my fingers deep into my ears, trying not to hear the answer to the riddle: going out, or staying in?

I was afraid to be home alone at night, like most children, I suppose. But what the cat dragged in was always even worse.

December 30

<u>a lonely summer</u>

when the sun is shining
nobody wants to be alone
nighttime passes
and the sun is shining
but not for me
i am alone
and it is the dead of winter

January 2, 2017

have been writing for one year now. It is hard to read my first entries. I was much happier then.

I think I will write more poetry. It helps.

It was new years eve two nights ago. Somehow, Claire convinced me to thorw a party here.

Somehow, I accepted.

The air was as heavy as lead. no one had much fun, i don't think.

There was Tom and Zandra and Laci, there was Robin and Claire. Rachel, as i learnt, was on holiday with Adil.

We sat around the living room, played a few board games and card. But everything seemed grey.

We went to sleep a few minutes after watching the ball fall in New York. Everyone stayed for the night.

I offered to make a nice breakfast yesterday morning, but everyone seemed to be in a hurry to go. Claire has not been home yet.

Will life ever have colour again?

January 14, 2017

My mother came by today: the woman I fled, the woman from whom I protected my children, but from whom I never learnt to protect myself.

"Sit, dear, let me make you some coffee," she said.

I was standing with my back against the wall. "I don't drink coffee, Shelley. Sorry. I have none on hand…"

"really? Not even that instant stuff? All tea drinker have that instant stuff," she said as she looked through my pantry.

"No, sorry."

"No matter," she said. "ill just have a glass of water."

"Okay," I said, getting a tall glass and filling the bottom with ice cubes. "Do you want to sit in here? In the living room? Solarium?" I filled the glass with water from the tap.

She rolled her eyes. "So many rooms!" she said. "*Pardon moi*, Nina dear. You've always been so damn fancy… Never have I owned a home with so many rooms. Never have I even spent a night in such a home!"

I placed her glass on the table, then turned my back to her, putting the kettle on the stove.

"So, anyways dear. Phil says hi."

"Who?" I asked.

"Phil? My fiancé?" said my sad, washed-out mother, while holding out her hand. *Notice the ring*, she screamed. I did not.

"Oh, I didn't know. Well, hi to Phil to," I said.

"Fiancé, dear! Didn't you hear that little piece of news?" she asked.

She was leaning against the kitchen table, almost sitting on it. I hate when people put their ass on my table. That is where food goes, not your ass. Seriously.

"Congratulations," I said for at least the twelfth time. "Good on you."

"Phil is a motivational speaker and yoga professor. He teaches an ancient form of yoga that is all about the merging of our own personal spirit along with the spirit of the world, and Our Sacred Mother, Nature," said my mother. And she was off.

"Oh..."

"You know, we are so silly to believe that we are separate from nature. well, Phil teaches that we are all a part of it, that our connection with the Divide Knowledge will lead us to the Higher Self." Capitalization mine for emphasis. "In this new Planetary Age, Nina, we have to look for old spiritual traditions to connect ourselves with the past. All diseases can be explained simply as a lack of spiritual connection. Heal the soul, you can heal the body."

That last statement bothered me. *All diseases?* That was the equivalent of saying that I had inflicted my Alzheimer's on myself, that my grandmother elected to die of pneumonia. I must have rolled my eyes.

"Nina, dear..." said my dear mother. "How do you think that I was finally able to cure my alcoholism?"

"You can't cure alcoholism, Shelley. You can only manage—"

"Open your mind, Nina..." she said, sighing.

"In a lot of ways, science lags far behind spirituality, Nina. Don't try to explain it away. I am cured, that is all I know. And I have Phil to thank for it. I met him – he was my teacher! – at a weekend getaway for people struggling with addiction."

"A cult?" Knives were drawn.

"Nina, grow up..." she sighed. "Cults, those only exist in movies. And in any case..." The end of her sentence was hidden behind the whistle from the kettle. I took it off of the stove and poured the water into the teapot.

"... teaches a kind of yoga that deals with the whole body, the spirit, and lifestyle. You may want to look into it, Nina. Take your jeans, for example..." she continued.

I looked down at my pants, almost spilling hot water on myself.

"Our clothes are the closest thing to our physical body. What type of message do you think that it whispers to our soul when we wear clothes without a conscious?" she asked.

I glanced over at her. Of course! Her outfit, had I paid better attention, would have been a dead giveaway from her new and improved *Lifestyle*. She was wearing loose fitting red pants with a beige elephant pattern and with elastics around the ankles and a white top, off the shoulders, with a scarf tied around her frizzy blond and white hair. No makeup. Never did I expect to see the day when my mother would be out without makeup. That Paul, what influence!

"How can clothes have a conscious?" I asked. It was not that I wanted to feed into her ridiculous game, but I was curious. She actually had me feeling curious.

"Well, not the clothes itself. I mean, the way that it is constructed. Image how it would feel to be wearing clothes made from an eco-conscious material, all natural fibres, made by a real artisan instead of an enslaved child. Imagine the wellness it would create. Mind, spirit, and body," she made a sign with her fingers, "all connected with the same goal: peace."

I held back some vomit that had crept up into my throat

"So what is it that you are lacking in the balance of life, Nina?" she asked.

"Pardon me?" I realized that I had forgotten to pour out the tea. When I finally did, it was bitter.

"Well, with that disease of your mind. What is it—"

"Shelley, please. I don't really want to discuss—"

"It is just that I asked Phil about it, and he said—"

"Shelley!" I shouted. "I really don't want to discuss this with you, and even less do I want to know what Phil has to say about it."

"Let me just say these two last things then: our fear of change is what stops us from accepting help, and when you are ready, I will help you through this."

"Oh, Jesus Christ, Mother!" I shouted. "What the fuck is wrong with you? I told you—"

"Be calm, Nina. And be still. Like a mighty oak. Trust me." She closed her eyes and put her hands together in prayer.

I walked into the living room and opened the window. My mother eventually followed me in.

"Anyways, what has happened to your boyfriend? Rachel was saying—"

"When did you speak to Rachel?" I asked.

My mother sat on the floor next to the couch, legs crossed. "Nina, I am certainly allowed to call my grandchildren every once in a while, aren't I?"

"I don't want to talk about it."

"She also mentioned that, in retrospect, your... your mental health degradation began to show even before Elvis passed away. May his soul rest in eternal peace, of course," said Shelley. "Rachel thought about how when you went into a room, sometimes you would—"

"You cannot be serious, Shelley!" shouted Nina. "What kind of thing is that to say?"

"Dear, is there a safe subject at all? My life bores you and your life is off limits."

She had a point.

"What happened to Gary?" I asked.

"Who?" she asked, looking over her shoulder at me with her phony face of calm and divine connection.

"Your fiancé. I mean, the last one. I thought he bought you the SUV you're currently—"

"Oh. Gary," she said, stretching the first syllable. "How should I put this? He is no longer among us."

"I'm sorry," I said. I was tempted to ask what he had done to qualify for his death, but I did not need to.

"He got hit by lightning, poor man. Playing golf."

"Really?" I asked. First my mother, then lighting? Gary was an unlucky man indeed.

"It was a tragic thing, especially because they thought that he would make it at first. I went to the hospital, he was in bed with his children around him... Let us say that their welcoming of me was not... outright."

"Due to something you said?" I asked. "Or something you did?"

"Oh, not me. Gary. Gary had his will changed, and they knew."

I grimaced, making the same face you make when you walk into a fish shop.

Anyways, she went on, "it would not have worked with Gary. He was too easy to manipulate. No challenge at all." she has always had quite the talent for ignoring the reactions of the people around her.

"Challenge?"

"You know. The way we do when we need affection, when we instigate an argument for no reason. When women make men feel badly about something without consequence."

I hated her for putting it into words, mostly because I recognized myself in what she was saying.

"Don't you think that men do the very same thing?" I asked.

She considered my question. "I imagine so. Paolo, for example, would initiate arguments for no particular reason. He was a gemini, so you can just guess what type of trouble he got into!"

"Certainly."

"He took more time looking after his appearance than I did!" she exclaimed. "Paolo Pauleau from Sao Paulo."

"That is amusing," I said, smiling.

"He was so much younger than me. He intimidated me so much!"

"Because of his age?" I asked.

"No, no. Because of his looks."

"Oh."

"I know," she went on. "I have no reason to worry about that department. I mean. Nina, look at me. I am 82. You are 66. We could be twins." She puffing out her chest.

I looked at my reflection in the glass door of the fire place. She was right. When had I gotten so... old?

"Don't you think that there is a reason for that?" she asked.

"You're not really going to talk about the holy spirit again, are you?" I asked.

"I just know what is good for my soul, which is good for my body."

"What did Gary do again?" I asked.

"Pardon?"

"For a living, I mean."

"He was an attorney," said Shelley. "He had his own practice. His biggest disappointment was that none of his four children – none of four! – went into business with him."

"What did you two talk about?" I asked. My mother, a first class gold digger with no education, sleazy as the day is white, and a lawyer. Curious.

"We made a lot of jokes together," she said. "We had a lot of fun. And we had similar pastimes."

"Really?" My mother, with a hobby?

"Sure," she said, touching my knee. "We both loved spending the weekend on his yacht. and when we would go to great restaurants. If only he knew that I am now transitioning to raw veganism!"

I had no idea that an 82 year old knew what veganism was. I hardly knew myself.

A thought occurred to me. "Coffee isn't raw."

"We had this private joke," she went on, ignoring my question which underlined the continued incongruence between her words and actions, "We liked to imagine what the world would be like if lawyers were replaced by wrestlers."

"What?" I asked, certain that I had misunderstood her. where is my mind going?

"Crazy, right?" she laughed. "But not so silly when you really begin to think of it."

I smiled. How long had it been since Shelley had made me smile genuinely?

"I guess it isn't so different, is it?" I asked. "Both are called upon to put on a show. And it is all very rehearsed..."

"Imagine, shopping for a lawyer by reading about stats, weight and height and number of knockouts?" she said.

"Video montages instead of resumes..."

"Belts instead of diplomas..."

"Knock outs instead of closing arguments..."

Shelley sighed. "He was one of the harder ones to loop in," she said.

"What do you mean?" I asked.

"It was one of those drag him in, cast him out again, repeat, repeat, repeat, situations," she said. "but oh, so worth it."

"Cast him out?"

"Invite him out for drink and chat up the waiter, take him to a party and dance with another guest, that type of thing."

"You do that on purpose?" I asked. "I mean, it is all planned?"

"Oh, Nina, be real!" said Shelley. "Of all of the debauched women I have known, you were the absolute most strategic. In your twenties? oh, I *remember*!" she said *remember* like it was the most powerful word she had ever spoken. Remember what? You weren't even part of my life in my twenties.

"I taught you well," she said, smiling at whatever she was reliving in her mind.

"So were you planning on staying for supper?" I asked.

"What time is it?" she asked.

"Half past—"

"Shit! I have class!" she exclaimed as she got to her feet. The trouble it took to stand betrayed the aura of youth that she had cultivated all about her exterior.

I followed her to the door.

"May I..." She stood below me on the doorstep, looking so tiny and frail. "May I say a mantra for you?"

I sighed. "If you insist..." I said.

She sang something with an excessive number of vowels and hard consonants from the back of her throat.

"Namaste, Nina," she said and she turned to go. "Call me, will you?"

I closed the door.

January 20

Claire was just over 10 years old. She called a family meeting, which was strange, because that was not a common occurrence in the Rossi-O'Connor household. we had never done anything so... wholesome.

"thank you for coming," she said as she stood in front of the four of us, squeezed onto the couch. I could see Rachel roll her eyes in my peripheral vision. "I have a big announcement to make. It is something personal, about myself, and I—"

"You change your mind about being a dog walker when you grow up?" asked Tom.

"New favourite colour?" asked Rachel.

"New boyfriend?" exclaimed Tom.

"Precisely where I was going with this." Claire spoke with the dignity of a middle-aged teacher. she always had though... She had the oldest soul I had ever met. "Do you all remember Lola, the girl in my glass who played Wendy in the winter *Peter P—*"

"The one who puked all over the stage?" said Tom.

"You let your sister talk. Or I'll..." said Elvis. He was never really very good with threats.

"That was Gerry. Anyways. Well, I have something to say about Lola." She took a deep breath. "I think that I'm in love with her." Such a bold statement coming from such a small, chubby child.

Rachel snorted. No one else made a sound.

"What I am trying to say is that I am attracted to females," said Claire.

Females. She must have read up about it somewhere. "And I thought that you should know."

"What?" said Elvis. "How do you know?"

"How do I know I'm in love with Lola? Well, I guess it is the way she makes me feel. Like my heart—"

"Thanks for the news bulletin, but I'm out..." said Tom as he stood up to leave. "Charles is waiting outside to go to the skate park." He left the room, quietly followed by Rachel.

"What were you saying, Claire?" I asked.

"I was saying how it feels to fall in love. But I guess that I don't need to explain that, now that Rachel and Tom are gone."

"Why is that?" I asked.

Claire chuckled. "Well, you two already know how. You're in love with each other!"

Elvis and I exchanged a strained smile.

"It's how you made me, isn't it?" asked Claire. She kissed us each on the cheek and went upstairs without saying any more.

"What do we do?" asked Elvis.

"What do you mean?" I asked.

"Did our ten-year-old daughter not just come out of the closet to our entire family?"

"It is a phase," I said. "She probably heard some older kids talking about it at school."

"What if it isn't?" asked Elvis.

"Can't we just cross that bridge when we get to it?" I asked as I stood up to leave the room.

"This certainly felt like a bridge to me..." I heard Elvis say from behind me.

"What?"

"I just think that she was serious," he said.

"I'm not suggesting that she isn't serious, Elvis. I'm just saying that maybe she only feels that way *at this moment,* but that in the future... who knows?"

"I think I'll stop by the library tomorrow to see if I can't find any books about parents who—"

"Mom!" shrieked Rachel from the doorway.

I ran to meet her.

"Tom got hurt," she said as she pointed out the door.

"Where is he?" asked Elvis at my heal

"On the street, they called an ambulance..." said Rachel.

I was halfway to the scene of what looked like a traffic accident when I realized that I was outside on a crisp fall day without shoes or coat.

"I just didn't... He was just... Out of nowhere!" shouted a short, middle-aged Asian man. He had one leg out of his SUV, the other still inside. He tried to pull himself to both his feet, but as i got closer, i realized that he was still wearing his seatbelt.

"Tom," said Elvis as he squat down by his side. "Where does it hurt?"

I was standing just over Elvis' shoulder. Tom was lying on the ground, face up, his left arm limp beside him perched at a rather strange angle.

"He came out of nowhere!" shouted the man from the SUV. He had apparently abandoned the idea of getting out of his car and was sitting in his seat, but with his head still sticking out the door, his glasses crushed on strangely against his face.

"Tom..." I whispered.

His eyes were open, but much like the confused driver, they were blank as the door of an unplugged microwave oven. He was in shock.

"Mom..." he finally said, looking over at his arm and the hair stood on the back of my neck. I got the sense that he was not looking at his flesh-and-bone arm, but at the pain that must have been pushing from it.

"Don't move, Tommy boy, help is coming," said Elvis.

indeed, there was a police car tunneling down the street, followed by an ambulance.

After that, everything happened in a quick blur. The policemen, the paramedics, Elvis in the back of the ambulance, the doors slamming in my face, the police interview, the phone call – only broken bones, just a cast, no other damage – the pacing for what felt like a year until their return...

I learnt a lot while I waited for Elvis to come home with Tom.

I learnt that motherhood is nothing more than a shit storm within a much larger shit storm. basically. From the moment your child is born, you are condemned to a constant state of worry. It the baby breathing? Did the baby drink enough milk? Does the kid have enough friends at school? Extracurriculars? Is my teenager suicidal? Do you smell like pot? Did you use protection, at least? get your finger out of your nose.

I spent so much of my life as a mother focused on what I saw to be the most important things: having a clean house, the kids' grades, car insurance, eating vegetables, working full time.

Motherhood is about so many things. I had so much trouble letting go. Living in the moment. Elvis was good for that, always telling me to relax...

Now that I am older woman, now that the kids have grown up and turned out to be reasonable taxpayers... now, I wish that I could just share a few words with Nina the Young Mother.

"Nina," I would say, "stop for a minute." I would look up at myself, wrinkles and white-blond hair. "They need you, Nina, not a clean floor. go eat a popsicle for breakfast. And for goodness sake, Nina, be good to Elvis."

How I miss that man.

January 31, 2017

The headshrinker suggested that I write down a list of things about myself.

"A general inventory," he said. "Something like the time capsules that we made when we were children."

I held back a sudden urge to chuckle. When we were children? *sweetheart, when I was a child, your parents were still wetting the bed...*

"Some studies have shown that identity-affirming activities can help to slow the progression of dementia," he said, focused more on listening to himself than on speaking to me. "When we are young, we are constantly trying to figure out who we are, both to ourselves and to others. Generally, when we get older, we move more into a contemplative phase, where we consider our past choices, beliefs, goals, values... We call this the transition between implementation and reflection. but what I am asking you to do is to affirm your personality. If you remember that you always loved to play cards, then write it down. After you have drawn yourself out with words," – what? – "then go ahead and schedule those activities."

The more I think about it, the more I think that it is not a question of age, but a question of expiry date. we do not go into the reflection phase when we notice a few grey hairs. It happens when we know for a fact that our decisions are no longer of consequence because there is simply no time left. There is more to think about in the past than in the future.

"How is it a time capsule?"

"Well, the way that I see it," he said, "it is a time capsule in that it is a catalogue meant to be examined at a later time, with the goal of informing the people of the future about something that is important today."

"Who will examine it later?" I asked. I was intrigued, bloody well despite myself.

"You will."

Anyways.

I'm going to write down some things that are important to me, not because buddy told me to, but because i happen to like the idea.

I always liked the feeling of running my finger on the edge of paper. It is the riskiest thing that you can do while sitting in your living room. I am doing it right now with this piece of paper.

adrenaline.

My dream job, had there been no restrictions in money, time or talent, would have been to write fictional novels. My character would have been a sexy lady detective. My books would have been like in the style of the film noir. her name would be Fox Ee. She would write poetry while she travelled on private jets and yachts.

I have never understood why people drink drinks with bubbles. The bubbles get stuck in my nose and it seriously hurts. With a straw makes it worse.

I love ballet, it is the one clean art form. There is something about the crisp movements, the chin-up-ribs-in, the tight bun on the top of the head... my mother enrolled me in ballet. It is the one gift from her that has ever meant anything to me.

I once competed in a spelling bee, I was about 10, and came in second. i don't know why. I have never been a gifted speller.

I like the smell of rain on wet pavement, the Atlantic ocean, fresh cut grass and the top of a baby's head.

My secret wish had always been – is still? – for my father to somehow materialize in my life. he would be a top marine, or a NASA scientist, or a famous actor, and he would apologize for having missed so much of my life, explaining that he had no idea that I existed, that my mother had lied about me for all of this time.

i have a weakness for reggae music, but know nothing about it and never listen to it.

i am afraid of forgetting everything about myself. i am afraid of withering away.

I am a person today, but have no idea what will be left of me tomorrow.

February 6, 2017

Sometimes I think that I may have been getting a little mixed up before the big incidnet that happened in October with the keys.

I have always been a forgetful kind of person, but I always imagined that it was because I didn't pay to close attention.

The small things would get me the most: what is that called again, that thing that toasts bread? The one that opens cans? The one that you use instead of stairs? Automatic stairs?

I just want to understand why this is happening to me. Is it somehow my fault? Did my father die of the same disease? Or is my case totally random?

Lightening does strike unpredictably.

When I was waiting for my psychologist appointment, I picked up an old magazine. I read a story about an Indian man being struck by a meteor. Four people who were around him at the time were injured. Now I don't know about the statistics from indian traffic accidents, but it seems to be that it must be quite high. And yet a 40-year-old Tamil Nadu bus driver ended up evaporated by a falling star.

February 10, 2017

WINDOWS AND DOORS

sometimes when you need a door, all you can find is a window
sometimes when you need a window, all you can find is a wall
sometimes when you need a wall, all youcan find is a staircase
sometimes when you need a staircase, all you can find is a door.

February 28

Lst night, a man broke into my house. I was in bed when I heard it happen.

He cut a thin hole in the glass of the front door, thin like an envelope. I don't know what tool he used or how he fixed it on his way out

I was terrified. I layed there in bed, pretending to sleep. I imagined that he was like a bear and I just played dead.

He came up the stairs. then he came into my bedroom. then he looked through my things. He really touched everything. I don't know what he was looking for it was hard to see his face... But it was definitely familiar to me.

I was so shocked and scared that i must have passed out.

I woke up this morning with a start. I did not know if the robber was still in my house. Claire was not home.

I got out of bed and looked around my room first. I had two pencils in each hand for protection.

Everything was exactly as I had left it.

"What the fuck was he lookig for?"

I looked around the entire house. Everything was where it was supposed to be

What the fuck?
What the fuck?
What the fuck?
What the fuck?

The man was gone, the door window somehow fixed.

All day has been a feeling of needing to clean my house. A strange man who came in and put his hands on my things... That is almost like putting his hands on me. The degrees of separation are minor. I feel so dirty. My whole house is dirty.

And who can I really talk to about it? If I tell Elvis, he will call the police. If I tell Tom or Claire, they will insist that it is not safe for me to live alone anymre.

Fuck.

Maybe I need to get an alarm system, or a dog or something.

March 7, 2017

I am very, very tired. It is taking all of my energy just to hold this pen. maybe, when I am done writing, I can sleep.

There is nothing funny about the stages in life when the deterioration begins. We grow, we stretch, we dig our roots deep and shoot out our brightly-coloured flowers into the world. blossom, share, glow, create.

But then...

The time comes when you stop getting better. You only aim to do almost-as-well-as-before. It only happens in a few parts of your life. then more, and more.

I called Thomas yesterday to tell him about the break in. i said I wouldnt... but I was so scared. That is how this all started. He was concerned and asked why I didn't call the police. It was a strange conversation, because I actually had no idea why I didn't call the police.

"Where was Claire?" he asked.

"Thomas, I don't know. In her own room? Out with her girlfriend? She's a little old for me to be keeping an eye on her..."

"Wasn't that the point of her moving in with you?" he asked. I heard Laci crying in the background.

"What?"

"She came to live with you to keep you safe, so that you don't have to go into a home so soon. But then she is never around?" said Tom. i actually felt my mouth fall open, my jaw hitting my chest.

"No, Tom. That was not the the pint at all."

I heard him talk to Zandra, the phone away from his mouth. "Sorry," he said, coming back after a few moments. "Laci is a little sick... it has been a rough few days." He cleared his throat. "Anyways, what exactly happened, Mom? Did you want to tell me again, and I can write it down for you? Then we can contact the police and ask them to keep a closer eye on your place? Did Harvey see anything from across the street?"

"Harvey!" I said, a little more loudly than I had thought that I would say it. "Tom, don't bring him up..."

"He is still your neighbour, you know..." said Tom. "You haven't fixed things up with him? I like him a lot, you know. Did you try to apologize maybe?"

"Jesus, Tom, are you a fucking idiot!" I shouted. "What can I apologize for? My brain? For my slow fall down the hole of sanity? i wasn't calling you for a lesson in—"

"No, Mom..." said Tom. "You could at least apologize for lying about it though," said Tom.

"Thomas, forget it, this is not what I called you for!" I said. I was feeling agitated. I stood up from the couch and tried to open the window, but it was stuck shut. My hands were shaking.

"Sorry, Mom," he said, taking a big breath. "So where is Claire now? Have you seen her since the break in? And how did the man get in?"

I tried to organize an answer to all of the questions at once. "I don't know! Yes! I don't know!"

"What?" asked Tom.

I could feel my patience going away.

"I saw Claire all week, but I don't know where she is at this very current *SECOND* because she is a grown person who came to live at my house until she gets married. She needed a place to stay, you know, Tom, and she actually begged me to take her in!"

"Okay, okay," said Tom. "You called about a man breaking into your house. When did it happened exactly?" he asked.

"It was night," I said, my memory shifting back to that night, "But I don't know what time. It was dark." I felt a cold shiver work its way up my back bones.

"Where were you when it happened?"

"I was in bed..." I said. "And the man broke into the house from the front door. He broke in through the glass—"

"Shit," said Tom. "That will cost an arm and a leg to repair!"

"No. I mean, that is how the robber *broke in*, but he did not actually *break* the widow. He must have used special tool, or maybe he fixed it on the way out..."

There was silence on the other end of the line. "That sounds strange," Tom finally said. "So the person just... came through the door?"

"Listen, Tom," I said, growing impatient with his tone. "I was in bed. I just know that is where the sound came from. Other than the robber—"

"You were in bed, in your room, on the second floor?" asked Tom.

"Yes, as I said..."

"What did you say was stolen?" he asked.

"That is the strange thing..." I said. Suddenly, I was afraid to tell Tom the rest of the story. i suddenly realized that he didnt believe me. Why didn't he believe me?

"Go on," said Tom.

"Well, I don't think that the man was a... he wasn't a thief... not really..."

"A robber but not a thief?" asked Tom.

"No, no..." I said. "Listen, Tom. I am tired. Can I talk to you later?"

"Just tell me the rest of the story," said Tom, putting emphasis on the word *story*. Had Rachel gotten to him?

"Well, the man – maybe not robber or thief, Tom, but the MAN – came into my room and... moved my things about," I said.

"So you mean that you saw him move your stuff, like he was looking for something? Did you take pictures of where he left things?" he asked.

Silence.

"Mom?"

"No. I... I didn't."

"What stuff did he touch? Like your jewelry box or something?" asked Tom.

"Mostly... everything." I said. It felt like second aggression, just having to answer all of Tom's questions.

Quiet breathing.

"Well, Mom..." said Tom. "Did you want us to pay for some kind of... security system? Or maybe one of those alert necklaces, you know what I mean? So that you can just press the—"

"No. Thanks for your time, Tom. I'm fine."

I hung up the phone without waiting for his reply. My hand was shaking. i was feeling sick, weak. I went to my bedroom, let myself fall onto the bed, and just lay there. I wasn't tired – not in the sleepy sense – but I felt like I had no power left in me, that it was impossible for me to do anything but breath.

i lay there for hours, watching the shadows move about the clock, but i did not sleep. i could not sleep.

I learnt two things yesterday: people treat the elderly like stupid toddlers, and lying in your bed without sleep or sex is as uncomfortable as lying on a lumpy floor.

March 17, 2017

It had been such a long time since I had been alone with Rachel... She finally decided to come over yesterday, for tea. i wasn't excited about the visit. Rachel is so difficult. it ended even worse than how it began.

"Mom, when is the last time that you've looked at yourself in the mirror?" she asked as she walked in the door.

"What?"

"You've got to do something about that hair, Mom. You look older that Grandma Shelley..."

"Grandma?" I said. We were still standing in the doorway and already her guns were blazing.

"Do you remember her?" she asked, her blue eyes colder than an iceberg. "Do you remember your mother?"

I ignored her and walking into the kitchen.

"Grandma Shelley said that I should come by and see you," she continued, carving at me with her knife. "I see why."

i put the kettle onto the top part of the oven a little harder than i had anticipated.

"Everything alright?" said Rachel. "Anyways, she was saying that—"

"Jesus, Rachel!" I shouted. "I get it. You're pals now. That's nice. Can we talk about something else?"

Her eyes shone. One point to Rachel. How many more times would she try to get under my skin?

"Actually, I wanted to talk about her a little. You know, you have told us so many terrible things about her. But at the end of the day... She isn't all that bad. I guess what I have come to realize is that no parent is perfect. She probably had the best intentions for you, but—"

"She is a drug addict and a compulsive liar. I can't believe that someone as smart as you, Rachel, could get caught up in her lies."

One point for me. Rachel has always been so easily disarmed when complimented...

"Oh, I know the tricks of a compulsive liar. I've seen them used often enough," she said, still fully engageged in battle. "But at the end of the day, she isn't all bad. I really think that she has turned a new lease," she said.

"That does bring me some hope for her," I said.

Rachel was surprised by my quick change of side. Well, fuck her. Fuck them both.

"Can I get you something to eat?" I asked.

"No," said Rachel. "I haven't got much time."

I nodded, helping myself to an almond biscotti. I prepared the tea then joined Rachel at the table.

"So, to what do I owe this visit, your royal highness?" I asked. "I haven't seen you in a while..." I said.

"Well, let's just say that things will be changing a lot in the next little while" she said. Her words were nutral, so why did her eyes look so bad?

"I heard. Congratulations," I said. "The pictures looked lovely. Let's see the ring!"

Rachel held out her left hand.

"That is beautiful sapphire stone," I said. "It matches perfectly with your eyes."

"It is a blue diamond, actually," said Rachel. "Adil's grandfather had it sent in from his mine near Golconda. A piece of his homeland. Such a precious symbol..." said Rachel.

"Your such a romantic. Your father would be proud," I said.

Rachel looked over at me, surprised. There was nothing bad in my comment, nothing mean, no irritation in my voice. Just melancholy.

Truce, then?

"That is a sweet thought," she said. "I do hope he is proud."

I offered her a biscotti from the cardboard package.

"No, thanks," said Rachel. "I'm literally on my way out."

"Okay," I said. "So when is the wedding going to be?"

"Oh," said Rachel as she took a sip from her cup. "Well, we're not sure. Adil's parents would want us to get married before living together, but we don't really want to spend the money and energy on planning a wedding right now."

I was confused. "It is just that you said something about many changes to come, so I thought that you were talking about your wedding," I said. "What is it? You aren't pregnant, are you? Rachel?"

She looked uncomfortable.

"No," she finally answered. "No, Mom. It's not that."

"What is it?" I asked.

no answer

"I am getting so tired of all of these big secrets and whispering sessions everywhere I go," I said. "The only person who has made me feel normal since I got sick was Harvey... And now he is gone too."

"Mom, you didn't just *get sick*."

"What do you mean I didn't just get sick?" I asked.

"I don't want to get into this, Mom," said Rachel. "But we are all pretty sure that signs of—"

"All pretty sure?" I said. "Now who the hell are *all* of these doctors that you've been talking to?"

"Doctors?"

"So what," I said in a mean voice, "you have all become Alzheimer specialists? Congratulations, how did you find the time to get such a special degree?"

"There's lot of literature on the subject, Mom.'

"So what, you all just sit around and talk about me, about my mental health and my falling appart? What is wrong with all of you?" I asked. Don't you have anything else to talk about?"

Rachel rolled her eyes. "So typical," she said. "You just love knowing that we're all talking about you, worried about you, don't you?"

"Serisouly, Rachel?"

"The centre of attention, even when you're not around. It's the dream, isn't it?" she said.

"Oh yeah. You're on to me. Alzheimer's. Ultimate glamour."

Rachel rolled her eyes.

"And by the way," I said, worried less and less about restraining my anger. "You owe me a serious apology."

"For what?" she asked. "I'm here so that you can apologize to me!"

"What for?"

"Everything!" shouted Rachel. "You are so damn self-centered. Why do we even worry so much about you?"

"I don't need your pity," I said in a very small voice

"What the hell do you want me to apologize about?" she asked. "I tried so hard. I came to your psych appointment. But you're impossible to—"

"You made Harvey leave me!"

"Harvey?" said Rachel. "What the hell does he have to do with this?"

"You need to apologize to me for making Harvey leave. He was the last good thing that I had in my life, Rachel. And you made him go."

"The last good thing? You mean like the three children that you neglected for all of their child and adolescent lives, the same ones who are working like maniacs to find a home that will take you in?"

"What?"

"Forget it, mother. I have nothing to apologize for. The day you realize that it was your lie, and not my truth, that was the problem, will be the day that we can continue this conversation. But it won't be any time soon. So to hell with it," said Rachel. "I have made my peace with how things are. Just now. I have tried..." she stood up tears in her eyes. "I have tried so hard to make things right. But I just can't. And now, in this very moment..." She smiled, but a tear rolled down her cheek. "I have made peace with that. I have gone as far as I can go without you meeting me along the path. Well. I will not compromise myself – my integrity, my pride, my feelings – anymore. The only thing that I am sorry for is you."

She turned and left the kitchen. I heard her walk through the living room and back out the front door. I did not follow.

March 26,2017

Thomas insisted that we make an appointment to see my psychologis together. I figured that Rachel had spilled the beans about our little 'conversation'.

So on Wednesday he came down to see him with me. I figured that he would have more important things to do, since he will being going back to school in less than two weeks, but whatever.

"Thomas," said the shrinker, "it so nice to finally meet you."

"Likewise," said Tom as they shook hands.

"Please, have a seat."

We did as we were told.

So tell me a little about yourself, he said, looking at Tom.

"I would like to know why you're here," I said to Tom.

Tom cleared his throat. "Well, I'm a teacher."

The psychologist nodded. "what subject do you teach?" he asked.

"History and geography."

The psychologit nodded again. "When did you know that you wanted to be a teacher?"

"There was no real *moment*," said Tom. "But I guess I just liked the subjects. And when you study history and geography, the only logical outcome is to teach it."

"You've always been interested in maps then?" he asked.

"There was a time when my dad had a job as a train conductor. He was going to be away for a while, chugging across the country. So he showed me the stops on a map. And I was so impressed..." said Tom, his hearth fondly set on the memory. "The thing that I couldn't was how Canada is surrounded by water."

"What is so surprising about that!" asked the psychologist.

"It wasn't that we're surrounded that surprised me," said Tom. "i was just confused because if Canada is surrounded by water, that makes it an island. But my dad said it wasn't, that it was a continent. And I remember thinking just how stupid grown-ups can be sometimes, giving calling an island one thing and a contident another thing when their the same thing: land surrounded by water."

"Do you have a lot of fond memories about your father?"

Tom nodded.

"You care deeply about both of your parents, don't you?"

Tom sighed. "My family is very important to me."

The psychologist looked in my direction for the first time since we arrived. "Mrs. O'Connor," he said, "Tom asked me if he could join you for this appointment because he cares deeply about you."

"I know that," I said uncomfortable. "But we didn't need to come here for you to tell me that."

"Mom, I wanted to talk to you in a safe environment."

The psychologist nodded approvingly. "Go on," he said. "Mom, you know that things have been getting harder at home for some time," said Tom. "You don't even live with me anymore," I said.

"Please, Mrs. O'Connor. you must listen to him speak"

"We have been worried about you, and we believe that it is time for you to live somewhere a little safer," said Tom. "Between the supposed break-in, or how you almost burnth dow the house when you the kettle on the stove, and went to bed, and the other small things that Claire has noticed, we—"

"Claire?" I said. "Claire doesn't even live with me!"

"Yes she does, Mom."

"I know that" I said. I was so frustrated that I was having trouble getting my point across clearly. "I didn't mean it that way. She sleeps at my house, sure, but that's about it. so she really can't be the one who is informing you of anything... she has no idea herself."

Tom shook his head. "Don't you trust me, Mom?"

I sat there in silence.

"Do you trust your son, Mrs. O'Connor?" asked the psychologist, "do you care about what he thinks?"

I suppose I do."

"Then perhaps you should hear what he is saying," he said.

"It has become quite clear to me," I said, quietly but clearly, "that it is a general belief from my children that I am a danger to myself."

"We only want what is best for you. If Dad were still here, it would be different."

"Is that so?" I snarled.

"Yes. Because he would make sure that you are cared for. He would be there to make sure that you are safe."

"That sounds nice," I said. "So where do I sign up?"

"That is not the reality of our situation, Mom," said Tom, ignoring me. "And so we have to deal with the reality of this real situation. We found a nice home for you, Mom."

"I have a home, Tom."

"It has a floor for autonomous people," he said. "But the apartments have no kitchens. That way, you don't have to worry about cooking for yourself. And you will be with lots of likeminded people."

"Likeminded?" I said. "You mean, other Alzheimer's patience? No, thank you!"

"Sorry, that was a clumsy word to use,"" said Tom. "No. not Alzheimer's pateints. Just other retirees like you."

It's not a hospice?

"No!" said Tom. "No, of course not."

"What about the other floors?" I asked.

"It is a very large centre. There are other floors for people with lots of different degrees of autonomy. People of all ages!"

"At the end of the day," pipped in the psychologist, "you are capable of making your own decision. No one can force you into selling your home."

"Selling my home?" Was it already a questions of that?

"Mom," said Tom. We just want you to be safe, to keep you in good hands. you know that.

Alyson Hope

"Dont you trust your sun, Mrs. O'Connor?"

April 1, 2017

It is April Fool's Day, and, in truth, I think that I am the biggest fool of them all.

I spent so much time trying to fill the deep holes inside my heart and mind with empty experiences and meaningless encounters. I spent so much time trying to ruin what I had. And I had so much...

What we find funny today, we certainly did not find funny before, and wont find funny later, either.

But what is NOT funny – wasting your life chasing greener grass, ignoring your closest friends and family, burdening yourself with things that have absolutely not significance – will not change.

This writing is getting ne down.

April 22

Finally, we have some respite after days and days of heavy rain.

This morning, I went into my backyard to pull some weeds and prepare the flourbeds for the spring. The soil was moist and warm, but the air was still rather cold.

I love digging up the old roots in the spring, sprucing up the perrennials and making way for new annuals. I know a lot of people complain about the spring because of dog shit and sleet, but I see so much more.

Aech spring is a chance for nature to renew herself. The tight little buds of leaves and flowers, just waiting for the right moment to embark upon their first – and final – journey. Maybe that is what I am doing, too.

When I was finished in the backyard, I went out in front, to the driveway, to assess the snow situation.

I began shovelling some of the soft snow around my driveway. Only a Quebecer will know what I mean: to take snow from the top of a pile and spread it out on the warm pavement to help it melt... It sounds like busywork – cleaning a dirty shoe on a clean shoe and then cleaning the dirty shoe on the clean shoe and then cleaning the dirty shoe on the clean shoe... – but it is actually quite affective.

May came outside to chat with me. Things have been kind of awkward between us, since Claire and Robin came home to us spending time together.

She made a few remarks on the weather, then sked how Tom is doing.

"Oh, he is well!" I said, not quite as convincingly as I would hav e liked. "Laci is growing up so fast." Of course, the visit we had with the psyc last month set us on a rocky path. But Tom, ever the diplomat, did an admirable job of remaining amiable.

"It was such a surprise to me, when he decided to move away," said MAy, smiling fondly, inwardly, at her memory. "He was always so close to you and Elvis. Rachel and Claire, they always ran around doing their own thing. But Tom... Tom preferred staying near home, didn't he?"

I held my shovel up, resting the tip on the ground and my foot on its step. "Yes," I said, returning the warmth. "That is very true. Oh, Thomas..."

"Remember the year that he had you pick him up from sleepaway camp?" asked May. "The kids were so cruel to him, in the fall, when they all went back to school!"

"Well," I said, grinning, "he was 12 or 13 at the time, wasn't he?"
May laughed.

"I didn't know that his classmates made fun of him," I said, shaking my head. "Oh, Tom..."

"What about Claire and Rachel? They're doing well too, I guess?" she said.

"Sure," I said, knowing that May would recognize my departed enthusiasm, but be too polite to ask. "Both engaged, apparently. So I guess, theyre doing well."

"Good," said May, nodded, with a hint of sadness in her eyes. "Good. Im glad to hear it. Ill let you get back to your work now."

May 3, 2017

Every time I looked in your eyes
Light was reflected true.
Vibrant heart and benevolent smile
In my heart I always knew.
Someties I wish it had been me, not you.

May 19, 2017

Lately, I have been so reticent to right. I pick up my pencil, sit in front of my journal, and do nothing. I get lost in my thoughts, in my mind. My mind, that inhospitable habitate for my soul.

In the pamphelts that Dr. Lee gave me, there was a link to a website giving general information about alzheimers.

There was a website with pictures of brains with and without the disease. Im not sure how I feel about it. Do I really need to know that my brain matter is shrinking and drying, while the pockets of fluid around it are getting bigger? I cant shake the feeling that my head is full of water. if I tilt my head too far one way or the other, I will become unbalanced and fall. Or maybe it will spill out.

I was thinking about what if I lived my life differently, like if I had another job, or moved somewhere warmer, or ate more fuirts and vegetables. Would I still have this dicease?

If I had known that I would get alzheimers, and that my children would have a greater risk to get it too, would I have had kids? I don't think so, honestly.

It is scary times. I would not wish this on anyone, not even Shelley.

Shelley who wont tell me anything about my biological father. I don't even know his name. Maybe he had this too, maybe we could have done some testing before. Been more vigilant. She will not stop trying to ruin my life until she wins. And it is looking like tthe wind is in her favour.

The doctor said that the earlier we catch this, the better things go.

Rachel was right, although it is painful to admit it. Things had started to slip even before Elvis died.

But how can you know that youre not just forgetting things because you forget? Because everyone forgets birthdays sometimes. Everyone learns a new card game and then forgets the rules before the next time they play. Everyone forgets an appointment, or shows up at the wrong time, or on the wrong day. Everyone forgets what day of the week it is, especially when theyre not working fulltime. Everyone missplacs their wallet.

But not everyone slowly forgets who they are entirely.

may 2017

Not long after I starting working with Marie's Mom, my own mother had a serious mental health break. this episode that left her in a psycheatric hospital for several months.

I went to visit her about once a week. She asked me to bring fashion magazines and cigarettes.

When I got to the part of the hospital where interned patients were kept, there was a big, ominous, metal door with a small slit of window through which employess could look.

The first time I went, I was taken aback. it was a scary place. first, you had to fill in a chart about you, who you were there to visit, the time and date. then, there was a search of your self. all of your extra clothing, like coats, bags, jewerly, or scarfs, had to be left in a locker behind the nurse's desk. no belts, and any shoes with laces were swapped for scratchy taupe slippers. They took the magazines and shook them, spine up, pages down, to ensure that there was nothing hidden isnide. they took the pack of cigarettes and opened it, pulling the cigarettes out and inspecting the box.

once I had passed the security check, an orderly guided me to my mom's room. we passed by an open area with several beds, then a long hallway with several doors, some open, most closed. I did not dare look inside.

My mom's room was the size of a shoebox, just big enough to to enclose a single bed and a highschool-sized locker, which was locked. Her personal items were all kept in the locker, and to go through them –

even to take warmer socks for cold evenings – she had to be supervised. even my visits were supervised: the door had to be left wide open, and ever few minutes, the orderly would pop thier head into the room and check on us.

"How did you get your hand on this room, instead of beig in the open area over there?" I asked, pointing towards where ei had come from.

My mother turned her head slowly towards me. she look like a goldfish: her face was swollen, her skin irritated and red-tinged, her blue eyes round and barely showing any intelligence behind them. she blinked, her eyelids staing closed for longer than what would appear as natural.

"Hi, Nina dear," she said. Her voice was raspy, as though she had just been crying. "My hand in which place?" she asked, looking at her hand.

I must admit that I felt a flood of uncomfortable emotions just then. It was a pile of pity, sadness, fear, disgust, and thankfulness, for not being in her shoes. "I brought cigarettes, I said, gesturing the pack towards her.

Shelley nodded slowly, but made no move to take them.

"Did... should I light one for you?" I asked. Again, the slow, painful nod. i lit a cigarette – my hands shaking slightly – and handed it to my mother. She reached out, so very slowly, took the cigarette, and brought it to her mouth. she pulled a drag, then let the smoke escape slowly from her mouth and nose, dragonlike.

"So, how are you doing?" I asked. It was such an empty question, but in reality, I had nothing else to say.

Shelley nodded.

I stood up, looking out the barred window. It was open, letting in a small breeze.

"Nina?"

I turned to my mother.

"Did... how did you get in here?" she asked. "Arent the doors all locked?"

I explained the route through which I had arrived.

"I came on a strecher, I think..." she said slowly.

I am not sure how long I stayed, but it was long enough for the orderly to visit three times.

June 4, 2017

I think tha t it is easy to judge people for their mistakes. But what is best is to ask why they made the mistakes in the first place.

why did I stray from Elvis, for example?

I had no doubts about our relationship, Elvis was always there for me, he complimented me, he was kind.

But despite all of that, I was lonely. i felt unloved. i needed attention. I wanted adventure, a change from the routine. I cheated for all these reasons, but also, because I could. the door was opened so many times, all I had to do was walk though it.

Gianni was not the first, but he was the last. there was no conscious decision there, I didnt somehow transform into some altruistic version of myself. it just stopped. And the longer it was done, the better it felt. like when youre in the middle of eating an entire chocolate cake. the longer you step away from the table, the less you want to go back. just the smell of the icing on your fingers is enough to make you sick.

June 17

Claire caught me in her room just now.

I told her I was checking if the window was open, as I thought it was about to rain.

She stared at me for several moments. "You were here to close the window?"

"Yes..." I said, checking the window In a cheap play-acting way. "In case it rains." I put my hands on my hips.

Claire nodded slowly. "Now, you're done?

"Yes," I said. "All done."

She watched me walk out of her room and closed the door bwhind me.

I went into my own bedroom and closed the door.

You see, I am still very suspicious about Claire. her grandmother is an addict, or recovering addict, but the point is... it could run in the family.

I check her drawers and her coat pockets regularly, but this is the first time I got cot.

Claire has a new job working as a guide in the museum. Sometimes, she works on a bizzare collection of paintings that she started in the basement. It based on a story she composed in her mind, based on a dream she had had a few months earlier.

on new years eve, 2020, on alien race came into contact with planet Earth. The vessel appeared as an orb that emitted a golden light. The spoke every language, and their message was diffused directly into each person's brain. It was something like

We have been watching how you treat each other. It is time for a fresh start. We will do to you what you do to each other. We will return in nine.

"Nine what?" I had asked when she explained her premise

Claire laughed. "I don't know!" she exclaimed. "And neither did anyone on earth. But one thing that they could agree upon was that they had reason for concern."

The largest canvas in the basement is propped up on a gigantic wood easel on metal wheels. something about the several clamps that braced the top of the tilted painting vaguely reminds me of a guillotine, so I dont look at it too often. the background looks like the milky way, and thre is a wisp of blue and green that is probably the Earth.

June 27

NO SADNESS

There is no sadness like the sadness
That will ever outweigh
The loss of a lved one
Who you took for granted
But for who youd give anything
Just to spend one more day

Jly 6

Once, I read on a tea tag something tacky along the lines of: when you hear a voice of doubt, doubt the voice and not yourself

It seemed like fine advice at the time, equalparts banal and poingnant.

We spend so much time in our society being obsessed with making ourselves better that we forget that if we just let ourselves be, that would be best. Im not sure any of this makes sense.

Another tag read something like this: everyone in an argument is both right and wrong. therefore, dont argue, discuss

That is easy for a little bag of tea to declare, when all it is concerned with in life is flavouring hot water. living, breathing, moving humans... there is a little emore complexity to the whole thing.

For excample: how could Harvey be angry with me over not sharing something so personal as a medical diagnosis that is sure to rob you of years of your life? Maybe decades.

Ive been thinking a lot lately: if it had been the other way around, would I have been angry with Harvey?

Speculation is cheaper than salt, but... I just cant see myself reacting as he did.,

Of course, I could have been angry... but not this angry.

Harvey was a break in the clouds after months of rain. He was a brief pause in my diminuendo. I cant say that I loved him, and maybe I never would have. but I cared for him.

And even if I had been afraid to stay in a romantic relationship with him.... I would at least have been his friend.

Another tag said that: wanting to repeat a past experience is the greatest source of human sufferig

July 11

Im not sure how much I can blame Rachel for what is happening between us, and how much I can blame myself, and how much I can blame Adil, for that matter.

I was talking to Claire, and it occurred to me: I think that Rachel was simply born to the wrong parent. Of course, I said nothing to Claire, as Claire would say tha ti am trying to drag her into things that have nothing to do with her.

Maybe, how could I know, my father felt the same about me.

Of course, when you spend as much time alone as I do, you come to learn some things about yourfself.

One thing I know is that what I hate in Rachel I would admire in others. Her drive. Her determination. Her intelligence. Her beauty.

So why is it that I cant stand to be in the same room as her?

I think it would be obvious to guess that I am jealous of her. Maybe I am. but that feels like a backpedal.

Im trying to remember how well Rachel got along with Elvis. I think she actually loved him.

Maybe she blames me for what happened.

I sure do.

July 18

I went to the psychologist today, this morning.

claire insisted on driving me there, even though I can absolutly drive myself.

he went on and on about things. I was annoyed: isn't it my space to speak?

He wanted to know what I love and appreciate in the moment. What brings me joy.

Lately, there isnt much, is there?

That's what I said to him. he nodded, then asked for more insight.

"I like gardening," I said after some time. "And visits with Tom and his family."

He just kept reminding me that he is there to support me. I don't need crutches, my leg isnt broken.

"Have you read anything recently?" he asked.

I nodded. I am in the middle of something. "It's the third or fourth time now that im reading it," I said. I didn't say that I am having trouble following the story, that it is the third or fourth time because I have been starting over.

He wants me to do more puzzles, listen to music.

I thanked him for his time and agreed to another appointment, although I was fully anticipating cancelling over the phone.

"Thanks for the lift, Claire," I said as I got out of the car. She stood up from the driver's seat and handed me back my keys.

"Yeah, no problem," she said with a tense smile. "did you want to... go inside and have some tea or something?"

Im pretty tired," I said. "I think I am going to go lie down."

I just felt like keeping to myself

July 30

Summer

When the summer blazes down
Your head is swimming in mist
Your body is so hot tha you stick to every surface
Your hair becomes burnt and frayed
Your mind becomes tipsy and dazed
Your skin becomes charred and tough and suede
You are half-crazed
You think things could not possibly get worse
And then
It rains.

August 26

It has been so long since I wrote because my hand was in a bandage and hur ttoo much to hold a pencil.

What happened was I fell asleep on the sofa. Napping isn not generally a big deal, but this time it was.

I fell asleep with a kettle on the stove. I was boiling water for tea.

I woke up to the kettle screeching and bumping about.

I ran to the kitchen to grab the kettle by the handle, but it was so hot tha ti burnt my hand. There was no more water in the kettle. The bottom was all bumped and groved. I dropped the kettle onto the stove in surprise.

I ran to the sink and stood there for several minutes with cold water running ovver my hand. It hurt a lot. The skin started to peel a little, wash away with the water. that felt like a bad sign.

"Claire!" I shouted. She was down in the basement. I waited a few minutes but heard nothing. I went to the door at the top of the stairs. "Claire!"

I heard her raced upstairs.

"What happened, Mom?" she shouted. Her favce was painted in concern and pity. Her eyes were wide as the moon.

"I... I burnt myself on the kettle," I said.

"Oh, Mom, I am sorry..." said Claire. "I should have been paying closer attention."

I shook my head. "It is my fault, Claire. I fell asleep. It bothered me that she felt responsible for my absentmindedness.

"I should have been here with you. im sorry, mom..."

We went to the hospital. Right away, they sanitiezed my hand and placed a cool compress on it. Then after several hours in the waiting room, they called me to have my burn cleaned more thoroughly and and bandaged. I had to go back to have the bandange changed twice.

August 29, 2017

I was reading over past entries. What a nightmare!

Last year, around this time, Harvey and I were in a budding, innocent relationship.

Last year, around this time, Tom was asking about my selling the house and moving into a hospice.

It is easy, I can only imagine, for young people to throw these terms around.

Home, hospice, retired living facility.

I even hear about people my age that are excitecd to go.

Don't they see things as I do? Basically, theyre taking a final leap into the last chapter of their life. Aren't they scared? Don't htye se that the curtain is about to fall?

Every night before I go to sleep, I htink to myself that I am one day closer to death.

I don't have much left. But I have my autonomy. And I plan to hold onto it for as long as I can.

Any old person can accidentally forget a pot of water on the stove, or forget to lock their front door at night. It doenst make them a danger to themselves and others,now does it?

When I think about how my mom was, how she could barely keep the lights on, or keep food in my belly, or keep me out of harms way... now that was a person who needed to be interned.

Sept.

When things get out of control
    you think you are on top of the world and one day you dont even
remember your own name
    Relief, when it comes back: oh no, the meomry, the confusion is still
to fresh
    to too two these things used to mean different things to me
    now does that really matter?
    rimes
    cat – fat – bat
    reading my own poems that i dont even understand myself
    my brain wrote this? or ! or...
    i get so SO angry
    why wont anyone help...

September 20

My eyes have been becoming so very tired lately it is so hard for me to write now okay.

So maybe mr psychologist would like to see this and say yes yes tests and so on, something has changed lately yes sir mam I feel it really.

Well... there is a voice deep in my head that I try to quiet that says 'is it possible?"

i always thought, when I was younger, that to die at 68 was okay: yea, that is a normal age to die. but now... i jus dont think so anymore.

Maybe I am not so mature as others. Maybe I just feel i have more to live?

i was looking out my window the other day just admiring my neiborhood no big deal and what did i see but a lady invited to Harvey's house!

okay, should I be jealos or not concerned at all, well who really can say, right? Harvey is not my belonging or anything like that so maybe your thinking yeah take it easy little lady.

Well that is easier to say than to say, you know! maybe a cousin or something right mhmm.

so why am i writing when I clearly have nothing to say?

Semptember

It is so hard sometimes to feel alone and live alone.

   i can see that my mind plays tricks on me sometimes and im not the one laffing.

   like i will think

   when will elvis be home?

   and get angry about it, and then remember that he wont

   or sometimes / this is the worst i will look at the clock and i cant read what it says. i know the numbers but i dont remember what each of the hands do.

   and sometimes I forget about what i was doing. i will go into a room and stand there staring at the light switch and not remember how to turn it on. or ill stand there and try to remember what i was there to do, but poof! nothing.

   i forgot my keys in the door a few times.

   i left the frige door open all night

   i used mayonaise instead of hair conditionner

   i called Tom, but forgot i called tom, so i called him back and then remembered

   mom, we just spoke...

   i know! (brilliant) i just wanted to say hi to Zandra too! i said.

   shes still in brazil with her family...

   yes

   is everything okay?"

   "yes"

October 22

This morning i wok up at 7.43 and i had a thought: 7.43 am smells like citrus. there is somthing very citrusy about that hour.

it was my first really good night of sleep in quite sometime.

Claire, Tom and Rachel brought me to the home yesterday morning. i guess that i dont know why i said NO for so long. this place isnt so bad! beside the old lady that sits on the bench in fromt of my room all the time. hahaha! she has long white hair that she chews on all of the time. she dosnt say much... she almost seems scared. that part is sad. who wants to live in a place where their scared? that is why i guess this place isnt sooo bad. you know no more breakin troubles. no responsibility to water flower or trim trees and no more HARVEY.

i tried to talk to the lady but no, she is scard of me to. or mabe she is deaf i just thought of that now. i am sitting up in my bed that is a very good position! and i am writing in my journal. but i am geting very tired of writing seriously im not sure how much longer I wanna do it.

it is nice to be here because i dont have to cook anymore that is nice. alos, this place feels more safe for me.

i really wanted to sell my hosue myself. But! Tomhas insisted that he would contact somone i used to work with. he really insisted so I accepted. but inside i am crumbling.

Elvis is gone. that house was a piece of him. i may have forgoten about a lot of stuff.but i did not forget about that tree in the backyard. Elvis is there.

we met in that house. we bought that house together. we lived there, laughd and cried there. ELVIS DIED THERE. it was a symbol for me to sell it. it was for me to close the book, new chapter.

   now that i didnt sell it myself what is left of me

oCTOBER 25, 2017

The home isnt so bad after all. i met some new frends that is pretty cool! my room is like a dorm i feel like a colege prep student ha!

the biggest problem is when i forget why i I am here. i wake up sometimes thinkign im in a hotel on vacation.. i look for elvis or for another man and i find myself in a old single bed with ramps so i dont fall off. where is the beach? where is the boardwalk? where is the jacuzi, the ski hill?

no no more time for that just lonliness

now

October 23

bad dream bad dream so i think of happy things
elvis when he proposed to me we were in a restauant
he actualy hid the ring in a pie! wow so sweet haha!
take a bite, somthing hard, spit..? A RING?
will you marry me Nina oconner?
yes, ELVIS!
then then the band began to play our song
where is elvis and wen will he come get me?

October 29

Last night a bad man brok into my house
now this morning i wake and i don no where i am
he did not steal? did not take a THING
            but he came in i sawwwww! Him
now where am i beacaus i recognise my cloths and some of my stuff
and my journal! ha! but not WHERE AM I
the door was not broken just fixed

March 1

a psychologis came to visit me today to talk. blablabla how are you doing

i decided that i want to get out of here

i donno wher ei want to go but i want to get out?

Last day i wrote that i didnt no where i was and that. is scary because i do no... and i just forgot..

Noviember 15, 2016

i smile but i dont no why
i laf but i dont no why
then the lit goes down
an i am scared
but i am brave
so i dont cry

December 17

Elviss chrismas party just made me so mad. okay.
   We Walk into the party for BLUS AND FORBS BUS COMPANY.
   i am pregnan with anothr babe girl.
   there were mostly men at hte party, a few big big women. I felt very out of place.
   I: I should not have worn this dress I said to myslf. i wen to the nose to ''powder my bathroom.
   i cam back,,so then i saw him having a VERY privat conversation with a lady, not lik the other ladies. they jus looked each other in the i and in a way full of sparkle and... and I NEW!
   oh elvis, why u do this to be elvis, write whn i needed u so badly
   he stil did not admit the real truth but! I will make him.
   HE WILL REGRET IT
   What did i ever do to deserve this? jus wait til he comes home

Decembr 20

i do remember that! the date.
except when i accidentaly call the police
maybe i will go to a new floor! n this hospital

Dec 25

My dear family ivited me to christmas! no idea, but there is snow outside and montreal is so white. i do no most of the people. They're were playing a game but tit is so complicate I cant follow. I somewhat skared of the people around me but it is o ok. I feel love and warm.

I think that they are feeling bad like not easy but they are the ones wo dont understand.

They jus don understand somehing about life that i do and that I cant really explain in words because it is hard for me today my mind needs sleep. our experiense is far bigger then what w e experience thru our own eyes. we ar so much more than our skin you know! elvis i am ready to see you agan, but at the same time

Decemver 31

Okay so the new year is here. not much to celebrate except rachel's high-school graduation oh wow so happy for her!!

she will be a famous ballerina one day, you no she is so graceful.

excep I am hungry an i dont understand why, why in a cafeteria like food you know!!

ha

December 32

Osoo my mom came by to see me today.
   she came in my room and said wow der Nina this place is nice
   she is always saying that my place. is so nice so faancy wow!! as like i always have betrr then her and she is jus jealous. well! i made a life for myself, oka mom, i will not apologise for it.
   Blablba it is so anoying to writ wen your hand is soar like me rit now..!
   but why did elvis put me heer when we wer supossed to live together for EVER
   and i miss him .

Januwary 12

The door knoked.
Hello?
Mom home?
Nope...
I am here about your front windows. Hav eyou noticed a problem?
I cant let you in mom said not to let people in-
its okay i work for the city
!
dont be scared little girl just here for the windows! with the city.

Jan 15

thought that it could be interesting to write a novel one day. not just keep a journal like i am. or a memoir! a lady on my floor said that there is a class about. WRiting a memoir about yourself that. could. be fun.

but not for me tho.realisitc? id forget what i was writing about half-way through.

January. 21

Every day is like the other day and i need to no what is the point.
?

come do puzzles, missrs oconner. well, fuck the puzzles i dont want to do puzzles or make finger panting im not dead am i?

abd my eyes are becoming to tired. so tired! why do i even rite? because i guess it will help me to remember.

becsuse lately i been forgeting

so some people visit me to sometimes that is fun.

my MOM even came once an also elvis jus onCe. my heart misses ELVIS

Febuary 2018

Yestrday, Tom came to get me at the home. He brought me to a beauti-ful. wedding.

there was a girl who walked down the isle and then another girl. To girls getting married. isnt that somthing. I suppose. love is love.

tThere were so mane flowers. Like all flowers evrywere. And candles to. it was a beautiful seen. just wow.

One of the girls was waerign a long, white wedding gown like a princes. she had red hair and

the othur girl wore a short whit dres like we wore. jus lik my wedding dress to elvis!. she had dark eyes and hair. She remind me of somone I usd to love. and it was TOm who walked her down!!

she was so bauetiful, I cried.

oh mom, she is so beutiful said Rachel

YES. She. is. i siad.

i love you all so much

1

I wonder when elvis will be home I really need. to sit him down! and explane. These constant business trips are getting out of hand. the children will hardly remember him if he goes on this way?

im scared. i

m sorry, elvis.

why did you stay with me all this time elvis when i was so BAD to you?

Nina, i promisedd to always take care of you.

i did not derserve you elvis

you stole my heart. and

sometimes i dont know where i am. Not at home. Not in our home..

writing takes alot of troble. now. Like tryng to read but without enouf light. and

IM tired.

but I dont want to go. Im not done here yet. and IM scared.

please elvis wait for me wereever you are

Acknowledgements

I would first like to recognize the wonderful people from Renaissance Press for giving me the opportunity to publish my first novel. Collaborating with you has been the most amiable of experiences.

To my mentor, Professor Fahmi, thank you for having seen in me what I was too afraid to see in myself. Your warmth and guidance have shaped my life in ways that I cannot adequately describe. Thank you for teaching me that magic is real, and that it happens when just the right words are penned to paper.

Thank you to my family for supporting my dreams, especially to Mom and Papa, who will always be my biggest fans. Josh, I would like to express a special appreciation for your thoughtful, thorough annotations of my manuscripts.

To my family of friends, namely Chloé, Christelle, Jess, and Josy, who received each manuscript with curiosity and enthusiasm, I am grateful for you feedback. On this fleeting journey between clusters of stars, I am forever thankful to have crossed paths with you.

Eric, thank you for these past two decades of camaraderie. Your love, patience, and kindness have influenced every single aspect of who I am today. When you look at me, your eyes say that anything is possible. And so, I believe you. I look forward to many more decades by your side, hand in hand with RJ.

My final thoughts are with Marguerite and Annette. I am grateful to these women for having welcomed me into the family with warm arms, cheerful stories, and plate upon plate of home cooking. You are the inspiration behind this narrative. I hope that wherever you are now, you are looking down on us with all the joy and serenity you both deserve.

About the Author

Alyson Hope is a writer who currently lives in Montreal, the island of Tiohtià:ke – unceded land of the Kanien'kehá:ka Nation.

In 2014, Hope received her Master's Degree in literature from the Université du Québec à Chicoutimi. Based largely on ecocritical theory, her thesis examines the multi-faceted relationship between nature and the characters in John Steinbeck's *East of Eden*. Hope's love and respect for the natural world is what drew her to the study of ecocriticism.

The Smell of Rain, published by the brilliant folks of Renaissance Press, is Hope's debut fictional novel.

About Renaissance

Renaissance was founded in May 2013 by a group of authors and designers who wanted to publish and market those stories which don't always fit neatly in a genre, or a niche, or a demographic. Like the happy panbibliophiles we are, we opened our submissions, with no other guideline than finding a Canadian book we would fall in love with.

Today, this is still very true; however, we've also noticed an interesting trend in what we like to publish. It turns out that we are naturally drawn to the voices of those who are members of a marginalized group, and these are the voices we want to continue to uplift.

At Renaissance, we do things differently. We are passionate about books, and we care as much about our authors enjoying the publishing process as we do about our readers enjoying a great Canadian read on the platform they prefer.

pressesrenaissancepress.ca

pressesrenaissancepress@gmail.com

Printed in the USA
CPSIA information can be obtained
at www.ICGtesting.com
LVHW012027161123
764185LV00009B/296